WITCHING YOU WERE HERE

A WICKED WITCHES OF THE MIDWEST MYSTERY
BOOK THREE

AMANDA M. LEE

WINCHESTERSHAW PUBLICATIONS

To Kylie, for walks in cornfields and countless mutual excuses – and for being the closest thing I have to a sister

Sic gorgiamus allos subjectatos nunc
We gladly feast on those who would subdue us.
The Addams Family Motto

ONE

*W*inter in Michigan sucks.

There's no other way to put it.

Sure, you have those romantics that think the white powder is beautiful – even when Mother Nature drops two feet of it on you in a twenty-four-hour period. Those are the people that live in warmer climates and only visit an area with actual seasons every once in a while, of course.

Then there are those people that actually like winter sports. Daredevils that think skiing and snowboarding sounds like a fun afternoon. I don't know any of those people and, frankly, I don't want to get to know any of them.

Then there's that deranged group that thinks snowmobiling through a huge drift at excessive speeds – actually going so fast that they manage to get air when they hit a drift at just the right angle – is a fantastical experience.

Okay, the snowmobiling thing *is* fun – as long as my Aunt Tillie isn't the one driving the snowmobile. She's hell on a Polaris. When the chief of police pulled her over last week for purposely spraying the other denizens of Hemlock Cove's senior center with the slushy snow that had accumulated in the parking lot (she swears they were cheating at euchre) she retaliated by running over his foot with her brand-new sled. It's okay, nothing was broken – at least that was her argument at the time.

In any other town, she would have been locked up and sent for a mental evaluation. Since Chief Terry has known my family – and her specifically – for more than fifty years he was easily bribed with a red velvet cake that my mom had made. Aunt Tillie still claims he purposely put his foot under her snowmobile. She's eighty-five, so you can't argue with her. And, if you do, you're taking your fate in a dangerous direction. She'll curse you – and I don't mean bad words here – without batting an eyelash.

My name is Bay Winchester, and I'm a witch. Not an evil witch, don't get me wrong – although Aunt Tillie has been called evil by at least half of the town (and every single member of our family). I come from a long line of earth and kitchen witches that have lived in northern Lower Michigan since – well, as far back as I've cared to track our family tree.

I'm the editor of the The Whistler, Hemlock Cove's weekly news-paper. A few years ago I moved down to Detroit to be a "real" jour-nalist – but when that didn't work out I found myself back home. Now I'm living in a small guesthouse with my cousins, Thistle and Clove, on the edge of the property my family has owned for centuries.

And the rest of my family? My mom lives with her sisters, Twila and Marnie, and they transformed the old family Victorian into one of Hemlock Cove's most successful bed and breakfast inns. The inn earned that distinction despite the fact that they named it The Over-look – yeah, I tried explaining about *The Shining*, but they didn't get it.

My elderly great-aunt Tillie lives with them. She doesn't exactly help with the day-to-day operations of The Overlook – but she thinks she runs everything, which is a constant annoyance to my control freak mother and aunts. Since you have to respect your elders, though, they often acquiesce to her demands. We all do. That woman can be evil when she wants to be – and she wants to be most of the time.

December has hit Hemlock Cove – and it looks like it's going to be a doozy. The day after Thanksgiving, a foot of snow dropped on the small hamlet. Two weeks later, another foot fell from the sky. In the past two weeks, the area has seen another six inches of snow – with very little break in the temperature. In other words: Hemlock Cove is literally a winter wonderland right now. Unfortunately, I'm wondering when spring will hit.

As for Hemlock Cove, I should probably explain a few things about the town. Several years ago, it was at a tough crossroads. Larger conglomerates forced all of the small industrial businesses in the area out and the tax base was practically non-existent. In an effort to keep Hemlock Cove viable, the town officials decided to rebrand it as vacation destination. Since everything supernatural was all the rage, they rebranded Hemlock Cove as a witch town.

Think of it like a Renaissance Fair, in a way. The storefronts are quaint and specific – pewter unicorns, collectibles, bakeries, tarot cards, and costumes – and there are a variety of townspeople that run tours, hayrides, and moonlit star walks. Almost every month, there's some sort of fair, whether it be corn mazes, murder mystery weekends or harvest festivals. It's kitschy, but it's kept Hemlock Cove alive.

Unfortunately for the townspeople – or fortunately, depending on who you talk to – they have no idea that my family is actually made up of real witches. I think some people have suspicions – especially about Aunt Tillie – but they usually keep those suspicions to hushed whispers when we walk by. We're not exactly embraced by the town, but we're not really shunned either.

Most of the business owners in Hemlock Cove make their money in the spring, summer and fall. Winter is more of a relaxed time. We get skiers and other cold weather enthusiasts, but the visitor traffic is a lot lighter. That's the one good thing about winter in my book.

Now, though we were in the middle of December, the weather forecasters (who are only right about fifty-percent of the time) were predicting that a blizzard was going to hit later in the week. Snow is one thing, but a blizzard is another. None of us were looking forward to it.

"I hate snow!"

I glanced up from the couch, where I was still happily ensconced in my pajamas and homemade afghan, and regarded my cousin Thistle dubiously. She had just walked back into the guesthouse from outside and her close-cropped hair – this month it was a violent shade of red in honor of Christmas – was dusted with fresh snow.

"It's winter, what do you expect?"

"We're witches, can't we just put up a protective bubble around our house," Thistle grumbled.

"Because no one would notice that," I laughed.

Thistle's brown eyes lit up with new indignation. "Why aren't you dressed? We have to go to the inn for breakfast."

"Why?" I noticed my voice had taken on a certain whiny quality. I love my family, I really do. They're just really taxing sometimes.

"It's homemade cinnamon roll morning," Thistle reminded me. "You're the one that promised to go up there for breakfast if your mom made cinnamon rolls. This is all your fault."

I had forgotten about the cinnamon rolls. I jumped to my feet in anticipation and reached for my coat excitedly. "Let's go. Where is Clove?"

"She's still getting ready," Thistle said. "You can't go up there in your pajamas. They'll pitch a fit."

I glanced down at my yoga pants and tank top and sighed. She was right. I would never hear the end of it. "I'll be quick."

Twenty minutes later, I had showered and changed into simple jeans and a sweater. Clove and Thistle were waiting for me in the living room. "The rolls are probably going to be cold now," Thistle grumbled.

I brushed my shoulder-length blonde hair out of my face and regarded her dubiously. "You're always such a crab in the morning."

"Like you're pleasant to be around before you've had your first cup of coffee."

She had a point.

Usually, since the guesthouse is only several hundred yards away from the inn, we would walk. Since there was so much snow, though, we had taken to driving to the inn over the past two weeks. It was easier than wading through huge drifts and then sitting through a meal in wet clothes.

We parked in the front parking lot, which had only three cars in it, and marched into the inn. We clomped our feet on the front rubber mat and pulled off our heavy parkas and hung them on the coat stand by the front door.

"Take off your boots, too."

I glanced up to the front desk and saw my Aunt Marnie standing behind it watching us. Marnie is Clove's mother – and they look almost exactly alike. They're both short – right around five feet tall – and they have dark hair. Clove has been growing her hair out, so it is halfway down her back these days. Marnie, who was getting her color from a bottle these days – something my blonde mom found hilarious – had cut her locks to a more manageable shoulder length.

"You want us to walk around barefoot?" Thistle asked irritably. "That's not very professional."

"It's better than tracking melting snow through the inn and making us clean it up," Marnie responded pointedly.

Thistle blew out a frustrated sigh, but did as Marnie asked. It was easier than an argument. Once we were all barefoot, we followed Marnie into the dining room. It was empty – which surprised me. "Where is everyone?"

"Breakfast won't be ready for another fifteen minutes," Marnie chided us.

"Then why did you tell us to be here at 8 a.m.?" I could have taken more time getting ready if I'd known the cinnamon rolls weren't ready yet.

"Because there's something we need to talk to you about and we knew that if we told you breakfast wouldn't be ready until 8 a.m. you would be late," Marnie said, glancing down at her wristwatch. "And look, you're fifteen minutes late."

"Menopause has made you mean," Thistle said as she regarded Marnie.

"I'm not going through menopause," Marnie bristled. "Your mothers may be going through menopause, but I'm not."

5

Clove, Thistle and I couldn't contain our chortles as we followed Marnie into the kitchen. Our mothers were notorious for their competitive natures. It didn't matter if it was cooking, gardening, decorating or, yes, menopause. One of them was going to win. In this case, though, I had no idea what winning constituted.

The kitchen at The Overlook is actually my favorite room in the house. No matter how old I am – and I'm in my mid-twenties, if you're wondering – I revert back to my adolescent years whenever I walk through the swinging doors and inhale the smells of childhood.

For their part, my aunts and mom added on an addition at the back of The Overlook a few years ago to use as their own private residence. The only way to access the residence from the inn is through the kitchen – and the guests would never dare.

We heard a flurry of voices in the kitchen before we actually saw what the most recent catastrophe was taking the form of today.

"I think you're being unreasonable."

My mom was the first person I saw when I entered the kitchen. She was standing behind the counter, hands on hips, and regarding Aunt Tillie with her patented "you're being a child" look. I was familiar with the gesture. She'd used it on me at least once a week for my entire life.

"I think you're being a pain in the ass, Winnie," Aunt Tillie barked back.

My Aunt Tillie was sitting in her reclining chair in the corner of the kitchen. A few weeks ago, the aunts had tried to remove the recliner – it had taken on a peculiar smell – and replace it with an antique rocking chair. Aunt Tillie had been so incensed she had taken to sleeping in the chair to make sure that they didn't try to sneak it out of the house again. Now it really smelled – like angry old lady.

"Let's try to remain calm," my Aunt Twila said, nervously wringing her hands as she watched the scene unfold. Just like her daughter, Twila had close-cropped hair that was dyed a bright shade of red. Thistle's hair was Christmas red, though. Twila's hair was Ronald McDonald red. She had been dying her hair for so long, I had no idea what her natural hair color was. She could have been darker like Marnie or fairer like my mom – but I had no idea which one it was.

"What's going on?" Clove asked curiously.

"Your Aunt Tillie is being impossible," my mom said.

"So? What else is new?" Thistle asked, jumping up and landing on the kitchen counter in a sitting position.

"You have a smart mouth," Aunt Tillie warned Thistle. "Someone should research a spell on helping you shut it."

Thistle regarded Aunt Tillie coolly. They had been in something of a cold war for the past few weeks (well, years really). Thistle had been getting bolder and bolder in her disagreements with Aunt Tillie, who had been getting more and more creative with the curses she cast on Thistle as retribution. The problem was, depending on the day, Aunt Tillie's curses weren't always relegated to Thistle alone. Clove and I were often collateral damage in their ongoing fight.

"Why don't you tell us what's going on?" I interjected quickly. I didn't want to go a week without being able to talk. Again. Aunt Tillie had stolen our voices for a week when we were teenagers because she thought we were gossiping about her. We had actually been gossiping about the fact that Twila was sneaking around with the gardener, but that didn't matter to Aunt Tillie.

"Your mothers are trying to kill me," Aunt Tillie said dramatically.

"They should try harder," Thistle grumbled.

"How are they trying to kill you?" I ignored Thistle, while hoping Aunt Tillie hadn't heard her. She was getting old. She missed a lot of things – or at least pretended she did.

"They took away my room."

"Your bedroom? Why? Because you're sleeping in this chair now?"

"We did not take away her bedroom," my mom said with a horrified look. "We would not take that away from her. We took away her wine room."

Uh-oh. Aunt Tillie's wine room was actually a closet in the basement where she illegally brewed some of the strongest wine in the county. Chief Terry looked the other way – even though he knew what she was doing – because he thought she wasn't selling it. That wasn't exactly true, though. Aunt Tillie had a thriving side business selling the wine. She just didn't make it public knowledge.

"Why did you take away her wine room?"

"We have to get a new furnace," my mom explained. "That's the only place it will fit."

"Can't you just move the wine room?" Thistle asked.

"We offered to build her a new shed in the spring, but she doesn't want that," Marnie explained.

"You want to make an old lady walk that dangerous path to a shed?" Aunt Tillie only called herself old when it benefitted her. When anyone else called her old, it was wise to duck and cover in anticipation of the explosion that would surely follow. For someone that resembled a wizened hobbit, she had a fiery temper.

"Isn't there another room she can have?" Clove asked.

"Why don't you just use the kitchen?" Thistle interjected.

"My recipe is secret," Aunt Tillie sniffed. "You just want me to use the kitchen because you want to steal my recipe."

"We're family," Marnie reminded her. "It's not stealing when it's family."

"You may share my genes, but you don't share my wine recipe," Aunt Tillie countered. "If you want to make wine, make up your own recipe."

"Maybe I will," Marnie said.

"Good. Do it. It won't be as good as my wine, though."

Thistle cocked her head to the side as she regarded Aunt Tillie's words. "That actually sounds like a good idea," Thistle said. "I'll help Aunt Marnie. I've always wanted to learn how to make wine. I bet it will be even better than Aunt Tillie's recipe."

Aunt Tillie narrowed her eyes in Thistle's direction. "I would expect as much from you."

"What's that supposed to mean?" Thistle asked, a challenge flashing in her determined eyes.

"You know what it means," Aunt Tillie sniffed. "But go ahead. Make your wine. We'll see who makes the better wine."

"Does that mean you're willing to give up your wine room?" My mom asked Aunt Tillie hopefully.

"I said no."

"Grow up and use another room," Thistle muttered.

Aunt Tillie glared in her direction. "Someone obviously needs another reminder of exactly who the matriarch in this family is."

Thistle visibly blanched. "That's not what I meant ... ."

"Oh, it's too late now."

"What are you going to do?" Thistle asked angrily.

"I'm just an old lady," Aunt Tillie said. "I have no idea what you're talking about."

Crap. We were all going to pay for this one. I just knew it.

TWO

*A*unt Tillie managed to sit through a pouty breakfast, although I caught her casting thoughtful – and decidedly evil – glances in Thistle's direction throughout the meal. Even though there were only a few guests at the inn, we all knew better than causing a scene in front of paying customers. That had been ingrained into us at a young age. You never made a scene in front of the guests. It wasn't a rule that always stuck, but it was a rule that had stiff retribution if you broke it.

After breakfast, Clove, Thistle and I moved to the front foyer to leave but Marnie stilled us. "By the way, we called you here for a reason."

I had forgotten that there was something they wanted to talk to us about before the Aunt Tillie drama took over – as it so often did. "Oh, yeah, what did you want to tell us?"

"It's not a big deal, but we've hired a handyman to do some stuff around the inn," Marnie said. "His name is Trevor. He's a nice boy. Very nice looking, too." Marnie looked at Clove knowingly.

"I don't want to be set up," Clove said quickly.

"It's not a set-up," Marnie corrected her. "He's an employee. He just happens to be a very nice and handsome employee."

Thistle and I rolled our eyes at each other. This had disaster written all over it. Clove was a hopeless romantic that always second-guessed her decisions. Marnie was a hopeless meddler that always pushed her own agenda. One of them would end up disappointed in this scenario – maybe both of them.

"Why are you telling us about the handyman?" Thistle broke in to save Clove.

"We're sending him down to the guesthouse to put in some new insulation," Marnie said. "I just wanted to make sure you guys wouldn't be taken by surprise when he showed up. And maybe that you would change your clothes," she added to Clove pointedly. "Maybe that nice pink sweater I got you for your birthday. It brings out your eyes."

"What's his name?" I asked.

"Um, Trevor Murray," Marnie said.

"Well, we'll be nice to him," I started to move toward the door again, but I was stopped when Marnie's hand shot out and grabbed my elbow to hold me back. "What?"

"He's for Clove," she whispered. "Not for you."

"Thanks for the update," I said irritably. "As you might well remember, I've sworn off men."

"I'm just making sure," Marnie warned.

"Why aren't you warning Thistle?"

"Because she's with Marcus," Marnie said. "You're the sad and needy one right now."

Well, that was a low blow. Apt, but low. My most recent love interest had walked (more like ran) away when Aunt Tillie had brought a storm down – literally – on a gun-wielding maniac down by the Hollow Creek. He had asked for answers that I wasn't ready to give and I had let him walk away. I was still wondering if it was a good decision.

"I am not sad and needy," I scoffed. What? I had only watched *The Notebook* once (okay, maybe twice) since Landon had walked away from me. Okay, I admit it; I've watched it like ten times. It's a great movie. Oh, leave me alone. The point is, I'm not sad and needy.

"What's going on?" Thistle asked suspiciously.

"Nothing," Marnie was suddenly studying her manicure as if it was the most interesting thing in the world.

"She was warning me that Trevor is for Clove and not for my needy ass," I said grimly.

"Bay wouldn't steal Clove's guy," Thistle said dismissively. "That's kind of a low thing to say."

Marnie looked horrified by Thistle's statement. "I wasn't inferring anything."

"I really think menopause has made you mean," Thistle said. "Hurting Bay's feelings like that is just a terrible thing for an aunt to do."

With those words, Thistle linked her arm through mine and flounced out the front door. Once we were outside, I turned to her. "I don't think she was trying to be mean."

"I know," Thistle waved off my concerns. "I just like messing with them. There's not a lot to do in the winter here and I have to get my fun somewhere. Especially since Aunt Tillie is being such a pill."

"You should be careful. She's got revenge on her mind."

"I'm not scared of her."

I gave Thistle a knowing look.

"I'm not scared of her," she repeated.

I knew that wasn't the truth. We were all terrified of Aunt Tillie.

BY THE TIME we got back to the guesthouse, Thistle had worked herself up into righteous frenzy – and a good and proper snit.

"I'm not scared of her," she said, throwing herself on the couch haphazardly. "You guys give her more power than she should have. If we all stood up to her she would back down. She's a bully. That's what bullies do."

"You're a bully, too," Clove reminded Thistle.

"I'm not a bully," she argued. "Bay is the bully."

"Hey! How did I get involved in this?"

"You're the oldest," Thistle pointed out. "Being a bully was your birthright."

"I am not a bully," I argued. "If any of us is a bully, you definitely fit the bill."

"How do you figure?"

"You're the stubborn one that digs your heels in," I said.

"She's got a point," Clove said.

"It's not bullying when you're a walking doormat," Thistle said pointedly.

"I'm not a walking doormat!" Clove's voice raised an octave when she said the words. She looked to me for confirmation.

I shrugged. "If any of us is a doormat, that would easily be you."

"I am not a doormat," Clove crossed her arms over her chest huffily.

"You're the middle child," Thistle said sagely. "You have Jan Brady syndrome. You're the people pleaser always looking for attention between Bay the bully and me the ... ."

"Baby," I supplied helpfully.

"I am not a baby!"

"If any of us is a baby, that would be you," Clove said snottily.

"You're both dead to me," Thistle muttered.

I decided to change the subject. "So, what are you guys doing today?"

"Just inventory at the store," Clove said. "There aren't a lot of people around. We're going to decrease our hours this winter. We might as well take advantage of it. We're too busy the rest of the year to take any time off."

"That's a good idea," I said.

"I am not a baby," Thistle said again. "And Bay is a bully. She's just like Aunt Tillie."

My mouth dropped open in surprise. "That's the meanest thing you've ever said to me."

"It's the truth. When you don't get your way, you bully Clove until she agrees with you. That's exactly what Aunt Tillie would do."

"You do the exact same thing," I argued.

"I'm serious," Thistle said suddenly, sitting up straight in her chair. "I want us all to band together against Aunt Tillie."

"That's okay," I said dismissively. "I like the ability to talk."

"She's the reason we don't have fathers," Thistle said.

The statement surprised me. This was obviously something Thistle had been stewing about for some time.

"We have fathers," I corrected her. "We just never see them." I didn't add that a healthy fear of Aunt Tillie could easily be a contributing reason why we rarely saw them.

"My dad sent me a card for Halloween," Clove said brightly.

The truth was, none of us had a definitive fatherly influence. All of our mothers had been married at one time. Actually, they had all been married around the same time. They had all married local boys and moved into small houses around Hemlock Cove – leaving Aunt Tillie and our grandmother alone in the big house. When our grandmother had died a few years later, Aunt Tillie had been left alone. Once alone, Aunt Tillie had nothing better to do than meddle – and that meddling often took the form of poking our fathers with a magical spear (or her forked tongue) until they cried for mercy.

One by one, each marriage had crumbled. Twila's went south first. My Uncle Teddy had been a kind man – from what I could remember – but he had also had some form of OCD. He needed things to be neat and orderly. Twila would be considered scattered on her best day. The marriage never really had a chance.

After the divorce, Uncle Teddy had moved to the Detroit area, and his visits with Thistle had steadily diminished throughout the years. Now they had a phone relationship – and by that I mean they talked on the phone every couple of months. He never came up to visit her – and since Thistle owned a business she didn't go down state to visit him either.

Aunt Marnie's marriage was the next to go. My Uncle Warren was a loser from the beginning, if you listened to my Aunt Tillie, that is. He was a local construction worker that had whistled at Aunt Marnie when she was crossing the street one day. They were married two months later.

The marriage wasn't exactly what I would call happy. Uncle

Warren was a patient man, but Marnie was a master at trying the patience of men. And women. And small animals, quite frankly. I don't remember a lot about the time they spent together, but what I do remember was fraught with some really loud fights.

When they divorced, Uncle Warren stayed in the area for a few years – seeing Clove on alternating weekends. He left the state for Minnesota when she was four. He still sent regular cards and gifts, but he didn't visit very often. He had remarried two more times – and divorced two more times – since his marriage to Marnie imploded.

And my father? He had a Type A personality that rivaled my mother's Type A personality. They just weren't a good fit. He had moved down state to the Grand Rapids area after the divorce.

We talked to each other on the phone every couple of weeks and met each other for neutral visitations – meaning far away from the Winchester witches – every couple of months.

Basically, the Winchester women are hard to live with – and Aunt Tillie was practically impossible. Ironically, she was the only Winchester woman – to my knowledge, at least – that had kept a husband until he died. By all accounts, my great-uncle, Calvin, had been some sort of saint. Apparently he had been the only person that could ever exert any control over Aunt Tillie – and that was, reportedly, a pretty limited control. It was more like he doted on her and she let him.

"You can't say that Aunt Tillie didn't have something to do with the divorces," Thistle said.

"I think Aunt Tillie is a pain in the ass to deal with, but I think all those marriages would have imploded on their own," I answered.

"My dad sent me a card for Halloween," Clove repeated.

"Yeah, we heard you the first time," Thistle said angrily.

"Don't be mean to her," I said. "That's something a bully would do."

Thistle reached over and pinched me. Hard.

"Ouch! What was that for?"

"I'm a bully. I don't need a reason."

Thankfully, things didn't have a chance to decay much further. We were interrupted from what was sure to be a righteous hair-pulling fight by the knock at the front door.

"It's probably the handyman," Clove said finally.

"Well, he was sent here for you," I said. "You should probably get the door."

"Oh, right," Clove jumped to her feet. Realizing we had tricked her into answering the door, she swung back on us. "I really am the doormat."

Clove's self-realization didn't last long. Once the door swung open her attention was entirely taken over by the hunk – no, I can't think of a better word – on the other side of the door.

Trevor Murray was six feet of well-muscled perfection. He had dark brown hair, deep blue eyes and just enough stubble to make him sexy and not disheveled. One look at his narrow hips – and the denim that snugly fit his muscular rear end – and I knew that Clove was actually happy with one of her mother's set-ups.

"I'm Trevor Murray," the man at the door introduced himself. I could tell he felt uncomfortable with the silence that had encompassed the room when the door opened.

"I'm Clove Winchester," Clove introduced herself coyly.

"Nice to meet you."

Thistle and I waited expectantly, but Clove didn't acknowledge our presence in the room. "I'm Bay and this is Thistle."

Clove shot me a dirty look and I took an involuntary step back.

"And we're going to work," Thistle supplied quickly, grabbing my arm. "I'll ride with Bay. Why don't you show Trevor around and come to work whenever you feel like it?"

Clove shot a shy smile at Trevor. "It's not a big place, but I'll show you were the attic entrances are."

"That's great," Trevor said, smiling down at her. Oh, man, he had dimples. Clove was a goner. "This is a great place."

"Oh, yeah, we've done a lot with it since we moved in," Clove said, ignoring Thistle and I. "I did most of the decorating."

"We'll just go," Thistle laughed, slipping out the door behind Trevor.

Once we got out to the car, I turned to her. "How long until she realizes we're gone?"

"Let's just say I doubt I'll see her at the store today."

THREE

I dropped Thistle off at Hypnotic, the magic store she co-owned with Clove on Main Street, and then headed toward The Whistler's office. Since the paper was only a weekly, there were only a handful of full-time employees. Basically there was me, the editor, a paginator that worked nights, an advertising representative and the owner, Brian Kelly.

Brian Kelly's grandfather, William, had actually hired me when I returned to Hemlock Cove from Detroit a few years ago. When he passed away a few months back, William had given the newspaper to his grandson with the stipulation that he keep me on as editor.

Brian Kelly wasn't a bad guy. He was a narcissistic guy. He was a fake guy. He was an obnoxiously flirty guy. He just wasn't a bad guy. He kept sniffing around looking for an in with me – even though I had made it pretty clear that he wasn't my type. That was annoying, but I felt it was pretty harmless – for now, at least.

When I got to my office, I sat down at my desk and started going through the weekly budget. If there was a lack of news in Hemlock Cove on a normal week, then the winter months were decidedly skimpy. I frowned when I realized that this week's top story was the remodel of Mrs. Gunderson's bakery.

"He's up to something."

I looked up to see the source of the voice, and was not surprised to find Edith – The Whistler's resident ghost. Edith had died almost fifty years before. She had taken a nosedive into her evening dinner – one I suspected was poisoned – and she'd been haunting the halls of The Whistler ever since.

Oh, yeah, I can see ghosts. That's kind of my witchy super power – if you want to call it that. Sometimes it is a helpful gift. Other times it is a big pain – like when I was a kid and people thought I was walking around talking to myself. My mom always lied to people that asked and said I had an imaginary friend – which made the town think I was even weirder than I actually was.

"Who's up to something?" I asked wearily, turning my attention back to my laptop. Edith was always coming up with some sort of nefarious conspiracy. Last week she had been convinced that Mrs. Little, the local pewter unicorn peddler, was really selling cocaine. In reality, she had just spilled baby powder on her bathroom floor. As a ghost, Edith had access to anywhere in Hemlock Cove she wanted to go. She usually stayed close to the paper, but when she was bored she made a few excursions into town. Since she had died so long ago, though, she didn't know many people in town anymore. Unfortunately, Aunt Tillie was one of them. And, since the two of them had not gotten along in life, Edith was now taking great joy in haunting Aunt Tillie in death.

Aunt Tillie wasn't taking it well. You can imagine, I'm sure.

"Brian," Edith hissed. "He's up to something."

"What do you think he's up to? You don't think he's a spy again, do you?"

A few days ago, after catching a rerun of *Alias* on the newspaper's small television, Edith had been convinced Brian was working for a covert terrorist organization bent on building a dirty bomb right here in Hemlock Cove. It had taken me two hours to talk her off that metaphorical cliff.

"No, I realized that setting off a dirty bomb in Hemlock Cove doesn't make a lot of sense," Edith said. "You were right on that front. That doesn't mean he's not evil, though."

"What does William think?"

"I haven't seen William in weeks. I think he moved on."

That was news to me. Last time I had seen William, he had been walking through the downtown with the son he had never claimed in his life. They were getting to know each other in death. Maybe they had moved on together.

"That's why you're so keyed up lately," I said, realization dawning on me. "You're bored without anyone to hang around with."

"I am not bored … and he is up to something."

"You're going to have to be more specific," I said. The truth is, since Edith is a ghost, she can haunt me whenever she wants. Sometimes it's just easier to listen to her than to try and get rid of her.

"He's been having secret phone calls," Edith said.

"With who?"

"I don't know; I can't follow the phone line through to the other end."

"You tried?" Explaining technology to Edith had proved to be an impossible feat.

"Once. It doesn't work. There's nothing to follow. It's like magic."

I didn't have the heart to tell her that technology wasn't magic. Now talking to a ghost? That was magic. "So, what was he saying?"

"He was saying that he would make sure you didn't find out about the meeting."

Well, that was interesting. "What meeting?"

"I don't know," Edith shrugged.

"But he specifically said to make sure that I didn't find out?"

"He said, and I quote, 'Bay doesn't know anything. I told you I would keep it a secret. I'm a businessman. I know how important this is.'"

"And you have no idea who he was talking to?" My distrust of Brian Kelly was rearing its ugly head again. Last month I had thought he was a suspect in the death of his own grandfather. As it turned out, I was wrong, but I was still suspicious of his motivations at times –

even if I was constantly reminding myself that I had no proof he was up to no good.

"I told you that I didn't," Edith said irritably. "I just know that he's had a few phone calls where he mentions secret meetings somewhere on the outskirts of town."

Hmmm. "Next time, why don't you follow him when he leaves the office?" I suggested.

Edith cocked her head as she considered my request. "Okay, maybe I will. That might be fun."

"Then report back to me and tell me who he is meeting with."

"I'm not your slave," Edith reminded me.

"I know that."

"If I occasionally help you, it's because I'm loyal and you've been nice to me," Edith continued. Plus, I was one of the few people in town that could see her, so she didn't have a lot of choice in whom she was going to interact with. I didn't say that out loud, though. "I'm not your employee," she reminded me.

"Fine, don't follow him then," I said. "I just thought you might want to get those investigative reporter juices flowing again." In truth, Edith had been the local Ann Landers – giving out pithy advice to housewives and teenagers. The way she told it, though, she was Hemlock Cove's version of Walter Cronkite. I was just baiting her, quite frankly. I had no doubt she would take the bait. She always did.

"No, I want to follow him," Edith said hastily. "I just think you should ask me nicely."

"Please follow Brian and find out what he's up to, Edith," I said, never looking up from my laptop.

"It would be my pleasure," Edith said.

When I glanced back up, she was gone. I could only hope she was on the job. I really did want to know what Brian was up to.

After double-checking the budget, I reread the lead story one more time and then emailed it off to the paginator. With the threat of a blizzard looming later in the week, I figured it would be wise to try to get the paper locked early this week.

I was shaken out of my menial task when my cellphone rang from inside the pocket of my coat. I rummaged around for it quickly, recognizing Chief Terry's phone number on the caller ID when I pulled it out.

"What's up, Chief? You missed homemade cinnamon rolls this morning, by the way. They were awesome."

Chief Terry was a longtime family friend and he was a visitor for meals at the inn several times a week. The truth is, Chief Terry was the subject of an ongoing competition between my mother and her sisters. They were all convinced they were going to be the one to land him. For his part, he seemed to bask in the attention. I wasn't actually sure what would happen if one of my family members actually managed to nab him. I had a feeling it wouldn't be pretty. I think he knew that, too.

"I didn't call about food," Chief Terry said gruffly. His voice sounded far away, like he was outside and near the water.

"What's going on?" Chief Terry may be the head of Hemlock Cove's small police department, but he was also my best source.

"I think I just found something that could change your weekly edition," he said. "Are you still looking for something to bump the Gunderson remodel off the front page?"

Was this a trick question? "Why, what do you have?"

"We're hauling in an abandoned boat that was found out in the channel a few minutes ago," he said. "If you hurry, you should be able to get some decent photos."

"Where is it?"

"It's being tugged in now," he said. "It will be here in a few minutes."

"Where are you?"

"Down on the docks."

"I'll be there in a few minutes," I said excitedly. "What kind of boat is it?"

"A big one," Chief Terry said. "That's all I know right now."

"I'm on my way."

"You don't have any of those cinnamon rolls with you, by any chance?" He asked hopefully.

"No, but I saw they had all the fixings out to make pumpkin pie tonight," I said slyly.

"I'll be waiting for you," Chief Terry said.

I disconnected and grabbed my gear excitedly. An abandoned boat was definitely a better story than the Gunderson remodel. My week was looking up.

FOUR

*H*emlock Cove, despite being a small town, has a lot of great aspects. The fact that it has mile-long beach access to Lake Michigan is just one of them. When I got out to the parking lot, I debated about driving to the docks but I quickly thought better of it. It would actually take me longer to drive there than it would to walk if I cut through the Wellington's livery property – which I had every intention of doing.

When I got to the livery, I saw that Marcus was working in the barn. I waved at him as I walked through the building. "Hey, Marcus."

"Hey, Bay. What's going on? Nothing's wrong, I hope."

Marcus was exactly what you would expect to see when you imagine a farm hand. He is handsome, with his overgrown blond hair and bright and sparkling eyes. He is always dressed in denim and flannel and – since he has been seeing Thistle for the past few weeks – I know that he is all lean muscle and bronzed skin under his clothes. Let's just say I accidentally walked in on them naked once – or maybe twice.

"No, nothing is wrong," I said hurriedly. "I'm just cutting through your property to get to the docks."

"What's going on at the docks?" Marcus furrowed his brow.

"They're towing in an abandoned boat," I said dismissively. "I'm just covering it for the paper."

"That's big news for Hemlock Cove," Marcus chuckled. "Well, at least when we don't have a murderer running around."

I laughed at Marcus' feeble joke, but suddenly I wasn't feeling as excited about the abandoned boat. A sudden wave of dread washed over me, but I shrugged it off. This was my job, after all, and just because a boat had been abandoned in the channel that didn't mean that dead bodies would follow. I hoped.

It took me about five minutes to get to the docks. When I turned the corner that led to the lake access, I was surprised to see that there was a handful of cars parked at the end of the dock. One of them was Chief Terry's cruiser, and another I recognized as belonging to one of his officers. I didn't recognize the other two vehicles.

Chief Terry was standing at the end of the dock waiting for me.

"Is it here yet?" I asked.

"No, it's about five minutes out."

"What do we know?"

"Right now? Just that a sixty-foot cabin cruiser was found in the channel by the marine patrol," Chief Terry said. "When they couldn't get anyone to answer them, they boarded the boat and found it was deserted."

"That sounds pretty ominous," I said. "I'm not an expert on boats, but I would think that there had to be a pretty good reason to abandon a sixty-foot cabin cruiser. They're pretty expensive, aren't they?"

"Let's just say you and I are never going to be able to afford one," Chief Terry said easily.

I noticed that he was looking anywhere but directly at me. Something was up. "Were there any signs of foul play?"

"I don't know," Chief Terry said. He finally glanced at me and then blew out a frustrated sigh. "I'm not technically in charge of the investigation."

"What do you mean?" A hard knot had started to form in the pit of my stomach. It was like I knew the answer, before he even uttered the words.

"The feds are here," he said warily.

Crap.

"They're very interested in the boat," Chief Terry continued. "And they're not telling me why."

I swallowed hard. "Why would the feds be interested in an abandoned boat?" That wasn't actually the question I wanted to ask, but I couldn't find the words to ask that question just yet.

"That's a pretty good question," Chief Terry nodded. His kind eyes met mine as I looked up warily. He knew what was bothering me. "Landon is in charge of the investigation."

There it was: The words I hadn't wanted to hear. Landon Michaels was not only here, but he was in a position of power. Landon and I had met several months ago when he was undercover with a group of local drug dealers. He had saved my family from a particularly unpleasant demise. Then, several weeks ago, we had crossed paths again when a local businessman was murdered in town. Landon and I had been circling each other like two teenagers in heat for several weeks, but when Aunt Tillie caused a lightning storm to come down in the middle of the woods – and a killer had disappeared into thin air – Landon had taken a step back. A really big one. He had asked me for the truth, but I was too scared to tell it to him. I hadn't seen or heard from him since.

When Chief Terry saw the sudden sorrow wash over my face, he put his hand on my shoulder in an effort to comfort me. "He's an ass. You don't have to talk to him. I'll give you all the information. If you want to leave, I'll understand. I'll come to the paper when I know more."

"Why did you call me here?" I said finally. "Especially if you knew he was here." I wasn't really angry with Chief Terry; I was just looking for any excuse to be mad at someone.

"They showed up right after I got off the phone with you," he said apologetically. "I was going to call you back and tell you not to come but … I didn't know if that was the right thing to do. I was sitting here trying to decide what was the right thing to do when I saw you walking this way."

"You did the right thing," I said suddenly. "I don't care about Landon Michaels. I'm a professional. He's a professional. We can have a professional working relationship." I almost totally believed that.

Chief Terry regarded me doubtfully. "Are you sure?"

"Of course I'm sure," I said defiantly.

The bravado I had been feeling – or at least projecting – immediately fled me when I glanced up and saw Landon walking toward Chief Terry and me. Even from a hundred feet away he was an imposing sight. Shoulder-length black hair – which he refused to cut in case he needed to go undercover again – piercing blue eyes, broad shoulders, narrow hips and a set of dimples that could turn me into a puddle of goo in thirty seconds flat. He was walking toward us with a purpose. When he saw Chief Terry wasn't alone, though, his pace slowed.

I clenched my jaw grimly. The confrontation I hoped would never happen was about to happen. I mentally cursed myself for being in such a hurry to get to the inn this morning. I had let my hair air dry into a series of uneven waves – which were poking out from underneath my knit hat – and I had put on the bare minimum of makeup before I left this morning.

What? I'm not shallow. I just would rather verbally crush him when I looked my very best.

Landon paused when he was a few feet away from the two of us. He turned to Chief Terry first. "The boat is almost here. I thought you would want to be the first one on it."

Landon wasn't an idiot – even though I had been calling him exactly that for the past month. The feds may have had more power, but he knew it was always a good idea to keep the locals happy and not tread all over them.

Chief Terry turned to me, at a loss. I could tell he didn't want to leave me alone with Landon, but he didn't know how to voice those concerns without making me look like a whiny mess. I squeezed his arm reassuringly. "Tell me when I can come take some pictures," I said.

Chief Terry nodded and stepped around Landon. He stopped long enough to give him a warning look. He didn't speak any words, but his message was clear: Make her cry and I'll make you cry.

When Chief Terry was gone, Landon turned to me warily. "How are things?"

"Fine," I said breezily. "Couldn't be better."

"How are Thistle and Clove?"

"They're good," I said. "Thistle is still out to get Aunt Tillie and Clove stayed home to drool over the new handyman."

"And your mom and aunts?"

I couldn't help but smile internally. He was going to run out of relatives soon. "They're good. They made homemade cinnamon rolls this morning."

"And your Aunt Tillie? Is she still causing trouble?"

"If by trouble, you mean is she sleeping in the kitchen in an ancient recliner so my mom and aunts can't throw it out, then yes, she's causing trouble," I said vacantly. "She's more worried about them stealing her wine room than anything else right now."

"Her wine room?" Landon looked confused.

"It's basically a closet in the basement where she brews that wine you drank the night in the clearing," I said. I immediately wished I hadn't brought up the night in the clearing. Landon had interrupted us doing one of our witchy séances. He hadn't seen anything, but he had known we were up to something.

Landon didn't seem bothered by the reference. "Yeah, that's some strong stuff," he laughed. "I'm guessing she doesn't have a license to make that."

"Chief Terry lets her slide as long as she doesn't sell it," I replied.

"And does she adhere to her end of that bargain?"

No. "Of course."

"I think you're lying," Landon laughed. He paused when he realized the weight of his words. He had thought I was lying when I told him I had no idea what had happened down at the Hollow Creek either. He had been right. "I didn't mean … ."

"It's fine," I waved off his concerns. "I am lying. She probably does sell a few bottles of it here and there. In fact, she's about to embark on a winemaking contest with Marnie and Thistle. I'm hoping that keeps her busy and out of everyone's business for the next week or so."

"Do you think that will actually happen?" Landon looked relieved that I hadn't been offended by the lying comment.

"Probably not. I can always hope, though."

We lapsed into an uncomfortable silence after that. Landon looked like he wanted to say something, but I couldn't be sure. "I'm glad I ran into you," he said finally. "I've been wanting to talk to you."

"You have my phone number," I reminded him irritably. "Although I can't imagine what you would want to talk about. I've told you everything I know about what happened at the Hollow Creek."

Landon gritted his teeth. "I know that's not true," he said carefully. "I also know you obviously have a reason for keeping it secret."

I shifted my gaze. "I don't know what you mean."

"Bay," Landon sighed. "I know something happened out there. I know that your Aunt Tillie did ... something."

"And what do you think she did?" I asked shrilly.

"What do I think she did? I think she brought a storm down and vaporized a man."

Holy crap, there it was. In the days following the incident at the Hollow Creek, Landon's rational mind had refused to believe what he had seen with his own eyes. He had insisted that the suspect must have run into the woods when we were all distracted by the lightning strike. Now he obviously thought differently.

"I don't know anything … , " I started and then stopped. I didn't want to keep lying to him. I couldn't tell him the truth, though. Instead, I just shrugged helplessly.

"I know you're protecting your family," Landon said, glancing around to make sure someone wasn't listening. "I also know that you're not ready to trust me. Yet."

I pursed my lips to ward off the words I wanted to say. The truth was, part of me wanted to tell him he was crazy and run home to my mommy. The other part of me wanted to admit the truth and see how he took it. Instead, I did nothing.

"You're not going to say anything," Landon pressed.

"I don't know what to say," I admitted.

Landon looked frustrated, but determined. "Why don't we continue this conversation over dinner tonight?"

My throat was suddenly dry. "I don't know," I said hesitantly.

"Too soon?" Landon looked amused. "Or perhaps you want to see what Clove and Thistle think about it?"

Well, that was insulting. Like I couldn't make my own decisions or something. Sure, it was true, but it was still insulting.

"How about I give you a call instead?" he offered.

"I guess that would be okay," I said grudgingly.

Landon smiled in relief. It was his full smile, dimples and all. "Good."

I glanced up when I heard footsteps on the dock. Chief Terry was returning. He didn't look happy. "Everything alright here?"

"It's fine," I said hurriedly.

Landon looked at Chief Terry questioningly. "What did you find?"

"Blood."

"Blood?" I asked in surprise.

"On the deck of the boat. There's blood."

"How much blood?" Landon asked.

"Enough to call the coast guard out for an aerial search," Chief Terry said.

Crap. Maybe an abandoned boat in the channel did mean a couple more dead bodies were about to turn up after all.

FIVE

I stayed at the docks long enough to get pictures of the crime scene crews working on the deck of the boat – *The Merry Minnow* -- and then made a quiet escape. When I got back to the parking lot, I glanced back in the direction of the boat to see if I could get one final glance of Landon. I blushed furiously when I realized he was standing on the bow watching me leave. I raised my hand and waved at him goofily. I felt stupid as I was doing it. When Landon waved back, I couldn't help but let a little rush of pleasure course through me. Yeah, I was a goner. No matter what Thistle and Clove said, I knew I was going to go on that proffered dinner date.

Instead of returning to The Whistler, I made my way to Hypnotic instead. I wanted to touch base with Clove and Thistle – although I had my doubts that the former would actually make it into work today. I cursed myself for my co-dependence, but I knew I would seek their advice regardless. Landon had practically broken my heart when he left, I wasn't sure that it was a wise idea to let him back in. I wanted to know what they thought, though.

Main Street was practically deserted as I made my way toward Hypnotic. I expected to find only Thistle inside of the magic store, but I heard raised voices the minute I walked through the door.

"I don't have a crush on him." Clove looked up from behind the counter when she heard the wind chimes above the front door of the store jangle. "Will you tell her I don't have a crush on Trevor?"

I sighed as I threw myself down on the couch in the middle of the store, searching the room for a sign of Thistle. I found her dusting shelves on the far side of the store, grinning wickedly in Clove's direction.

"She doesn't have a crush on Trevor," I offered lamely.

"Oh, please," Thistle scoffed. "You know she has a crush on him. You saw it the minute she opened the door. We talked about it the whole way into town."

"You talked about me behind my back?" Clove practically screeched.

"Of course we did," Thistle said. "You were our main topic of conversation – even though you obviously forgot we were even in the room the minute you saw him. Not that I blame you."

Clove shot me a dirty look. "How could you?" She's so dramatic sometimes.

"Oh, please," I sighed. "Of course we talk about you behind your back. We also talk about our moms behind their backs. And Aunt Tillie, too. We all talk about each other. Lying about it is pointless."

"We were talking about Bay twenty minutes ago," Thistle said pointedly to Clove.

"What were you saying?" I asked suspiciously.

"Nothing," Clove said hurriedly. "We weren't talking about you."

"She's lying," Thistle said. "We were both wondering how long it would be before you got over Landon."

I bristled at the statement. "What do you mean?"

"I mean that you've spent the last six weeks moping about and it's starting to get annoying," Thistle said truthfully. "If I have to watch *The Notebook* one more time I'm going to burn the DVD."

"That's terrible," Clove hissed. "Why did you tell her that?"

"Because it's the truth, and she needs to hear it," Thistle responded airily.

"I have not been moping about Landon," I said indignantly.

"What would you call it?"

"I haven't been thinking about him at all," I lied.

"You are such a liar," Thistle teased. She sobered after a second, though. "I'm only joking. You should take as much time as you need to get over him. I know you liked him."

I was about to explode and tell her that I didn't like Landon when my mind drifted to the image of him waving from the boat. Who was I kidding? "It's funny that you bring up Landon ... ," I started.

"Why?" Clove asked curiously. I think she was just glad that my arrival had derailed Thistle's Trevor interrogation.

"I just saw him," I said, in what I hoped was a neutral tone.

Clove's mouth dropped open and Thistle dropped the book she had been dusting back on the shelf – in what I was sure was not its proper placement. They were both beside me on the couch in seconds.

"Where?"

"How did he look?"

I told them about the call from Chief Terry and the abandoned boat that was towed into the dock. When I got to my conversation with Landon, Thistle and Clove were totally entranced.

"So, what did he say?"

"He said he thought that Aunt Tillie brought down a lightning bolt and vaporized his suspect," I said nervously.

"Well, she did," Thistle said thoughtfully. "I thought he was denying that happened. That's a big step forward."

"The last time I saw him he was," I said.

"He's had some time to think about it," Thistle said sagely. "He knows what he saw. He just didn't want to believe it. After some time, though, he realizes there's no other explanation."

"You don't seem upset by this little tidbit of information," I said.

"Why would we be?" Clove looked confused.

"Because that's our big family secret," I said simply.

"It's not that big of a secret," Thistle reminded me. "Everyone in town thinks we're off."

"Not everyone," I protested.

"Bay," Clove started gently. "You've always been the one to fight what we are. You even ran away to Detroit to get away from it. I thought when you came back you would realize that you can't hide from it, but you still try to and I don't understand why."

I was flabbergasted by her comment. "I don't try to hide from it."

"Yes, you do," Thistle agreed. "We've never said anything about it because we thought you would grow out of it. You're still scared of our birthright, though."

"I don't see you telling Marcus," I challenged her.

"He knows," Thistle shrugged simply.

"How?" I was floored by her admission.

"What do you mean how? Everyone in this town knows. You can't tell me you haven't heard the whispers? That you haven't felt the stares on your back? That you haven't known in your heart that they all know?" Thistle was trying to gauge my reaction.

"I know they know," I said finally. "It's just that no one admits that they know."

"That's their problem," Thistle said dismissively. "I don't care who knows."

"You don't care who knows? What if they found out that Aunt Tillie charcoaled a guy at the Hollow Creek?"

"You don't think they're already gossiping about that? I mean, they don't know exactly what she did, but they do know that she did something."

"Mrs. Little asked me if Aunt Tillie used a voodoo doll to dismember him," Clove said.

"Mrs. Gunderson asked me if Aunt Tillie shot fire out of her eyes and burned him alive," Thistle added.

I bit my lower lip as I considered what they were telling me. I didn't tell him that Brian Kelly had asked me if Aunt Tillie boiled him in a cauldron and used him as a secret ingredient in her wine. "Still, those are just rumors," I said. "They don't actually know anything about us."

"I think you'd be surprised," Thistle said. "Callie White once came in and asked us if we carried love potions. When we said we didn't, she told us we should consider it because that would make us rich."

"Callie White is an idiot," I grumbled.

"You're just saying that because you found her making out with your high school boyfriend under the bleachers at homecoming," Thistle chided. "That's not the point, though. I'm just saying that everyone knows about us, no matter how much you want to pretend otherwise."

"Landon is different, though," I said finally. "He's an outsider. He hasn't heard all the rumors. He doesn't think we're evil."

Clove patted my hand reassuringly. "He knows we're not evil, Bay. He also knows he's drawn to you and he can't figure out why. He knows there's something special about you. That's why he's back. He doesn't want to let you go and he's willing to give you the time to come to him with the truth."

"Do you think?" Part of me hoped that was the truth and part of me was terrified at the prospect.

"Of course," Thistle laughed. "Aunt Tillie knows, too. When he left, she told me he would be back. And she was right. God help us, that crazy old bat was right."

Clove looked around nervously. We were all convinced that Aunt Tillie could hear us talking about her – even when she was miles away. "Bay, the thing you have to ask yourself is if you are ready to tell Landon the truth?"

"I don't have to tell him right away," I said irritably.

"No, you don't have to tell him right away," Thistle conceded. "But, eventually, you're going to have to tell him. You can't truly move forward unless you do."

"We don't even know if he'll stick around long enough to find out," I said pragmatically.

Clove and Thistle exchanged knowing looks. "He's going to stick around," Clove said finally.

"He can't make himself stay away," Thistle laughed. "I'm surprised he managed to stay away this long, frankly. He's here for the long haul now, though."

"How do you know that?" I asked suspiciously. "Have you seen something?"

"I'm not the one that sees things," Thistle reminded me. "Sometimes I channel things, but not usually anything to do with your love life. When I channel, it's usually a life or death situation."

I turned to Clove questioningly. "Have you seen something?" She did see things. That's why she was the one who read the tarot cards at the shop. People swore up and down about her abilities, even though Clove only saw half the stuff she predicted. She was just really good at reading people.

"About you and Landon?" Clove asked teasingly. "No, I haven't seen anything. That doesn't mean I don't know."

"Know what?" I asked fearfully.

"That he's the one for you," she said simply.

"That's not what you two were gossiping about earlier," I reminded her.

"We're not omnipotent," Thistle said. "Despite what Aunt Tillie would have us believe. Sometimes, though, you just know. And I know he's the guy for you."

"And it's not just because he's really hot," Clove said earnestly. "It's because he has a good heart and I know he'll always be there when you need him."

"What else could you want?" Thistle asked honestly.

"I don't know," I admitted finally. "I think I'm just … ."

"Afraid," Thistle supplied. "You're afraid of letting him in because you're afraid he'll run again. You have time; take it."

Clove patted my knee affectionately. "He'll be here when you're ready. I promise."

Crap. I hated it when they thought they knew everything. I loathed it, though, when I thought they were right.

SIX

$\mathcal{I}$ was more than a little relieved when my cellphone buzzed in my pocket. When I pulled it out, I wasn't thrilled to see the name Brian Kelly pop up on the caller ID. "Crap," I muttered.

"What's wrong?" Clove asked curiously. "I thought you were getting along with him better?"

"That was before Edith told me that he was having secret conversations with someone behind my back."

"Edith needs more to do with her day," Thistle said. "I think you should suggest a few more visits with Aunt Tillie."

"I'm trying not to piss her off this week," I said. "I'd like to have a clear complexion when I have dinner with Landon."

"So, you've decided to go?" Clove asked with a mischievous twinkle in her eye.

I answered the phone instead of acknowledging her question. "Hey, Brian. What's up?"

"I have a new advertiser at the newspaper," Brian answered. "He's going to be throwing a lot of business our way, but he wants to meet with the editor of the paper first."

"Why?" I knew most of the paper's advertisers. They usually didn't want one-on-one meetings with me.

"I don't know why," Brian said. "I just think you should do it. We could use a good influx of cash."

Despite the dire straits the news industry currently found itself mired in, The Whistler made a solid profit each year. We had a stable advertising business, and tourists bought up as many copies of the paper as possible because they thought it was quaint. They used it as mementos for their photo books and, I imagined, to laugh over with their friends during cocktail hour when they got back to the "big city." Still, I knew that Brian wanted to make as much money as possible. I didn't see the harm in agreeing to his request.

"I'll be there in a few minutes," I said. "I'm at Hypnotic. It won't take me long to get there."

"Good," Brian said and then disconnected.

When I put my phone back in my pocket, Thistle and Clove were watching me expectantly. "He wants me to meet with some new advertiser."

"Who?" Thistle asked. She had never liked or trusted Brian.

"I have no idea," I said honestly.

"Have you heard of any new businesses coming to town?" Thistle turned to Clove.

"No, but that doesn't mean anything," Clove said. She had been nursing a backdoor crush on Brian Kelly since she'd met him. I was hoping that crush would disappear now that Trevor was on the scene. Clove was too good for Brian, quite frankly.

"I'll tell you who it is when I get home tonight," I said, dismissing Thistle's concerns outright. "How bad can it be to meet with an advertiser, right?"

Clove looked me up and down dubiously. "You probably should have straightened your hair this morning. You look like you've spent time in a wind tunnel."

"The air is really dry," I reminded her.

"That doesn't explain your hair."

"Oh, good grief," I huffed. "Go back to talking about me behind my back while I'm gone."

"Don't worry," Thistle winked. "We will. I might even call my mom and get her in on the action."

"Don't you dare! If you tell your mom, she'll tell my mom and Landon will be forced out there for dinner."

"I told you," Thistle said blithely. "Winter bores me. I have to get my entertainment where I can."

"Don't worry," Clove said placatingly. "I won't let her use the phone."

"If you do," I threatened. "I'll tell Aunt Tillie it was your idea for them to use her wine closet for the new furnace."

"That's not true," Clove protested.

"Aunt Tillie doesn't know that," I said as I strutted out of the store.

"I think Bay is catching Marnie's menopause madness," I heard Thistle say before the door shut behind me.

When I got back to The Whistler, I dropped my coat and hat off in my office before heading to Brian's office. Edith was waiting for me when I got there. "Who's in there?" I asked.

"I don't know," she admitted. "He looks familiar, but I just can't place him."

"He doesn't look evil, does he?"

"What does evil look like?" Edith asked.

"Kris Jenner."

"Who?"

"Never mind."

I raised my hand and knocked on Brian's door, waiting for an invitation before I entered. Nothing could have prepared me for who I found inside. The man sitting in the chair, wearing a pressed suit and wringing his hands nervously, was someone I hadn't seen in years. I recognized him, though, from Thistle's photo book and my own weak memories. "Uncle Teddy," I said breathlessly. "What ... why ... what are you doing here?"

"Bay, this is Ted Proctor," Brian started to introduce me.

"I know who he is," I said irritably. "He's Thistle's dad."

"Oh, right," Brian looked properly chastised. "He was worried you wouldn't remember him."

"Thistle has a picture of him up in her bedroom," I said warily.

"She does?" Ted spoke for the first time since I entered the office.

"What is he doing here?" I pointed the question at Brian.

"He's a land developer," Brian said easily. "He's looking at some property in the area for a group of businessmen that want to invest."

I glanced back at Ted. He looked different than I remembered – and yet the same. His dark eyes were deep pools of concern, and his brown hair – which had a little more gray at the temples than I remembered – was still slicked back in the manner he had worn it all those years ago.

"So why do you need to see me?" I asked finally.

"I thought it was best," Ted said. "Brian and I are going to be doing some business together. Instead of hiding from you, I thought it would be best to just announce my presence."

"To me?"

"Yes," Ted looked confused.

"What about to your daughter?" My mind traveled to the conversation that Thistle, Clove and I had had this morning. I had been surprised when Thistle mentioned her dad. Maybe I shouldn't have been. Maybe she knew her dad was in town and she'd been keeping it a secret. Somehow, I doubted that was the case.

"I plan on seeing Thistle," Ted shot Brian a nervous look. "I'm just not sure how to do it."

"Well," I said angrily. "Her store is a couple blocks down the road. She's there right now. I was just with her."

"Still joined at the hip, I see," Ted said, flashing me a bright smile. "The three of you were more like sisters than cousins. Even when you were little."

"Which is the last time you saw me," I reminded him.

"Yes," Ted nodded. "I would recognize you anywhere, though. You look just like your mom."

"I do not."

Ted looked confused. "Yes, you do. You always did. I would imagine Clove still looks like Marnie, too."

Well, that was true. "I wouldn't open with that," I said. None of us wanted to admit we looked like our moms. If that was true, I couldn't help but picture us all still living together and fighting over the same guy in thirty years. I shuddered at the unwanted thought.

Ted laughed, despite himself. "Yeah, I remember how mad Marnie used to get when people told her she looked like Tillie."

That still infuriated her.

"How is your Aunt Tillie?" Ted asked. I think he was just trying to fill the awkward silence.

"She's fine," I said. I didn't miss the fact that Brian had coughed the word "evil" into his hand, though. "She's as ornery as ever."

"I would expect nothing less." I think Ted was trying to charm me. It wasn't going to work, though.

"So, what property are you interested in?" I changed the subject.

"I'm still looking," Ted said, shifting his gaze laterally to Brian, clasping his hands behind his back. I knew he was lying, his body language confirmed it, but I couldn't figure out why. "I just didn't want to keep hiding while I was in town."

"I'm not the one you have to hide from," I reminded him.

"I'm not hiding from Thistle either," he said hurriedly. "I'm just not sure how I should approach her."

"I wasn't actually talking about Thistle either," I said. "I was talking about Aunt Tillie. She's the one you should be afraid of. It's not like you're one of her favorite people. She tortures the people she loves, so what do you think she's going to do to you?"

Ted visibly blanched. I could tell that thought hadn't occurred to him during his meticulous planning. "She can't possibly still be mad?"

"You've met her, when *isn't* she mad? Your timing is great, by the way. She was in a right snit this morning because she's losing her wine closet. Your arrival will just be icing on her ... witchy cake."

Ted swallowed hard; the meaning of my words wasn't lost on him. "What do you suggest?"

"Why should I suggest anything?"

"Because you love Thistle," he said pointedly. "You want to make this as easy on her as possible."

41

That was true. If I could go back in time and not answer my phone when Brian called, I would gladly do it.

"I suggest you go down to Hypnotic and see her now," I said harshly.

Ted didn't look like that was the scenario he had in mind. "I'm going to ask you to do something, Bay, something you're probably not going to like."

"Well, that sounds great," I said sarcastically.

"I need you to let me approach Thistle," he continued. "I don't want you to tell her before I have a chance to."

I opened my mouth to argue and then snapped it shut, mulling the thought over in my mind. I shook my head as I considered it. "I can't lie to her."

"Not lie, just avoid her until I have a chance to talk to her."

"I live with her."

"Well, just don't bring it up," Ted begged.

Crap.

"I can't promise anything," I said bitingly. "You had better handle this – and you'd better handle this today."

Ted pursed his lips, clearly resigned to the situation. "I'll think about it."

"You do that," I said angrily. I swung around on Brian. "How could you keep this from me?"

He held up his hands to ward off my anger. "To be fair, I had no idea you would be this upset about it."

"I'm not upset," I snapped. "I'm ... confused."

"That's understandable," Ted said in his most placating voice.

"I don't understand," Brian said blankly.

"I would expect nothing less," I seethed. Then, for lack of something better to do, I stormed back out of the office. The last thing I wanted to do was continue this conversation. I slammed the door behind me for good effort.

Well, this day had gone to crap pretty quickly.

SEVEN

When I left Brian's office, I felt myself inundated with a nervous energy that I couldn't quite contain. Normally, when I was this keyed up, I would go to Hypnotic to vent. That wasn't really an option in this particular case.

"What's wrong?" Edith was curiously watching me pace my small office.

"You know that guy you didn't recognize in Brian's office?"

Edith nodded, concern etched on her ethereal face.

"It's Thistle's father."

Something clicked in Edith's mind. "Twila's ex-husband. Of course, now I remember."

"How do you know him?"

"I saw them together when they came into the paper to place their wedding announcement," Edith said thoughtfully. "And Thistle's birth announcement. I remember that they seemed so happy. I was a ghost, so they didn't see me. I just remember thinking how grand it was for them to be so young and in love. I wondered what it would be like to be that happy."

"Yeah? Well he happily disappeared from her life, for all intents and purposes, when she was a kid. Now he's slunk back into town and he's asked me not to tell her until he gets a chance to."

"And you don't think you can do that?"

"I can't lie to her."

"Don't lie to her," Edith suggested. "Just don't tell her the truth."

"No, you don't understand," I said angrily. "I really can't lie to her. She always knows. She's going to make me eat a pound of yellow snow if she finds out."

"What are you going to do?" Edith asked, ignoring my yellow snow comment.

"I'm going to go for a walk and clear my mind," I said. "I need you to keep an eye on them and see what they're doing."

I expected Edith to remind me that she wasn't my slave. Instead, she nodded perfunctorily and winked out of my office. I was hoping she had gone to Brian's office to eavesdrop on him and Ted – or maybe haunt them into leaving town. I could live with either option.

"Crap!" I slammed my fist down on my desk.

Once I was out on the street, the frustration that had been welling inside of me didn't dissipate. As an earth witch, the outdoors is supposed to clear my channels and open my mind. Instead, I felt the prospect of lying to Thistle closing in on me like a shrinking coffin.

I had no clear direction as I walked. Before I realized what was happening, I noticed I was in front of the Wellington stables. I stood outside the fence to watch the horses play in the snow for a few minutes, hoping that would calm me. I didn't notice the two figures walking out of the barn, though, until it was too late.

"What are you doing?"

I recognized Thistle's voice before my eyes took in her slight frame. She was still a decent ways away, though, her fingers entwined with Marcus' as she watched me curiously. I couldn't let her get too close to me, I realized. The minute she did, she would know I was hiding something.

I took a step away from the fence uncertainly. "I'm just going to see Chief Terry about the boat," I yelled across the paddock. "The horses distracted me."

"Come help us feed them before you go," Thistle offered. She knew I loved feeding the horses even more than I loved riding them.

"Maybe on my way back," I said, turning to walk down the street and away from the stables. I didn't look back. I didn't have to. I could feel Thistle's suspicious brown eyes boring a hole in my back as I trudged down the street.

I didn't really have anything to talk to Chief Terry about, but the police station was only a block down the road. I knew Thistle was still watching me, so I had no choice but to go inside the building.

Once I entered, I greeted Chief Terry's secretary at the front desk and wandered down the hallway without waiting for her to announce me. I had been doing this long enough to know that Chief Terry would always welcome me.

When I got to his office, I found the door wide open and voices emanating from inside. He wasn't alone. Unfortunately, I recognized the other voice. Landon was there, too.

"There's no need to eavesdrop," Landon said with a small laugh. "We're not talking about anything that you can't hear."

I wandered into the office, offering Chief Terry a wan smile as I slid into the open chair next to Landon. I could feel his eyes on me as I studied my shoes intently.

"What's going on," Landon asked worriedly.

"Nothing," I said blandly. "Why do you think something is wrong?"

"Because you look like someone killed your favorite cousin," Chief Terry answered for him. He looked as concerned as Landon.

"I'm fine," I lied. "I just wanted to see if you found out anything about the boat."

Chief Terry didn't look like he believed me. "We've ran the registration," he said quietly. "It belongs to a Canadian couple out of Vancouver named Byron and Lillian Hobbes."

"What were they doing down here?"

"We don't know. We haven't been able to get that far yet."

"Has anyone reported them missing?"

"We have a call in to the authorities in Canada," Landon said. His eyes never left my drawn face. "We haven't heard back yet."

"Is there any reason to believe that someone would want them dead?"

"All we know is that they were in their late sixties and they bought the boat a little over a year ago," Chief Terry said. "We don't know if they had any enemies. We don't know anything about their financial situation. We don't really know anything except that the boat was empty and that there was blood on the deck."

"We just got the case an hour ago," Landon reminded me.

"I know," I said testily. "I was just checking."

Chief Terry leaned back in his chair and regarded me doubtfully. "I think something else is going on."

"Why do you think that?"

"Because you have that same guilty look on your face that you had when you got caught shoplifting lipstick when you were twelve."

Landon tried to hide his smile. I didn't find the situation amusing.

"I didn't shoplift it," I said. "It fell in my bag." Actually, Thistle had dropped it in there, but I had no intention of dragging her down, too.

"I didn't believe it then and I don't believe that nothing is going on now," Chief Terry said gently.

I looked up at him forlornly. "Brian Kelly called me into his office for a meeting," I started.

"Did he do something to you?" Landon looked incensed. He and Brian had gone toe to toe several times when Landon hadn't liked Brian's interest in me.

"He wasn't alone," I continued. "He had a new advertiser there. The thing is, I know the advertiser."

"Who is it?" Chief Terry looked concerned.

"Ted Proctor." I blurted out the name before I fully considered the ramifications of my actions. I trusted Chief Terry, but my mom and aunts could sweet talk just about anything out of him with just the promise of cookies and homemade pot roast.

"Ted Proctor?" Chief Terry looked confused.

"Who is Ted Proctor?" Landon looked like he was ready to jump into action, although he had no idea why.

Realization dawned on Chief Terry's face. "Teddy Proctor?"

"Yeah," I nodded miserably.

"Thistle's father?"

I nodded again.

"I don't understand," Landon started. "Why is everyone so worked up about Thistle's father coming to town? Is he a bad guy or something?"

"He's not a good guy," I said.

Chief Terry sighed. "He's Twila's ex-husband."

"Is that supposed to mean something to me?"

Chief Terry regarded me warily. "Teddy Proctor left town, abandoning Twila and Thistle when she was still a little girl. As far as I know, he hasn't been back since."

"Abandon is a strong word," I said.

"What would you call it?" Chief Terry asked bleakly.

"He left town and ... yeah, he abandoned them."

"So why are you so upset?" Landon asked curiously.

"He asked me to let him approach Thistle."

"So, that seems like a reasonable request."

I had to remind myself that Landon wasn't being purposely obtuse. "He doesn't want me to tell her that I've seen him."

The fog cleared from Landon's face. "And you don't want to lie to her?"

"I can't lie to her," I admitted. "She always knows."

"Maybe you're just a bad liar," he said pointedly.

"I'm a terrible liar," I said, ignoring the pointed barb. "Especially when it comes to Thistle and Clove. When I was thirteen I broke Thistle's favorite doll and tried to blame it on Clove."

"What did she do?"

"She burned down my tree house."

Landon looked stunned, while Chief Terry chuckled to himself. "I remember that. You were crying like someone had died."

"I loved that tree house," I said.

"I know," Chief Terry said. "Every time you ran away as a kid and your mom would call me all panicked that was the first place I looked."

"And you always found me there," I said. "And you never told them where I was hiding."

"I figured you had your reasons to run away," Chief Terry said fondly.

"I'm guessing that reason usually had something to do with Aunt Tillie," Landon said.

"I can't lie to Thistle," I said.

"Then tell her the truth," Chief Terry said gently.

"Uncle Teddy asked me not to."

"Are you loyal to him or Thistle?"

I met Chief Terry's gaze evenly. "Thistle, of course. That's why I'm so torn, though."

"What do you mean?"

"Thistle brought up her dad this morning," I explained. "She's clearly been thinking about him. I don't want to ruin their reunion by forcing a confrontation before either of them is ready."

"Then I would suggest booking a room at another inn," Chief Terry said honestly. "Because one look at your face and she's going to know something is up."

I knew he was right, even if I didn't want to acknowledge it.

"You can stay with me," Landon said brightly.

I could hear Chief Terry grunt from across the table. "Don't even think about it."

"Excuse me," Landon met Chief Terry's consternation with a flash of his dimples.

"Don't make me beat you, boy," Chief Terry said.

"She's a grown woman," Landon pointed out.

"Not to me," Chief Terry smiled. "To me she'll always be the little girl that bribed me with apple fritters in a tree house."

EIGHT

J excused myself from Chief Terry's office a few minutes later. I still wasn't sure what to do. On one hand, I could try to avoid Thistle – which would undoubtedly end with one of us pulling a clump of the other's hair out of her head. On the other hand, I could tell her I saw her father and that he had been hiding from her – which would undoubtedly end with her trying to scratch his eyes out.

It was a tough choice.

Landon followed me out of Chief Terry's office. He didn't invade my personal space, but he didn't walk away either.

"You probably think I'm a whiny baby," I said finally, glancing out the front window of the police station when we got to the front vestibule.

"No," Landon smiled. "I think that the loyalty you share with your cousins is fairly impressive. It reminds me of me and my brothers."

"You have brothers?" I realized I didn't know very much about him.

"Two," Landon said. "Both younger."

"And where are they?"

"One of them lives in Traverse City," Landon said. "I see him every couple of weeks. We get together for a football game and beers."

I could picture him hanging out with his brother and watching football. It was a nice image.

"And your other brother?"

"He lives in Saginaw," Landon said. "He's a Baptist minister."

Well, that was surprising. "Really?"

"Yeah, every time I see him he tells me I'm going to go to Hell because I'm plagued by impure thoughts."

The statement was pointed, and I could feel myself blush under his sudden scrutiny. "So, what would you do in my situation?"

"I don't know," Landon said honestly. "My mom and dad are still married so I don't know what I would do in your situation. Something tells me, though, you're worried about more than Thistle's reaction to seeing her dad."

"What do you mean?"

"I mean that you're also worried about Twila. And if you're worried about Twila and Thistle, that means the rest of your family will be worried about Twila and Thistle. And if the rest of your family gets worked up, that means that everyone in town should be worried about Twila and Thistle."

I think Landon was going for levity, but his words carried a trace of truth that I couldn't deny.

"Aunt Tillie is a concern," I said carefully. "She didn't like Uncle Teddy when he was married to Twila. She downright hates him now."

"And we don't want her getting mad," Landon said seriously. I could see he was really concerned.

"She wouldn't kill him or anything," I said hurriedly.

"Then what would she do?" Landon asked curiously.

I pictured Ted's face full of boils for a second and then shook my head. "Nothing that would have permanent ramifications."

"I guess that's something to be happy about," Landon said dubiously.

"This is such a mess," I sighed, rubbing the bridge of my nose to ward off the migraine that was threatening to overtake me.

Landon took a careful step toward me and then pulled me toward him, wrapping his strong arms around me to comfort me. I considered pulling away, but it felt so good to be in his protective circle – even if it couldn't last – that I willingly stayed there and rested my head on his shoulder for a minute.

When I finally broke away, I looked up into Landon's clear eyes and saw the comfort I so desperately wanted. I could tell he wanted to kiss me, but one look at the curious secretary at the front desk told him that he didn't want to do it here. I wanted him to kiss me, too, but I didn't exactly want an audience.

"I'll walk you back to the paper," Landon said finally, shooting an irritated look in the secretary's direction.

"That sounds nice," I said with a warm smile. I meant it, too. It did sound nice.

Unfortunately that sentiment didn't last long. When I exited the police station, Landon close on my heels, I found Thistle standing in the middle of the sidewalk with her hands on her hips. She was waiting for me.

I inadvertently pulled back when I saw her, slamming backwards into Landon as I did so. He wrapped an arm around my chest to steady me. "Hey, Thistle," he greeted her with faux enthusiasm.

Thistle ignored Landon's greeting. "Why did you walk away from me when I was talking to you at the stable?"

"I didn't," I said, avoiding Thistle's angry gaze. "I just needed to talk to Chief Terry about the boat."

"It's been like an hour," Thistle said dismissively. "You knew they wouldn't have any real information yet. Plus, The Whistler is a weekly. You don't have to turn your story in for days."

"That doesn't mean that I didn't want to get up-to-date information," I lied smoothly.

"You're full of it," Thistle challenged me. "You're hiding something."

"How's Marcus?" Landon was trying to deflect the conversation. I wanted to kiss him – again – right there.

"He wants to know why Bay is avoiding me," Thistle said, shooting a pointed look in Landon's direction.

"I'm not avoiding you," I lied. "If you must know, I was trying to find a reason to invite Landon to dinner up at the inn tonight." The minute I said the words, I regretted them. The last thing I wanted to do was spend time with Landon – with my mom and aunts hanging around, that is.

If Landon was surprised by the invitation, he hid it well. "I'm looking forward to a home-cooked meal," he said brightly.

Thistle shifted her gaze from my face to Landon's. "That's funny," she said. "Because when you were at Hypnotic, not an hour ago, you said that you didn't want me to tell my mom about you running into Landon because that would mean they would force him into a family dinner."

I could feel Landon shaking with silent laughter behind me. "You really told her that?"

"You're not funny," I muttered. All the warm feelings I had been basking in where he was concerned a few minutes ago were suddenly gone.

Landon returned to the task at hand. "I'm really looking forward to dinner tonight. I think it sounds like fun."

"Really?" Thistle challenged him. "I never realized you were crazy."

"You don't want me to come to dinner?"

"Oh, no, I want you to come to dinner," Thistle said. "In fact, I expect your phone to ring with an invitation from my Aunt Winnie at any moment. I just don't think that was what Bay was doing here."

I frowned at Thistle. "I told you not to tell your mom."

"I didn't," Thistle waved off my concerns. "I told Marnie."

"That's the same thing."

"No, it's not," Thistle said. "My mom and Marnie are different people."

"Barely," I grumbled.

"I'm not letting you change the subject," Thistle plowed on. "I want to know why you're avoiding me."

"I'm not avoiding you," I said, trying to step around Thistle so I could get to the sidewalk that led back to The Whistler. "You're just being paranoid."

Thistle moved in front of me to block my way. "I know when you're lying. You're horrible at it."

"I'm not lying."

"Oh, you're *lying*, I just can't figure out why. You were fine when you were at Hypnotic. You were even excited about Landon being back in town. Then you went to meet the new advertiser at the paper and now you're being all ... weird. Who was at the paper?"

"No one," I lied. "Just some guy."

"What guy?"

"I have to get back to work," I shifted my gaze to Landon. "I'll see you at the inn at seven?"

Landon nodded, although I could tell he was worried. "I'll see you then."

I didn't get a chance to move down the street. The next thing I knew, I was in the snow bank in front of the police station and Thistle was on top of me. She might be slight in frame, but she's powerful in determination.

"Get *off* me," I ordered.

"Not until you tell me what's going on," Thistle argued back. I could feel her pulling my parka back as she started shoveling snow down the back of it.

"That's cold," I said as I tried to shift her off of me.

"It's snow, what did you expect?" Thistle replied.

I could feel the ice trickling down my back, lodging underneath my shirt and even into my pants. "Stop it!" I bucked up angrily, managing to catch Thistle off guard and dump her into the snow next to me. I rolled over on top of her and started shoveling snow onto her furiously. "Why can't you just let it *go?*"

"Why can't you tell me what's going on?" Thistle sputtered, coughing as she tried to spit the snow off her face.

"I'm trying to *protect* you," I said as I shoveled a particularly big mound of snow on top of her.

Thistle rolled over, taking me with her as she did, and I was at the disadvantage again as she started sliding snow down the front of my shirt. I could see Landon still standing on the sidewalk watching us, clearly unsure of how to handle the situation.

"Protect me from what?" Thistle's voice was coming out in ragged breaths.

Landon must have decided this was the time for action, because he swooped in and grabbed Thistle by her tiny waist and hoisted her off of me. "This is ridiculous," he said. "Can't you guys act like grownups?"

Thistle started kicking wildly when she felt the air between us. She landed a vicious blow to Landon's knee, causing him to drop her back into the snow bank next to me. He didn't look even remotely amused now.

"Don't make me shoot you," he threatened.

"Oh, you're not going to shoot me," Thistle scoffed, scooping up a pile of snow and tossing it in his direction.

Landon dodged the pile of snow and fixed Thistle with a pointed glare. "What makes you so sure?"

"Because, if you shoot me, Bay will never sleep with you," Thistle said knowingly.

"Even if I do it to protect her?" Landon didn't look so sure.

"You're not going to shoot her," I grumbled from my spot in the snow.

Thistle smiled at Landon triumphantly. I smashed a pile of snow into her face when she wasn't looking and rolled back on top of her. "It won't be necessary," I gasped. This snow fight was really draining my energy.

"Get off me," Thistle whined. "You weigh a ton."

"I do not," I shot back. "We wear the same size pants."

"In your dreams," Thistle grumbled from beneath me. She couldn't muster the energy to buck me off, though.

"What the hell is going on here?"

I froze when I heard the new voice. Thistle peered around me curiously, her face glazing over in a confused mask when she took in the figure standing on the sidewalk behind us.

"Dad?"

NINE

J don't know what I expected at this moment. The truth is, I was hoping that I wouldn't be there when Ted and Thistle laid eyes on each other again. I glanced at Thistle, worry etching my face. I figured she would be fighting off tears – or fighting off the urge to throttle Ted with her bare hands. Imagine my surprise when her murderous gaze fell on me.

"Is this what you were hiding from me?"

"No," I lied, trying to scramble through the snow to get away from her.

"You're *unbelievable*," she snapped as she rolled to her knees and attempted to follow me.

"I didn't know!"

"You're lying," Thistle panted as she crawled through the snow behind me. "You're lying and you're doing it badly."

I gasped when she managed to not only get a hold of my winter boot, but pull it off as I struggled to get away. I swung around in surprise when I realized that I was missing a shoe and looked back at her angrily. "Give me my shoe."

"Come and get it," Thistle taunted me.

"Girls," Ted began nervously. "I don't think this is how you should be acting in public."

Thistle and I both ignored him. "Give me *my shoe*," I repeated."

"You want your shoe?" Thistle arched her eyebrow suggestively.

Uh-oh.

"Here's your shoe." Thistle launched my black boot back in my direction, but Landon slipped in between us and caught it easily.

"I've had it," he said angrily. "Enough is enough." He kneeled down next to me and slammed my boot back on my foot, grabbing my hand and pulling me to my feet when he was done. "You two are acting like children."

I opened my mouth to argue with him, but I forgot what I was going to say when I saw the snowball make contact with the side of his face. Thistle had tossed it from her spot on the ground.

Landon wiped the snow from his impressive jawline and then turned back to Thistle angrily. "Really?"

I realized what Thistle was doing. She was trying to engage Landon in an argument so she wouldn't have to deal with Ted. I put my hand on Landon's chest to stay him. I didn't want to explain what was going on. I was just kind of hoping he would magically get it.

I reached down and helped Thistle up to her feet. She met my apologetic gaze with her own furious one when she was back on the sidewalk next to me. "I can't *believe* you didn't tell me," she hissed.

"I don't know what you're talking about," I lied again.

Thistle looked like she was ready to toss me into the snow again when Ted quickly took a step toward us. "I asked her not to tell you," he said.

Thistle narrowed her eyes in my direction before turning to her father. "And why would you ask her that?"

"I wanted a chance to approach you on my own terms."

"So you had Brian Kelly call her down to the newspaper? That makes a lot of sense," Thistle shot back sarcastically. "That's really, really creepy."

"I didn't think that far ahead," Ted admitted. "I was really just worried that Bay would stumble on me when I was at the paper one day. I didn't realize you two lived at the inn together."

"We don't live at the inn," Thistle corrected him.

"Bay said you live together," Ted looked confused.

"We live at the guesthouse," Thistle said. "Clove lives there, too."

"That old rundown shack at the edge of the property?" Ted furrowed his brow in concern. For some reason, though, I couldn't help but wonder if the concern was real or not. If he was faking, he was doing a good job.

"It was updated and modernized years ago," Thistle said as she brushed snow from the back of my coat. "It's really nice now."

"I can vouch for that," Landon said after a second.

"And you are?" Ted turned his attention to Landon.

"Landon Michaels," Landon introduced himself easily.

"And how do you know my daughter?" Ted looked Landon up and down suspiciously.

Landon was taken aback. "I . . . ."

"Why do you care?" Thistle interjected. "It's not like you've made me a priority in recent years – or *ever*."

"Thistle, I'm going to be in town for the next few weeks for sure and probably the next few months, as well," Ted said. "I was hoping we could spend some time together."

"Why would I want that?"

Ted looked uncomfortable under Thistle's sudden scrutiny. "I'm your father."

"Since when?"

"There are a lot of things you don't know," Ted tried another tactic. "What I did, it wasn't right," he conceded. "There were mitigating circumstances, though."

"*Mitigating circumstances?*" Thistle's voice was suddenly shrill. "Like *what*? You were trying to broker world peace?"

I started to take a step toward Thistle to comfort her, but Landon caught my arm and pulled me back to him. "This isn't your fight," he said.

"I've done this all wrong," Ted said, shaking his head from side to side ruefully. "Bay warned me."

Thistle slid a glance in my direction. "What did Bay warn you?"

"She said she couldn't lie to you and I should just march down to your store and tell you I was in town."

"You told him that?"

"Of course I did."

"And why didn't you listen?" Thistle turned back to Ted.

"It's complicated, Thistle," he said. "I don't exactly have the best relationship with your mother. And your aunts hate me."

"Don't forget Aunt Tillie," I offered with faux brightness. Landon snickered behind me. "I don't know why you're laughing. You're stuck at dinner tonight and she's not exactly thrilled with *you* right now either."

Thistle choked back a laugh. "You're lucky you still have balls."

"What?" Landon looked a little green.

"Nothing," I said soothingly. "She's joking."

"She doesn't look like she's joking," Landon replied.

"Trust me, if she was going to go after anyone's balls, it would be Ted here."

Ted swallowed hard.

"Which gives me a great idea," I said suddenly.

"No," Thistle shook her head. I hadn't even said what the idea was and she was already vetoing it.

"What's the idea?" Landon asked curiously.

"I said *no*," Thistle repeated.

"Come on," I prodded her. "You know you're kind of interested to see how all of this will play out."

"I know how it will play out," Thistle said. "That old bat is going to go crazy and take whoever tries to get in her way down."

"It's also a way to reintroduce Uncle Teddy to the family in a way that's going to keep you clear of the drama," I suggested. "Well, maybe not clear of, it but safe from it. They'll be mad at him, not you."

Thistle thought about it silently.

"What are they talking about?" Ted asked Landon nervously.

"I think they're talking about you going to dinner," Landon said, a small smile tugging at the corner of his mouth.

Ted started to shake his head vehemently. "Girls, I don't think that's a good idea."

"I thought you wanted to spend some time with Thistle?" I said.

"I do," Ted looked trapped. "I thought that time would be just the two of us, though."

"Well, Thistle is going to be at the inn for dinner tonight," I explained. "I think, since you've been slinking around town and hiding from her for days, that you should probably be the one to make the bigger concession. And that would be dinner at the inn."

Thistle cast a sidelong glance in my direction. She didn't argue with me, which I was relieved to see. I could also tell she knew exactly what I was doing.

"I think it's a good idea," Thistle said finally. "I think that, if you *really* want to take a step forward here, that dinner at the inn is the best way to start."

"Your mom will be there, though," Ted whined.

"You know Aunt Twila doesn't hold a grudge," I interjected quickly.

"Winnie and Marnie will be there, too."

Now they held a grudge. "They probably won't make a scene," I said. "They have guests at the inn. They won't do something in front of them."

While Ted wasn't completely placated, he did seem relieved to know that there were currently guests lodged at the inn.

"One of them is Brian Kelly," I added. "He's been staying at the inn for several weeks until he finds a place that he likes."

"I think he just likes everyone cooking for him and fawning over him," Thistle disagreed irritably.

"He could like that," I acquiesced. "He couldn't possibly like the way Aunt Tillie treats him, though."

"That's true," Thistle nodded her head before turning to glance at her father. "Last week Aunt Tillie told him that if you eat certain mushrooms then your manhood will shrink. She told him that after he ate three bowls of pasta – with mushrooms he couldn't stop raving about."

Ted shifted his gaze between the two of us. "What will your Aunt Tillie say?"

"I'm sure it will be ... colorful," I said finally.

"At least there will be other people there," Thistle said. "Including an FBI agent," she gestured toward Landon.

Ted narrowed his eyes as he regarded Landon this time. "You're with the FBI?"

"Yeah," Landon said. His attention wasn't focused on Ted, though. He was clearly enjoying the tag team Thistle and I were currently engaged in.

"What are you doing here?"

"Huh? Oh, just investigating a boat that was found abandoned in the channel."

"Why would the feds be interested in that?"

Landon turned back to Ted curiously. "We just are. I really can't talk about an open investigation."

"And why would you be having dinner at the inn?" Ted pressed. "Are you staying there while you're in town for the investigation?"

"No," Landon shook his head. "I have a place in Traverse City."

"That's an hour away," Ted pointed out.

"Yeah," Landon agreed. "I'm hoping someone takes pity on me and offers me a spot on their couch."

I could feel the color rush to my cheeks. "I wouldn't press your luck."

"Sorry," Landon laughed. "I thought I would try."

"You're with Bay?" Ted asked the question warily.

"Is that a problem?" Landon asked.

"No," Ted said hurriedly. "I was just clarifying the situation."

That was a weird statement, I thought. Thistle didn't give me a chance to follow up with another question, though. Instead she took a decisive step forward and fixed her father with a harsh look. "So, we'll see you at seven for dinner, right?"

For his part, Ted still looked unconvinced. One look at Thistle's implacable face and the grim set of Landon's jaw, though, and he knew that he couldn't possibly say no. "I'm looking forward to it," he squeaked out. He reached forward and hugged Thistle awkwardly and then moved back down the street.

Once he was gone, Clove entered our line of sight. "Was that who I think it was?"

"If you mean Uncle Teddy, yeah."

"Holy crap!" She looked Thistle and me up and down for a second and then shook her head. "Have you two been having a snow fight?"

Thistle and I exchanged wary glances. "No," she said finally. "We both just slipped and fell into the snow bank."

Clove didn't look like she believed us. She turned to Landon for confirmation of her suspicions. "Are they telling the truth?"

"I didn't see anything," Landon said with a heavy sigh. He turned to me, though, after a second. "Does this mean I'm off the hook for dinner?"

"Oh, no," I said quickly. "If you don't show up, that just means my mom and aunts will hunt you down and you don't want that."

"Besides," Thistle said evenly. "With my dad there, you'll probably slide right under their radar."

Landon's face brightened considerably. "I hadn't considered that."

Clove watched the exchange curiously. "Do you think we should tell everyone that Uncle Teddy is coming to dinner?"

"Absolutely not," Thistle said hurriedly.

"Why?" I asked. "We should probably give them time to freak out before he gets there."

"That also gives them time to poison the food," Thistle said ominously.

She had a point.

"Yeah," Clove blew out a sigh. "We should probably let it be a surprise."

Landon regarded all three of us incredulously. "Are you saying that you're legitimately worried that someone in your family will poison this man if they know ahead of time that he's coming to dinner?"

"Of course not," Thistle scoffed. When Landon looked away, though, she frowned at me worriedly. Neither of us would say it out loud, but that was exactly what we were worried about.

TEN

*I*f a normal family dinner at the inn was enough to spark dread in Thistle, Clove, and me, the prospect of tonight's dinner was enough to cause outright terror. We all met in our small living room a full half hour before we were due up at the inn – something that was practically unheard of – and then perched on the furniture nervously as we waited.

"Do you think we should go early?" Clove asked wistfully, visions of fresh cookies floating through her head.

"No," I shook my head. "They're going to know we're all lying the minute they see us."

"She's right," Thistle said wearily. "We've got guilt written all over our faces. They'll know we've done something wrong."

"I'm hungry," Clove whined.

"You can wait a half hour," I chastised her.

"We should be up there before Landon and Uncle Teddy arrive," Clove tried again. "If they show up before we do, things will actually be worse than if we were there too early."

Thistle cocked her head to the side as she considered Clove's statement. "We're damned if we do and damned if we don't," she said finally.

"Let's just tell them that Clove is pregnant," I suggested. "We'll tell Marnie that sending Trevor over here was a great idea and that will distract them until Uncle Teddy walks in. Once he's there, we'll be off the hook."

Clove looked scandalized. "You'd better not tell them I'm pregnant."

"We wouldn't do that," Thistle said winningly. When Clove wasn't looking, though, she flashed a thumbs-up sign behind her back.

Since our nervous energy was too big for the guesthouse to contain, we finally gave up and headed toward the inn. We decided to walk, since that would take at least seven minutes. If we drove, we would only eat up four minutes of time. Hey, three minutes is three minutes.

When we got to The Overlook, we entered through the back door and found ourselves in the cozy living area that housed our mothers and Aunt Tillie – when she wasn't sleeping in a recliner in the kitchen, that is.

We paused in the empty living room to catch our breath and discard our coats. We were relatively safe – for now – because Aunt Tillie was obviously in the kitchen. If this had been a normal night, and if she hadn't been fixated on protecting her recliner, she would have been in her other cherished chair and watching her favorite show – *Jeopardy* – all the while trying to shush us until we left the room.

"We could just hide in here," Thistle whispered hopefully.

"No way," Clove argued. "I smell fresh bread."

Thistle and I inhaled quickly, our stomachs growling in response to the heavenly smell emanating from the kitchen. "I bet it's still warm," Thistle said finally.

I give up. No one can say no to Marnie's fresh-baked bread. "Let's go," I sighed.

Thistle and I deliberately followed Clove into the kitchen. We were hoping that, since she was the first one through the door, she would warrant the most attention. It worked – at least at first.

"Oh, girls, you're here," my mom said excitedly. "Clove, how are things going with Trevor? How was everyone's day?"

Uh-oh. She was far too chirpy.

"We're here," I said warily. "Why are you so excited?"

"What makes you think we're excited?" my mom asked evasively.

"Because we're not stupid," Thistle replied.

"Of course you're not," Twila patted her daughter's hand absentmindedly. "No one thinks you're stupid. Although, you do look tired. I think it's because your hair is so red. It washes all the color out of your face."

"Your hair is red."

"Yes, but my color enhances," Twila explained evenly. "Your color distracts."

This wasn't the first time that Twila had cast aspersions on Thistle's hair. Thistle usually responded by picking the most obnoxious color she could to retaliate with. I had a feeling the holly green Thistle had contemplated to honor Christmas – before deciding on the Santa red, that is – was going to make a triumphant comeback within the next few days.

Thistle's lips pursed first and then thinned. I could tell she was biting her tongue to keep from acting out. I stomped on her foot to make sure she got the message: This was the last thing we needed.

The gesture wasn't lost on my mom. "What are you guys up to?"

"Us? We're not up to anything." Clove's voice had taken on an unnaturally shrill tone.

"Well, that's convincing," Marnie said wryly.

"What are you guys up to?" Thistle countered.

"Nothing," my mom said innocently, turning back to the pot roast she was dishing up onto serving trays on the counter.

"Why don't I believe you?" I asked.

"Probably because you're naturally suspicious," my mom said evasively. "That's probably why you're always so tense."

I exchanged a wary glance with Thistle. Something was definitely up. I peered around my mom and gazed at Aunt Tillie, who was reclining in her chair and happily watching the spectacle unfolding in front of her.

"What do you know?" I asked her.

"Pretty much everything," Aunt Tillie smiled evilly.

"What do you know about what they're planning?" I narrowed the scope of my question.

Aunt Tillie pinched the bridge of her nose to keep from laughing out loud. That was disheartening. I felt Thistle move in behind me and put her hand on my wrist. "Don't play her game," she said forcefully. "That's what she wants. She gets off on it."

"What did you say?" Aunt Tillie straightened up in her chair and leveled a dark look on Thistle.

"You heard me," Thistle challenged her.

Crap. This wouldn't end well.

"You've been sowing your oats a lot lately," Aunt Tillie said calmly. Too calmly, if you ask me. "I like a witch that thinks for herself."

Thistle narrowed her eyes at Aunt Tillie. I didn't blame her. It was a weird time for a backhanded compliment.

"I also like a witch that respects her elders," Aunt Tillie said ominously.

And there it was. The real Aunt Tillie.

Thistle sighed dramatically. "I do respect my elders. I just like my elders to respect me, too."

"You don't think I respect you?" Aunt Tillie asked.

"Is that a trick question?" Thistle asked.

"That depends on who you ask."

"I'm asking you," Thistle pushed on.

"She's not going to answer you," I said, breaking into the standoff that I knew would continuously loop around if I let it move forward. "She wants to play, and you're letting her do it."

"Do you really think you should be getting involved in this?" Aunt Tillie turned her attention to me.

"I don't want to get involved in this," I said honestly. "I just want to know what my mom and her sisters have planned."

"Oh," Aunt Tillie said brightly. "They just invited Landon to dinner."

"Aunt Tillie," my mom chided. "You promised you wouldn't tell. You were the one that said she was going to freak out, so we shouldn't tell her until right before dinner."

Like mother, like daughters. Whoa, that was a freaky thought.

"I forgot," Aunt Tillie shrugged.

"That's what you guys are keeping secret? The fact that you invited Landon to dinner?"

"It wasn't a secret," my mom lied. "I just hadn't had a chance to tell you yet."

"I already knew that," I scoffed. "I invited him first."

"You did?" My mom looked surprised. "He didn't say that when I called him."

"When did you call him?" I regarded her suspiciously.

"A few hours ago," my mom looked thoughtful. "I wondered why he didn't seem surprised by the invitation."

"It's because he knew that Thistle told Marnie he was in town and that told us an invitation was imminent. We just beat you to the punch."

"Huh, well, see," my mom patted my arm happily. "No harm done. I wondered why you had done your hair and fixed your makeup."

I wasn't sure, but I was fairly confident that was an insult.

"Is dinner ready yet?" Clove changed the subject, sneaking in to grab a fresh slice of bread from the basket that Twila was readying.

"Close," Marnie said. "Go make sure all the guests are in the dining room."

The Overlook had one hard and fast rule: Dinner was served at 7 p.m. sharp. Most of the guests were seated at the table fifteen minutes before the cutoff time. The Winchester cooking gene – which had apparently skipped Clove, Thistle, and me – was well known throughout the entire county. No one wanted to chance missing a meal.

Clove, munching on her slice of bread, peered around the swinging door and then turned back to the room. "There's an older couple sitting at the end of the table. Brian Kelly is sitting next to them. Landon is also sitting on that side of the table and then there's two younger guys sitting on the other side of the table. They look a little uncomfortable."

"Yeah, they just checked in this afternoon," Marnie said. "I think they're names are Sludge and Wreck."

"What?" I raised my eyebrows questioningly. "Who names their kid Sludge?"

"Who names their kid Thistle?"

"Thistle is a lovely name," Twila corrected her daughter.

"Thistle is what you take when you have a hangover," Thistle grumbled.

"Was anyone else out there?" I interrupted what could have turned into a righteous snark-off purposefully.

Clove furrowed her brow. "No."

"No one?"

"Are we expecting someone else?" My mom asked as she continued to arrange her pot roast platter.

Thistle and I exchanged a worried look. It was going to be bad enough when they found out Ted was coming to dinner. If he was late? Everyone get ready to duck and cover.

"There might be someone else coming," Thistle admitted.

"Who?" Marnie asked.

"Oh," Clove said, her eyes widening. "Oh! I forgot."

"How could you forget?" I chastised her.

"I was hungry. I told you. You know when I'm hungry that I get forgetful."

Yeah, that was it.

"Who is coming to dinner?" my mom interjected worriedly.

"Oh, it's probably Trevor," Marnie said. "I invited him."

Well, that would make things really interesting.

"Or Marcus," Twila winked at Thistle knowingly.

"Marcus isn't coming," Thistle said.

"Then who is it?" My mom asked, shifting her gaze between the three of us suspiciously. She didn't trust us. She had years of history on her side to back up that feeling.

I couldn't help but notice that Aunt Tillie, who had been reclining lazily just seconds ago, was now in a sitting position and regarding us with her most serious glare. "I'm not going to like this, am I?"

"I don't know," Thistle said evilly. "Let's find out."

I put my hand on her arm in a warning motion. This had to be done tactfully. "Guess who is in town?"

"I don't want to guess," my mom said irritably. "Why don't you just tell me?"

"It's Uncle Teddy," Clove blurted out.

Thistle and I didn't have a chance to smack the back of her head – even though I could tell that was what we both wanted to do. Suddenly, all the oxygen had been sucked out of the room and Aunt Tillie was on her feet in front of us.

"You invited him to dinner?"

"That depends," I swallowed hard. "How ticked off are you?"

"Pretty ticked," Aunt Tillie grunted.

"Thistle invited him to dinner. Blame her."

Hey, in situations like this, it's every witch for herself.

ELEVEN

etween Aunt Tillie's murderous gaze and Thistle's mutinous glare, I knew it was time for me to escape from the rapidly shrinking kitchen.

"Don't you *dare* leave!"

I ignored Thistle's rather loud request and slipped through the swinging door and into the relative safety of the dining room. Everyone seated at the table looked up at me expectantly when I cleared the threshold.

"Where's the food?" One of the young guys at the end of the table asked worriedly. I looked him up and down, trying hard to suppress the mad laughter that was threatening to bubble up. He was your typical hipster, with denim jeans that were two sizes too big and some rock and roll T-shirt from a band I had never heard of. He was also wearing his knit hat at the table – something that would infuriate Aunt Tillie on a normal day. He might get away with it today, if he was lucky.

"It will be out in a second," I said with a smile.

I walked around the table and slid into the open seat next to Landon, sliding a tight smile in his direction. For his part, he looked a little too amused. "What?" I asked nervously, running my fingers over my mouth to make sure there wasn't any food or errant makeup marring my lips.

"You know we can hear everything that goes on in that kitchen, even with the door shut, right?" Landon asked.

I actually hadn't known that.

Brian nodded his agreement from the seat next to Landon. I was actually surprised they had decided to sit in adjacent seats given their general disdain for each other.

"What did you hear?"

"Someone named Uncle Teddy is coming to dinner," the other young guy said.

"And you like the dude with the cool hair," the first guy supplied.

"And your Aunt Tillie is angry," the elderly lady at the other end of the table said helpfully.

"And you threw your cousin with the wild red hair under the bus just to get out of the kitchen," her husband added.

"How do you know she has wild red hair?" I asked curiously.

"Her mother said that it looked awful," the man replied.

"You heard all of that, huh?" I turned to Landon ruefully.

"We did," Landon smirked.

"You should have come and told me that," I whispered under my breath.

"And risk getting Aunt Tillie pissed at *me*? Not a chance."

I didn't blame him. "You haven't seen Ted, have you?"

"No," Landon shook his head. "If I were him, though, I would be eating my dinner as far away from this house as possible."

"Why didn't you flee then?"

"I'm charming," Landon explained. "I figure I'll win them over pretty quickly. That's my super power."

"Not Aunt Tillie."

"We'll see."

Landon was pretty sure of himself. I had to give him that. Thankfully for everyone – I think – the swinging door opened again and the rest of my family trudged into the dining room carrying plates of food.

Once everyone was seated, Thistle looked around nervously. "I guess he's not coming," she said finally.

"Good," Aunt Tillie grumbled.

"Maybe he's just running late," Landon suggested.

"No one asked you," Aunt Tillie shot back, leveling her most terrifying "shut up" look on him.

Landon glared back. "It's good to see you again, Tillie."

"Speak for yourself."

My mom smacked Aunt Tillie on the shoulder petulantly. "Don't be rude."

"Don't tell me what to do."

"This smells good," the woman at the end of the table said, flashing the brightest smile I'd ever seen.

"Of course it's good," Aunt Tillie said. "I cooked it."

"You didn't cook it," Twila said. "I did."

"Well, I baked the bread."

"I baked the bread, Marnie countered.

"Wait until you taste the dessert," Aunt Tillie smiled at the woman.

"I made the dessert," my mom said.

Aunt Tillie cast a dubious gaze in Landon's direction. "You see the way they treat an old lady?"

The next few minutes were filled with the sounds of food hitting plates and thankful murmurs of happy customers as they tasted the meal before them. I was starting to relax and enjoy the meal when I heard someone clear their throat behind me. I didn't have to turn around to see who it was.

"Dad, take a seat," Thistle said nervously.

"I'm sorry I'm late."

"It's fine," Thistle waved off his apology. "We just started."

"It's not fine," Aunt Tillie said. "Dinner starts promptly at seven."

"It's fine," my mom gritted her teeth, placing her hand over Aunt Tillie's to make sure she stayed seated. I couldn't help but notice that Aunt Tillie was gripping her knife a little too tightly. Thankfully, it was just a butter knife. I didn't think she could do too much damage with such a dull weapon.

Ted looked around the table for an open place to sit. The only available spot was between Thistle and one of the slackers. Ted slid into the seat and started doling food out onto his plate immediately. It was a nervous gesture. "This smells great," he said.

I realized that my mom and aunts hadn't said anything yet. They hadn't greeted Ted. They hadn't started him on fire either. That was a good sign. I think. Despite that fact, though, the silence at the table was deafening.

"So," I turned to the slackers. "What are you guys doing in town? Snowboarding?"

"Yeah," one of them nodded. "They have some gnarly hills out this way. How did you know?"

Who says gnarly anymore?

"I think your clothes tipped her off," Aunt Tillie said unhappily. "And the fact that you call yourself Fudge."

"Sludge," the kid corrected her.

"That's *better*?" Aunt Tillie didn't look convinced.

"Well, that sounds fun," I said hurriedly, hoping to cut any more of Aunt Tillie's insults off before they exited her mouth. I turned to the older couple. "What are you guys planning on doing while you're in town?"

"We're antiquing," the man said. "We like antiques."

"In the winter?"

"We're retired," his wife explained. "We can antique all year."

That sounded fairly hellish. "Well, there are lots of great stores around here."

"That's what we've heard," the woman nodded happily.

Back to silence. I glanced over at Landon for help. "Say something."

"I'm good," he said, shoveling another forkful of food into his mouth. "This is really good, by the way."

"Yeah, Twila makes really good pot roast."

"She always did," Ted said from his spot at the table. He didn't raise his head when he spoke, but I couldn't help but admire him for having the guts to not only show up at dinner but actually say something as well.

"Thank you," Twila said warily. She was quiet for another second and then turned to look at Ted with a bright smile. Sure it was a fake smile, but she was trying, at least. "How are you?"

"I'm good," he said.

"That's good," Twila said. "That's really good."

"What are you doing in town?" Aunt Tillie asked.

"I'm helping some business partners find a piece of land for a new venture. They've been looking all over the area and I've been helping."

"What kind of venture?" Thistle asked curiously.

Ted swallowed and took a sip from his glass of water. I couldn't help but wonder if he was buying time so he could think of an answer. I pushed the thought out of my mind, though. That was ridiculous. Why would he do that?

"They're not a hundred percent sure yet," Ted said. "I'm just supposed to find a bunch of empty buildings and show them to them when they come to town in a week or so."

"That doesn't sound like a good way to run a business," Marnie said pointedly.

"I agree," Ted said. "I wouldn't be very successful if I told my clients that, though." He winked, and I flashed back to the charming man I remembered from my childhood.

"And are you? Successful, I mean?" Twila asked.

"I'd like to think so," Ted answered. "I'm not rich or anything, but I do okay."

"Well, how great for you," Aunt Tillie said sarcastically. "Too bad you didn't have the same success with your marriage."

"That was a long time ago," Twila said. "Let's not bring it up now."

"In front of guests," Marnie muttered.

My mom turned to Landon with a big smile – and an obvious agenda. "And how are you, Landon?"

Landon paused with his fork halfway to his mouth. "I'm good," he said warily.

"That's good," my mom said. "I hear you're working on a case here in town."

"I am."

"So you'll be sticking around for a while?"

"I should be," Landon replied. "I don't live that far away anyway."

"You must have been busy then," my mom said.

"It's been a busy couple of months," Landon glanced over at me. I shrugged. I had no idea where she was going with this either.

"That must be why you haven't been able to get a haircut," my mom said.

"I like his hair," Thistle interjected.

"You would," Twila said. "Look at your hair."

"Look who's talking," Thistle grumbled.

"I like it, too," I interjected.

Landon slid me a lazy smile. "You like my hair, huh?"

"It's nice," I said noncommittally. "It's very hair like."

"If you're about to steal something," Aunt Tillie scoffed.

Landon frowned. "I'm not generally the law-breaking type. No arrests on my record. No bootleg DVDs. No illegal wine-making endeavors."

"Just the heart-breaking type," Aunt Tillie countered, ignoring his wine jab.

I sucked in a breath.

Landon put down his knife and fork and turned to Aunt Tillie brazenly. "Is there something you want to ask me?"

Aunt Tillie looked surprised by his boldness. "I haven't decided yet."

"Well, until you do, let's go back to talking about Ted here," Landon said.

Aunt Tillie smiled – the first real smile of the meal. "That's probably a good idea," she said. "You'll be around long enough for me to torture next time. If history holds, Ted will disappear when no one is looking and slink away."

Everyone at the table turned to watch Ted curiously. This was dinner theater at its finest for them, possible disaster for Thistle. They probably didn't realize that, though.

"You look really good, Tillie," Ted said finally. "I'm glad to say that you're holding up so well. You've helped take care of my daughter in my absence, and I'll always be grateful for that."

Well, that was an interesting tactic. It wouldn't work, but he was obviously trying to distract her.

"Someone had to take care of them," Aunt Tillie said obstinately.

"Even if you helped drive him away," Thistle muttered.

Uh-oh.

"What did you say?" Aunt Tillie looked incensed.

"I said, even if you helped drive him away," Thistle repeated.

"Who told you that?" Aunt Tillie turned on Twila as she asked the question. "What did you tell her?"

"I don't know what you're talking about," Twila said uncomfortably, never moving her eyes from her empty plate.

"It's no one's fault but Ted's that he left," Marnie swooped in. "Blaming Aunt Tillie isn't fair."

"Don't you blame her for Warren leaving?" Thistle challenged.

"No, I do not," Marnie said stiffly.

"That's not what the family gossip mill says."

Landon leaned in closer to me. "This is about to get ugly, isn't it?"

"You have no idea."

"Really?" Aunt Tillie raised her eyebrows. "You all sit around and blame me for your husbands leaving?"

My mom shot me an angry glare. "This is your fault," she hissed.

"How?"

"You invited him here."

"It wasn't just me," I protested. "He's Thistle's father. She has a right to spend time with him if she wants to."

"And you thought a family dinner was the best way to reintroduce him?"

"I certainly didn't think it would be this bad."

"I think you just invited him so we wouldn't focus on Landon."

A pang of guilt tugged at my heart. Is that what I had done? Pretty much. "Fine, this is all *my* fault," I threw up my arms in defeat.

"Oh, it's not her fault," Aunt Tillie protested. "It's my fault. Everything that goes wrong around here is *my* fault. That's why you took my wine closet. You're trying to drive me to an early grave."

"You're eighty-five," Thistle shot back. "It's not an early grave when you're eighty-five."

"Well," Aunt Tillie got to her legs shakily. "Maybe I'll just end it all now and make everyone happy. I'll put myself out of my misery and you can all go on your merry way." She turned on her heel and strode angrily into the kitchen, leaving a wake of uncomfortable silence behind her. "You better get me a nice coffin," she screeched from the kitchen when she was out of sight. "No particle board."

"She's not *really* going to kill herself, is she?" Brian looked horrified.

"No," I said, shaking my head vehemently. "She's just going to make us all wish we were dead instead."

"I'm opening the aspirin bottle right now!" Aunt Tillie was still screaming from the kitchen.

Everyone watched the sliding door for a sign of her return – or another instance of Aunt Tillie drama -- but neither happened. "You're sure, right?" Landon looked worried, despite himself.

"Trust me, she's been threatening to off herself since I was a kid," I said. "When I was twelve she actually threatened to throw herself in the river if Thistle, Clove, and I didn't shut up. She said she wanted to drown out the sound of our voices."

"That's a little different, I think," Landon said.

"Not really. She actually walked us down to the river and jumped in. We thought she was dead. "

"Where was she?"

"She swam to the other side of the river and hid in the reeds and watched us freak out."

"That sounds mean."

"It was. Once we had screamed ourselves hoarse she walked us back to the inn. She said it was worth it because we couldn't talk anymore."

"So, you're sure that she's not killing herself in the kitchen?"

"Absolutely."

"I'm taking six aspirin at the same time!" Aunt Tillie yelled from the kitchen again. "With a bottle of wine!"

"She sounds serious," Landon laughed. "Six aspirin couldn't hurt her, right?"

My mom exchanged glances with Marnie and Twila. We were all pretty sure this was just another attention grab. The problem was, Aunt Tillie was known to take things to extremes to prove a point.

"Isn't anyone going to come in here and make sure I'm not dead?" Aunt Tillie's voice echoed from the kitchen.

"See, I *told* you."

Landon chuckled to himself. "Have you guys considered putting her in a home?"

"No home would take her," I said as I watched my mom and aunts reluctantly get to their feet and go into the kitchen. "Her reputation precedes her, believe me."

"You wouldn't really put her in a home, would you?" Landon watched me curiously for a reaction.

"Not today," I said grimly.

"But some other day?"

"Probably not," I blew out a deep sigh. "It's just one of those threats we pull out from time to time."

"So, it's an empty threat."

Mostly.

I glanced down the table and saw that everyone else was just sitting there and watching the door expectantly. I figured they thought more dinner theater would follow.

"So," one of the slackers finally spoke. "What's for dessert?"

"I'm guessing a big slice of humble pie," Clove replied irritably.

"Does that have apples?"

TWELVE

The end of dinner couldn't come fast enough. My mom and aunts managed to wrangle Aunt Tillie back to the table for dessert – but it sounded like a few things had been broken during the melee in the kitchen that followed their "intervention."

When she got back to the table, I couldn't help but notice that Aunt Tillie seemed a little too happy with herself – which wasn't an uncommon emotion coming from her.

When most of the guests had cleared out, Thistle walked her dad to the front door. I couldn't hear what they were saying, but Thistle didn't look happy with the direction of the conversation. Whenever she used big gestures you just knew things were going downhill.

Landon moved up behind me, watching the scene in the next room unfold for a few minutes before speaking. "Are you trying to read lips?"

"No," I scoffed. "Thistle will tell us what happened once she gets back to the house."

"Then what are you doing?"

"Just making sure that everything is okay."

"Are you going to rush in there and beat him up if it looks like things are going south?"

"I haven't decided yet," I said honestly.

Landon chuckled. "I think Thistle is capable of taking care of herself."

"Yeah, maybe I'm here to make sure Uncle Teddy actually leaves the house," I said. "There's snow outside. It's not so easy to hide a body when there's snow."

Landon shook his head. "Come on. I'll walk you home."

"I live on the property," I reminded him.

"It's dark," Landon countered.

"Clove and Thistle will probably walk back with me."

"Thistle looks busy," Landon replied smoothly. "And I don't see Clove."

"She's in the kitchen helping with dishes." Which is where I should probably be.

"So I'm helping you out," Landon smiled. "I'm saving you from another uncomfortable encounter with your Aunt Tillie."

He had a point.

"My coat is in the back," I said, a hint of mischief on my face.

"Where in the back?"

"The living room."

"Where's the living room?" Landon looked confused, glancing around at the various rooms of the inn that were visible.

"Through the kitchen, in the family living quarters," I said sweetly.

Landon remained stoic, but I thought I saw a hint of the color wash from his face. "I guess I just assumed everyone lived in the rooms upstairs. I think I knew better, but for some reason I blocked it out."

"Nope," I smirked. "They have their own area that's only accessible through the kitchen.

"So you're saying that if I want to walk you home I have to see your family again?"

"Yup."

"Let's go," Landon said resolutely.

"You still want to walk me home, even knowing that?"

"I still want to walk you home."

I shook my head but started moving toward the kitchen anyway. Part of me was going to enjoy this.

When I opened the kitchen door, no one looked up from what they were doing. Landon followed me. I could tell he was nervous, but he was also set in the path he had chosen to take this evening. You had to admire him for his determination – especially in the face of the Winchester witches.

"So, this is where all the magic happens."

My mom paused from the pan she was cleaning and looked up. If she was surprised to see Landon in the kitchen, she didn't show it.

"I guess it depends on the kind of magic you're referring to," she said carefully.

Landon suddenly realized what he had initially said. "I was talking about the cooking," he said hurriedly.

"Of course you were," Aunt Tillie said from her recliner.

"It's okay, dear," Twila patted him on the arm as she walked past. "You'll get used to it."

"If he sticks around," Aunt Tillie said pointedly.

Landon fixed Aunt Tillie with an unreadable gaze. "I'm just going to walk Bay home."

"She lives on the property," Marnie pointed out.

"I've noticed," Landon said dryly.

"I think it's nice," my mom said with a knowing smile.

I led Landon through the rest of the kitchen and into the back of the house. He cast a final look over his shoulder before the door swung shut and then turned to me. "Why is your Aunt Tillie getting ready to sleep in a chair in the kitchen?"

"If she doesn't, she's afraid that they'll throw her recliner out because it's old."

"Have they threatened to do that?"

"They had it out at the curb when she found it and dragged it back inside two weeks ago."

"She dragged it back inside herself?"

"Yeah, she's stronger than she looks."

"I guess so."

I shrugged into my parka, letting Landon look around the living room curiously. He had his immovable cop face on. The home was cozy, warm and inviting – at least when Aunt Tillie wasn't around. I wasn't sure what he was looking for, but he seemed to have found something of interest. I watched out of the corner of my eye as he walked up to the wall of photos on the far side of the living room.

I wandered up behind him and looked over his shoulder.

"Some of these are really old," he said.

"Yeah," I said, pointing to a black-and-white photo of a blonde woman that looked suspiciously like my mother. "That's my grandmother."

"And what happened to her?"

"She died when we were all really little," I said.

"Do you remember her?"

"Not really," I replied. "Aunt Tillie was always kind of our grandmother."

"Your evil grandmother?"

"She's not evil," I said. "She's got evil tendencies, but she's not evil."

"You love her," Landon said with a knowing smile.

"Most of the time," I acknowledged.

"You love her all the time, even when she's being difficult."

"She's always being difficult," I said.

"She wouldn't be Aunt Tillie if she wasn't. Right?"

"Pretty much," I agreed.

The walk back to the guesthouse only took a few minutes, but it seemed longer in the brisk night air. When we got there, Landon waited at the door expectantly. "Are you going to invite me in?"

"Not tonight," I said with a laugh.

"But some other night?" Landon asked hopefully.

"I haven't decided yet," I teased.

"Well, maybe I can help you decide." Landon closed the distance between us quickly, grabbing me by the lapels of my coat and pulling me up so my lips were pressed firmly against his.

The kiss was brief, but intense. When I pulled away, our breath mingled together in misty goodness for an added second before disappearing.

"Now you want to let me in," Landon said sagely.

"I do not," I lied.

"It's only a matter of time," Landon smiled, letting go of my coat, and starting to walk back toward the inn.

"Where are you going? You haven't gotten enough of Aunt Tillie?"

"My car is back at the inn," Landon reminded me.

I had forgotten. "Don't wake up Aunt Tillie," I warned him.

"I'll walk around the outside of the inn to the parking lot," Landon laughed. "I like your family, but I've had enough of them for one night."

"I don't blame you."

I watched as Landon turned back down the walk. I saw him step to the side to let Clove and Thistle by him. They were walking awfully fast and I could hear Thistle griping from where I stood.

"Aunt Tillie is unbelievable."

"You sound like a broken record these days," Clove chided her. "Goodnight, Landon," she said when she walked past him.

"Goodnight, Clove," Landon said. "Goodnight, Thistle."

"What's good about it?"

"Night, Bay," Landon said as he continued on his way. I could hear him laughing from the front porch.

"What's wrong?" I turned my attention to Thistle.

"Were you at the same dinner?"

I opened the front door of the guesthouse, letting Clove and Thistle trudge inside before I closed the door behind me. I knew Thistle was just getting wound up.

"It was an unpleasant dinner," I agreed. The walk home had been nice, though. "It's not like Aunt Tillie's attitude was a surprise, though. She's done way worse things."

"Not when my dad was there."

"It's not like your dad didn't know what to expect either," I reminded her.

"I know," Thistle said, blowing out a frustrated sigh. "This is all just such a mess."

"Maybe you should spend some time together away from the family," Clove suggested.

"I don't know if I want that either," Thistle grumbled.

"Maybe you should sleep on it?" I said.

"Maybe," Thistle agreed. "Maybe Aunt Tillie's recliner will swallow her up during the night and one of my problems will be solved."

"You can always hope," I said sagely.

"Tomorrow we start planning our revenge," Thistle said obstinately.

"On Aunt Tillie?" Clove asked squeakily.

"On Aunt Tillie," Thistle agreed grimly.

This wasn't going to end well for any of us.

THIRTEEN

"Get up!"

It took me a second to realize where I was. I was hoping I was still dreaming until a pair of blue jeans hit me in the head. I rolled over and looked toward the door of the bedroom and saw Thistle standing there, hands on hips, glare on face. Did I mention she was in her underwear?

"What's going on?" I glanced at my bedside clock. It was 7 a.m. How could she possibly be having a freak-out before morning coffee?

"None of my pants fit," Thistle seethed.

I propped myself up on my elbows and regarded Thistle irritably. "You woke me up to tell me your pants don't fit? Pick a different pair. I had another fifteen minutes before I had to get up."

"It's not just one pair of my pants that don't fit," Thistle shot back. "It's all of them."

"How is that possible?"

"I'll give you a hint," Thistle said sarcastically. "She's four foot eleven, she's got a mouth like a trucker and a vindictive streak as wide as the Grand Canyon."

Aunt Tillie. *Uh-oh.*

"Well, wait a second," I struggled to get out of bed. "Maybe you gained weight or something?"

Thistle shot me a withering look. "Overnight? I tried on the same pants I was wearing last night and I can't get them buttoned."

"What about Clove? Do her pants fit?"

"I don't know," Thistle said. "She's trying them on now."

I was still half asleep, but Thistle's words were really starting to sink in. *Crap.* I jumped to my feet and slipped into the pants that I had discarded on the floor when I climbed into bed the night before. I was relieved to find that not only did they slide up easily but they buttoned and zipped up easily, as well.

"Mine still fit," I blew out a sigh of relief.

"Well good for you," Thistle's tone was biting. She marched to my closet and pulled a pair of jeans off of a hanger. I watched with grotesque curiosity as she stepped into them and tried to pull them up. Things were going well until they got to her hips and then all forward momentum ceased. There was clearly enough extra fabric to keep going up, and yet the jeans just refused to move.

I slid over to her side and tried to help tug them up. They wouldn't budge, though.

"I'm going to kill that old woman," Thistle grunted out.

I looked up when I saw movement out of the corner of my eye. Clove was standing in the door wearing her own set of jeans. "Mine still fit."

"It's just Thistle," I said.

"Do you think it is Aunt Tillie?"

"Who else?" Thistle barked.

"We can't be sure," Clove wrung her hands frantically. "If you go after her and we're not one-hundred-percent sure then she'll strike back even worse."

"You wouldn't be thinking that if your pants didn't fit," Thistle shot back.

She had a point. "Maybe she did that on purpose?" I suggested after a second.

"What do you mean?" Thistle asked distractedly. She was still trying to tug the jeans up.

"Maybe she went after Thistle and left the two of us alone because she knew we'd be less likely to go after her?"

Thistle narrowed her eyes. "That would be just like her."

"You're not suggesting we go after her, are you?" Clove asked.

"Stop being such a Pollyanna," Thistle grumbled. "We have got to present a united front."

"None of our revenge schemes ever go as planned, though," Clove said. "Every time we try to think of something it backfires and then she just goes on a rampage that we end up regretting."

This was true.

"Then we're going to come up with a really good plan," Thistle said.

"Or, you could just apologize," Clove suggested.

"*Over my dead body,*" Thistle shot back. "Or *yours*, if need be."

Clove visibly blanched. She looked to me for help. "You don't agree with her, do you?"

"I haven't decided yet," I said grimly.

"Well, you better decide," Thistle said, her dark eyes flashing with fire. "Because starting today, Operation Takedown Aunt Tillie is on."

I SHOWERED and got dressed once Thistle and Clove vacated my room. When I exited into the living room, I found the two of them sitting at the kitchen counter drinking coffee. Clove was dressed for work and Thistle had changed into a pair of jogging pants. At least they still fit.

"Are you going to work wearing that?"

"Do I have a choice?" Thistle asked bitterly.

"She can do inventory in the back room," Clove said helpfully. "No one will see her there."

"What's wrong with what I'm wearing?" Thistle asked pitifully.

"Nothing, if you're going to the gym," I said brightly.

"You're dead to me," she grimaced, taking a big swig of coffee.

"That's just coffee, right?"

"I might have put a little something in it to take the edge off," Clove said evasively.

Thistle chugged some more of her coffee, muttering to herself as she did. I couldn't understand her, but I did hear something about Aunt Tillie and getting what she deserved. "Don't let her drive to work."

"I already confiscated the keys," Clove said blandly.

Any further conversation was cut short by a knock at the door. "It's probably Trevor," Clove said, suddenly sitting up straighter. "He didn't finish yesterday and said he would be coming back today."

"You have to drive Thistle to work," I reminded her as I moved toward the door.

"I know," Clove said sarcastically. "I'm not stupid."

"I didn't say you were stupid," I admonished her. "I was just making sure you didn't get distracted by anything handsome and forget what you were supposed to be doing."

I opened the door, expecting to find Trevor, but I found Landon standing there with a box of donuts instead.

"What are you doing here?" I blurted out.

"Bay!" Clove jumped to her feet and ran to the door. "Don't be rude to our guest. Oh, it's *Landon*."

Landon couldn't miss the disappointment in Clove's voice. "Is now a bad time?" He asked.

I opened the door and let him in. "That depends on who you ask."

"I'm asking you."

"What kind of donuts do you have in there?"

"Freshly baked cake donuts with chocolate and sprinkles from the Gunderson bakery," Landon said. "I wasn't sure about the sprinkles, but she said that they were your favorite."

That's what happens when you grow up in a small town. "Thistle doesn't like sprinkles," I said. "And she's the one having a bad morning."

"There are two apple fritters in there, too," Landon said. "Mrs.

Gunderson said they were Thistle's favorite. She said Clove liked the chocolate and sprinkles."

"I do," Clove agreed, digging into the donut box enthusiastically. She handed me a donut – which was still warm – and then took the box over to Thistle. I watched as Thistle grudgingly dug through the box and pulled out an apple fritter. I waited until she had taken a bite before I spoke.

"Are you sure you should be eating the empty calories?"

Clove's mouth dropped open in disapproving surprise. "That was mean."

Thistle rounded on me, never leaving the stool she was sitting on. "I wouldn't start, if I were you."

"What's wrong with Thistle?" Landon asked breaking a piece off of my donut and popping it into his mouth. "These are really good."

"Hey, that's mine!"

"Clove ran away with the rest of them."

"Bring the donuts back," I ordered.

Clove dropped the box on the coffee table between us, bending to whisper in my ear as she did. "Don't push her too far. She's going to explode soon, and we don't want her exploding all over us."

Clove straightened back up when there was another knock at the door. "I'll get it."

"Are you expecting someone else?" Landon asked curiously.

"Clove's boyfriend," I teased.

"Clove has a boyfriend?"

"Don't sound so surprised," Clove shot back. "And no, he's not my boyfriend. He's a handyman that is doing some work here."

Landon turned to me questioningly. "Why is she so excited about a handyman?"

"Wait until you see him," I said, grabbing another donut from the box.

Landon watched Clove curiously as she answered the door. "She's not very good at the flirting thing, is she?"

"Not really," I agreed. "So, what's going on?"

"Can't I just bring you warm donuts in the morning?"

"You don't usually."

"Well, maybe I'm turning over a new leaf?"

"This is a really yummy leaf."

"Would you have let me in without the donuts?" Landon asked curiously.

"Probably not," I said. "Thistle is having a bad morning."

"I noticed," Landon said. He was watching Trevor as he unpacked his tools and chatted with Clove across the room. "What's wrong with her?"

"None of her pants fit."

"I don't understand."

"She woke up this morning and none of her pants fit."

"How does that happen? Has she gained weight?" Landon looked Thistle up and down dubiously.

"No, she hasn't gained weight," I said evasively.

"Then why don't her pants fit?"

"Aunt Tillie," Thistle seethed from her spot at the counter. "That evil old lady has cursed me. Again."

I glanced at Landon to gauge his reaction. I wasn't sure how he would react.

"She cursed you so your pants wouldn't fit? She can do that?"

"She can do more than that," Thistle said grimly. "I'm going to do worse to her in retribution, though."

"Like what?" Landon seemed genuinely curious.

"I haven't decided yet," Thistle said. "The three of us have to put our heads together and come up with something."

"You're going to help her?" Landon turned to me.

"I haven't decided yet."

"Aren't you guys all about family loyalty?"

"Yes," I nodded. "Aunt Tillie can be ... unpleasant, though, when you go after her."

"More unpleasant than making it so your pants don't fit?" Landon actually seemed to be enjoying this.

"When I was in college, she cursed me so I could only make left-hand turns," I admitted. I figured I might as well go for broke. He was taking things relatively well, at this point.

"How does that work?"

"Let's just say it took me a long time to get to class," I said.

Thistle joined me on the couch, reaching inside of the donut box and pulling out another apple fritter. "She once cursed me so that every time I bent over my pants ripped and it sounded like I was farting."

I laughed silently at the memory. "That one was kind of funny."

"Not when you're sixteen," Thistle shot back.

"She once cursed Clove so her eyebrows fell out and she had to draw them on for two months," I interjected.

"Shhh!"

Thistle and I glanced across the room at Clove, who was frantically waving for us to keep our voices down. Thistle shook her head irritably.

"So, what you're saying is that your Aunt Tillie has made a practice of torturing you since you were kids?"

"Pretty much," Thistle said.

"And your moms let her?"

"They're just glad she's not doing it to them anymore," I said.

"She's still doing it to them sometimes," Thistle corrected me. "Last month she cursed Twila so every time she cooked something it burned."

"That's true," I said.

Landon couldn't help himself, he started laughing hysterically. "I thought my family was bad."

Thistle and I exchanged a look and then we joined him. Sometimes, all you can do is laugh. When we all sobered up, I turned to him. "Why did you stop by this morning?"

"To bring you donuts," he said simply.

"And?"

"I just thought you would want to know what we've found out about Byron and Lillian Hobbes."

"Did you find them?"

"No. We actually don't have much. We've talked to their family and they haven't heard from them in almost a week," Landon said evenly.

"That doesn't sound good," Thistle said.

"I agree," Landon said.

"So, what's next?" I asked.

"We'll just have to wait and see," Landon said. "We're continuing the search in the channel, but we have no idea if anyone is actually out there."

"They couldn't still be alive, could they?" Thistle asked.

"That's extremely doubtful," Landon said. "Unless they got on another boat, or something. I would think we would have heard about that, though."

"So, you're assuming they're dead," I supplied.

"That's the overriding theory for now," Landon said carefully.

I glanced up at the clock and realized it was after 8 a.m.. "Crap, I have to get to work."

Looks like I was the one that had gotten distracted by something handsome after all.

FOURTEEN

When I got to the newspaper, I was stuffed from the three – yes, three – donuts I had consumed this morning. I was starting to feel like my own pants were getting a little too tight. I was hoping that was just the donuts and not a delayed curse.

When I got to my office, Edith was pacing – or rather floating -- back and forth in front of my desk.

"He was on the phone again this morning," Edith said.

"With who? My Uncle Teddy?"

"I don't know, but he was acting sketchy," Edith replied.

"Define sketchy."

"He said that an offer had been made and the only thing left was for it to be accepted," Edith whispered.

"Why are you whispering?"

"He's just down the hall."

"He can't hear you, though," I reminded her.

Edith pursed her lips disapprovingly. "Thanks for reminding me."

"I'm sorry, Edith," I blew out a frustrated sigh. "It's been a long morning."

"What's wrong?" Edith asked. She actually looked concerned.

"Aunt Tillie cursed Thistle this morning."

"She swore at her?"

"No, she made it so none of her pants would fit."

Edith narrowed her eyes suspiciously. "She can do that?"

"Yeah. She's done that and a lot worse throughout the years," I said wearily.

"Has she ever done that to people outside of your family?"

That was a pretty good question. "I don't know," I shrugged. "Are you asking for a specific reason?"

"It's just that … ." Edith looked like she was biting her lip. "Back when I first started working for the paper your Uncle Calvin came in one day to buy an ad."

I had no idea where she was going with this.

"Anyway, the next day I woke up and I found that all my shoes were too small," Edith continued. "And not just too small. They really pinched and hurt. When I put my feet in them, it felt like I was step-ping on nails."

"Why would you think that had anything to do with Aunt Tillie?"

"Because she came in after your Uncle Calvin left and accused me of trying to seduce him."

Yep, that would do it. "Were you? Trying to seduce him, I mean?"

"Of course not," Edith looked scandalized, and a little guilty. "I just baked him some cookies. He was always so thin, I didn't think your Aunt Tillie was cooking for him."

That was probably a safe bet. Aunt Tillie had many talents, but cooking wasn't one of them. My grandmother had been the great cook of her generation. My Aunt Tillie would have starved if my mom and aunts weren't good cooks.

"Well, I don't know what to tell you," I said finally. "Just for refer-ence, though, how long was it before your shoes fit again?"

"About a week, why?"

"I'm just wondering how long it's going to be before Thistle can fit into her pants."

After getting settled for the day, I decided to go and have a little talk with Brian Kelly. It wasn't just Edith's tip about the phone call, it was also the fact that I had a feeling that Brian knew more about Ted's business dealings than he was letting on.

Brian's door was open so I walked in without knocking.

"Good morning, Bay." Brian greeted me like he hadn't been a witness to the catastrophic dinner the previous evening.

"Morning," I said shortly.

"How are you doing today?"

"Great."

"That's good," Brian looked up from the file he was nose deep in. "Do you need something?"

As openings went, it wasn't the best, but I wasn't going to let that dissuade me. I sat down in one of the wingback chairs across from the desk and fixed Brian with a hard glare. "I want to know more about your dealings with Ted."

"I've told you everything," Brian said evasively.

"I don't think that's true."

"I don't know what you want me to say. Ted is looking to invest some money in the area, including advertising. It's not like I was going to turn him down."

"You didn't have a problem hiding it from me, though," I pointed out.

"He's a business associate that asked me to keep his private business private," Brian said blithely. "He has that right."

"That's all you're going to say?"

"That's all I'm going to say. I wish you would just let this go. Don't you have an edition you're supposed to be working on? A missing couple? I don't see why this is such a big deal."

"You're right," I said tightly. "I do have some things I should be doing."

What Brian didn't know, though, was that I wasn't giving up on this. When I got back to my office, I was relieved to find that Edith was gone. I could only hope she was out haunting Aunt Tillie in retribution for the Great Shoe Escapade of 1965.

I fired up my laptop and started doing a search of land deeds in the county. I fed Ted's name into the search engine and came up with three different properties. When I pulled up the deeds on the parcels, I found that one was an old farmhouse with about a hundred acres of land attached to it. If the picture of the house was any indication, he was clearly more interested in the land.

The second piece of property had riverfront acreage on the Hollow Creek. Most of the Hollow Creek was encumbered with dense underbrush and trees. It wasn't fit for construction. There were small pockets, though, that were beautiful and flat enough for small buildings. I couldn't be sure, but I thought the parcel Ted had bought was one of those flat areas.

The third property record was the most interesting one. It was the Dragonfly, a dilapidated old inn that had been abandoned almost two decades before. In fact, if I remembered correctly, I thought that a portion of the inn had burned down at one point. The inn was only five minutes out of town. The road that led to it was still unpaved. The original owners had abandoned it after a failed insurance scam – yep, the fire – and the bank had owned it ever since. Now why would Ted want that old inn?

I closed my laptop, but continued to mull over the three pieces of property that Ted had bought in the past six months. They seemed to be quite a hodgepodge. I decisively got to my feet and left the newspaper to head down the street to Hypnotic.

When I got there, I found Clove working at the front desk and Thistle sulking on the couch.

"What's going on?"

"I'm doing the ordering for next week and Thistle is plotting revenge," Clove said, never looking up from the catalogue she was perusing.

"Any good stuff?"

"There are Christmas voodoo dolls? Did you know they made those?"

"Do they look like Santa Claus?"

"Yes. And Mrs. Claus. Actually, the Mrs. Claus one kind of looks like Aunt Tillie."

"Order it," Thistle barked out. "I want to stick pins in something and, she might be old, but I think Aunt Tillie might still be able to put up enough of a fight that I can't do it to her in the flesh."

"So," I sat down on the couch next to Thistle and changed the subject. "I did a little research."

"About how to get back at Aunt Tillie?" Thistle asked hopefully.

"No," I shook my head. "About Uncle Teddy."

Thistle looked surprised. "What kind of research?"

"I pulled up the county's land deeds and found out some interesting stuff about the property he's been buying."

"Like what?" Thistle asked.

I told them about the three pieces of property. When I was done, the room was awash with confused silence.

"Why would you buy property on the Hollow Creek?" Clove asked finally. "It's not like you can put a business out there. A house, maybe, but not a business. I thought he was all about developing businesses."

"Maybe he plans on building a house out there," I shrugged.

"Wouldn't he mention it, if he planned on staying, I mean," Thistle said. I couldn't help but note the hopeful – and concerned – tone of her voice.

"Maybe it's for someone else," I said. "That's not actually the piece of property that piqued my interest, though."

"The inn?" Clove asked knowingly.

"That thing is a wreck and half burned out," I nodded.

"What do you think he's doing?'

"I don't know," I admitted. "I'm curious, though."

"Maybe some company wants to buy the inn and renovate it. This area has a pretty solid tourist population."

"That's a possibility," I agreed.

"But you don't think so?" Clove queried.

"I think I want to check it out," I said finally.

"The inn?"

"Yeah."

"What do you think we'll find out there?" Thistle asked.

We? "You're coming with me?'

"Of course," Thistle said. "When have you ever known me to miss out on an adventure?"

Good point.

"Plus," she added evilly. "Maybe we can dump Aunt Tillie's body out there when I kill her."

"Maybe," I agreed. "It's at least worth a look."

Thistle looked thrilled with the idea, while Clove looked anything but. "We're going at night, aren't we?"

"Of course," Thistle said. "You can't sneak around during the day."

"Why don't we just ask him if we can see it?" Clove hated sneaking around, especially when it was in the dark.

"That would defeat the whole purpose," Thistle scoffed.

"You think the best way to make up with your dad is to sneak around and spy on him?" Clove tried a different tactic.

"I'm not sure I want to make up with him," Thistle admitted. "I do want to know what's going on out at that inn, though."

"You just want something to do," Clove grumbled.

"Oh, come on, it will fun."

"It's never fun," Clove exploded. "We always do this and it always gets us into trouble. Don't you guys remember looking for gold at the Hollow Creek and finding a body? Or how about sneaking around a cornfield and finding ghosts? That was fun."

"This time will be different," Thistle promised.

"It will be," I agreed.

Clove sighed and walked behind the curtain that led to the storage room at the back of the store. "It better be."

Once she was gone, Thistle turned to me. "It's not going to be any different."

"Nope."

FIFTEEN

*W*hen you're sneaking around at night and doing something nefarious, you have to dress the part. Usually that means all black. When there is snow on the ground, though, you have to be a little more creative. Half white and half black is generally the best mix for winter. It's like natural camouflage. Or cotton camouflage. You know what I mean.

When we were all in the living room and ready to leave, Thistle couldn't stop herself from laughing out loud. "We look like idiots."

I couldn't help but agree with her. We were all wearing black jogging pants and white hoodies. We had several shirts underneath the hoodies for layering, but it was still going to be tough to stay warm.

Clove grabbed a thermos off the counter and started heading for the door. "Let's get this over with. I want to come back here as soon as possible – and you two are going to buy me pizza for making me do this."

"We're not making you do this. Stay here if you want."

"No way," Clove shook her head. "You guys will be telling stories about this for a week and I don't want to miss out."

"See, then we're not making you go. What's in the thermos, by the way?" Thistle asked.

"Hot chocolate."

"No liquor, right?"

"No liquor," Clove acknowledged. "One of us has to drive. I'm saving the liquor for when we get back. I bought stuff to make chocolate martinis."

I loved chocolate martinis. Now I didn't want to go on our little adventure. A roaring fire, chocolate martinis and pizza sounded heavenly. Thistle looked like she read my mind. "We're going," she said. "If we hurry, we can be there and back in less than an hour."

I sighed. She was right. This was my idea, after all.

Thistle drove to the Dragonfly, mostly because she had the best night vision but also because her car was black. It wouldn't be as easily seen or recognized as my red Range Rover.

When we got near the property, Thistle killed the lights and pulled off to the side of the road. "There's nowhere to hide the car."

"We'll just tell people it broke down if they ask," I said finally.

"That will work," Thistle agreed.

We all got out of the car and walked the remaining quarter of a mile to the inn. It looked deserted. Of course, it was almost pitch black, but there were no other vehicles in sight and the inn was completely dark.

"We should have brought flashlights," Clove whined. "How are we ever going to see anything?"

"We're witches," Thistle reminded her. "We don't need flashlights."

Thistle opened her hand and whispered a short spell. A ball of light appeared in the palm of her hand and lifted into the air above our heads. Despite how small it was, it let off a decent amount of light. We walked toward the inn, letting the light lead us.

"The front porch doesn't look safe," Clove shifted beside me.

She was right. "Let's walk around toward the back," I suggested.

"We'll leave tracks," Thistle said.

I glanced down at the ground. Now that she mentioned it, we should have been looking for evidence of footsteps in the snow from

99

the beginning. Thistle followed my gaze. "It looks like two different people have been here at least," she said.

"Yeah. Those are big footprints. That means men."

"Or women in big boots," Clove said.

"Maybe." I wasn't so sure about that, though.

I glanced at the front of the Dragonfly curiously. All of the tracks led up to the front porch and it didn't look like anyone had fallen through. I shrugged as I regarded Thistle. "We should keep on the other tracks."

We climbed the steps mostly without incident. Clove slipped on the accumulated ice and grabbed on to Thistle to keep from falling at one point, but no one took any big spills. When we got to the front door, Thistle tried to turn the knob but it was locked.

"Well, we tried," Clove said nervously. "Let's go home."

Thistle rolled her eyes. She moved her hand over the knob for a second and then we heard the unmistakable click of the lock tumbling on the other side. "Did you forget how we used to get into the locked wine closet as teenagers?"

One look at Clove told me she had. "This is officially breaking and entering."

"We didn't break anything," I reminded her.

"Well, it's officially entering without permission."

"You never used to be such a prude," I said. "Remember when we were teenagers and the principal looked down your shirt and we retaliated by toilet papering his yard and starting the toilet paper on fire? That was your idea."

"It was Thistle's idea to start it on fire."

This was true. "Still," I said. "You were gung-ho to go out on that little adventure."

"That was different," Clove argued. "That was in the middle of spring and nowhere near as dangerous."

"How is this dangerous?"

"What if someone finds us out here?"

"Then we'll just say our car broke down and we were looking for a phone," Thistle said.

"We have cell phones."

"The longer you sit here and argue, the longer this is going to take us," I said.

"Fine," Clove said. "Just know that I'm doing this under duress."

"Duly noted."

We let the ball of light lead us into main foyer of the inn. The room was completely empty except for the curtains covering the windows – and they looked new.

"Why would you buy new curtains when there's no back wall to the property?" Thistle asked.

"To hide something," I replied.

"There's nothing in here, though."

"Not in this room," I agreed.

Thistle set her jaw grimly and nodded. We moved further into the dark inn. The room behind the foyer led to the dining room. It was also empty. We all looked at the staircase that led upstairs and wordlessly turned away from it. None of us felt comfortable enough to go upstairs. We would be cut off from any avenue of escape if we did.

Instead, we headed for the room behind the dining room – which we all assumed was the kitchen. When we got there, though, we were understandably confused. "This is the kitchen?"

"I think it used to be."

"There's nothing here."

"What's over there?" I pointed toward a door at the back of the room.

"Probably the larder," Clove said.

"What's a larder?"

"This is an old inn. Larders were for keeping food before refrigerators and stuff," Clove said knowingly. "They probably just used it for storage."

Thistle moved toward the small room, the ball of light moving with her. Clove was right on her heels. She didn't want to be away from the light. "Is there anything in there?"

"No," Thistle said. "But it looks like there was."

"What do you mean?" I peered around the corner and into the

101

small storage closet. There was a layer of dust on the floor that had clearly been disturbed sometime recently.

"It looks like big crates," Clove said finally. "What do you think was in them?"

"How should we know?" Thistle asked irritably. "You've been with us since we got here. Do you think we magically know something that we're not telling you?"

"No need to get snippy."

"I'm not snippy. You're just being dippy," Thistle shot back.

"You're a poet and you didn't know it," I sang out.

"No one needs that," Thistle chastised me.

"There's obviously nothing here," I said finally.

"Not now, at least," Thistle agreed.

We all froze when we heard the sound of a car door slamming somewhere outside. I glanced around the kitchen for someplace to hide. Thistle and Clove were right behind me.

"What do we do?" Clove hissed.

"We can't get trapped in this house," Thistle said.

I knew she was right. Instead of heading back through the house the way we had come I turned toward the door at the back of the kitchen instead. When I looked on the other side, I found what I assumed used to be a laundry room. The back of the room was missing, though. It was clearly the part of the inn that had been destroyed by fire. There was only a tarp keeping the elements from claiming the rest of the house.

Thistle quickly doused her ball of light and we all slipped into the laundry room, being careful to shut the door quietly behind us. I knelt down, pressing myself to the wall on the other side of the kitchen. Thistle and Clove did the same, all of us trying to control the ragged tempo of our own breath.

"Why don't we just leave?" Clove whispered.

Thistle clamped her hand over Clove's mouth to shush her. It was just in time, too, we could hear voices entering the kitchen. There were three distinct ones to differentiate from.

"Are you sure about this?"

I didn't know who was talking, but I could hear grunting as something big slid from behind the counter – the area we hadn't previously looked – and out into the open kitchen. Whoever was inside had flashlights, but I didn't want to risk standing up to look inside in case they caught a glimpse of me through the glass door separating us from them.

"I told you already," the other voice said. "If you want to back out, you have to do it now."

"Do you want to back out?" The third voice asked.

"No. We've been planning this for three years."

"I just want to make sure that we're not in over our heads here," the third voice said.

"We're not. Everything is going just as we planned. This town isn't going to know what hit it."

SIXTEEN

The three men didn't stay in the kitchen very long. They were gone within a few minutes. Clove, Thistle, and I stayed crouched in the laundry room until we were sure they were gone, waiting until we heard the car fire up and then drive away. Once they were gone, I turned to Thistle incredulously.

"I told you something was going on."

"No, I told you."

"I was the one that said it first," I argued.

"I was the one that insisted we come out here," Thistle countered.

"You both told each other," Clove interjected irritably. "Let's get out of here."

Neither Thistle nor I had the energy – or the inclination – to argue with Clove. The arguments could wait until we were safely home.

Once we got back to the car, Clove passed the thermos around and we wordlessly drank from it until we were a few miles away from the Dragonfly. Once we were almost home, Thistle broke the silence.

"I think one of those guys was my dad."

"Are you sure?" Clove asked.

"No," Thistle shook her head. "Maybe I just think it was because I know he's the one that technically bought the property."

"That's possible."

"Or maybe it's him and they were hiding something terrible in that house?"

There was that possibility, too.

"What do you think was in the box?" Clove asked, finally voicing the question that none of us really wanted the answer to.

"I don't know," I said. "Whatever it was, we had a chance to find it and we missed out."

"Do you think it's drugs?"

I shrugged. "I don't know."

"Do you think it was a body?" Clove asked.

"In a crate?" Thistle asked dubiously.

"We don't know it was a crate. We know that it looked like crates were in the larder, but we don't know what was behind the counter because we didn't look," Clove shot back petulantly.

She had a point.

"It was probably a coffin," Clove said excitedly.

"A coffin?" Thistle looked agitated. "I knew we shouldn't have brought you."

"How does thinking it's a coffin equate to you thinking you shouldn't have brought me?" Clove looked hurt.

"Now you're going to give yourself nightmares."

"I am not."

"Are too."

"Am not."

"Are too."

"Bay!" They both yelled my name in unison.

"What?"

"Tell her it wasn't a coffin."

"It wasn't a coffin."

"How do you know?" Clove asked.

"I don't. I just think we would have noticed a coffin. It had to be something small enough to fit behind the counter without being obvious."

"Oh," Clove seemed placated. "That makes sense."

"We still don't know what was in the crate," Thistle pointed out.

"Let's just get home," I sighed.

ONCE WE WERE BACK at the guesthouse, we all stripped down to simple T-shirts to pair with our matching jogging pants.

"Let's order pizza," Clove said. "I'm starving."

"I lost my appetite," Thistle muttered.

"I could eat," I said.

A knock at the front door distracted us all. We exchanged worried looks and no one jumped to their feet to answer the door right away.

"You don't think they followed us, do you?" Clove looked like she was about to pass out.

"We left after them," Thistle said.

"Maybe they were hiding in the woods?"

"How did they hide their car?"

"Maybe only two of them left as a decoy and the other hid in the woods until we left and then they picked him up and they all followed us? Or maybe whatever was in that coffin came to life and followed us?"

Thistle was right, there was no way Clove was going to sleep alone tonight. She'd be crawling into bed with one of us around 2 a.m.

There was another knock on the door.

"One of us has to get it," Thistle said finally.

"I nominate Bay," Clove said hurriedly.

"Why me?"

"You're the oldest."

"You're sleeping with Thistle tonight," I grumbled.

I got to my feet and slowly plodded toward the door. I had images of masked assailants on the other side. I knew it was ridiculous, but that didn't stop my imagination from running wild.

"Who is it?" I asked when I got up close to the door.

"Pizza delivery."

"We didn't order any pizza."

I tried to peer out the side window and see who was standing on the front porch but it was too dark. I flicked on the light, bracing to run as quickly as possible, but I found that the sight of the figure on the front porch was more welcome than I would have liked to admit.

I threw open the door and greeted Landon with a welcome smile. "You brought pizza?"

"Three of them."

"I guess you can come in then."

"Am I always going to have to bring food when I want an invitation beyond the front door?" Landon teased.

"So far."

Landon pulled up short when he saw Thistle and Clove. "Why are you all dressed alike?"

Uh-oh. I most definitely didn't want to tell Landon about our little excursion in the dark. Not only had we broken the law, but Thistle's dad may also (or may not, who knew?) be involved in something underhanded.

"This is how we dress when we want to get comfortable," Thistle said.

Landon handed me the three boxes of pizza and shrugged out of his heavy coat. Clove jumped to her feet and went to the kitchen to get plates and napkins. We were all settling around the coffee table to eat when there was another knock at the front door.

"Get out your gun," Clove hissed at Landon.

"What?"

"Nothing," I waved Clove off. "She's just high strung tonight."

"She's on her period," Thistle said.

"I am not," Clove protested. "That's not even a good lie. We're all on our periods at the same time. You know that."

"That sounds like a fun week," Landon said, clearly uncomfortable with the turn in the conversation.

I opened the front door without looking outside this time. I felt a lot braver knowing Landon was only a few feet away. I found Marcus standing on the front porch with a paper bag in his hands.

"Hey," I greeted him.

Marcus looked surprised when he came in and found Landon sitting with us. "Hey man, I didn't know you were back."

Landon and Marcus knew each other from a few months ago. They hadn't spent a lot of time together, but they had seemed to get along well enough.

"I'm back," Landon agreed. "You hungry? I brought pizza."

"Cool. I'm starved."

Once we were all grouped around the coffee table, the conversation stalled for a few minutes while everyone relished the hot pizza. Once we were done, though, Marcus handed the bag he had brought to Thistle.

"What's this?"

"I thought you wanted chocolate martinis?'

"Clove bought the ingredients earlier," Thistle explained.

"Well," Marcus shrugged. "Now you have more."

Thistle and Clove set about making the martinis while Marcus and Landon got comfortable in adjacent chairs. They were soon discussing the state of the Detroit Pistons and how they thought the Lions were going to do next season – both topics of conversation that pretty much bored me to tears.

Once Thistle pressed a fresh martini in my hand, though, I didn't care what they were talking about. I just let the chocolate goodness wash over me while Clove built a fire.

Once everyone was settled, the topic of conversation turned to the missing Canadian couple.

"We don't know anything more than we knew this morning," Landon said.

"A boat like that doesn't just get abandoned," Marcus said.

"No, it doesn't."

Marcus turned to Thistle. "So, how did your little adventure turn out tonight?"

"What adventure?" Landon turned to me curiously.

"No adventure," I said evasively. "We were just doing some recon on Operation Make Aunt Tillie pay."

"That's not what we're calling it," Clove scoffed. I could tell she was already half drunk.

"And how is that little endeavor going?" Landon asked.

"We're going to order Mrs. Claus voodoo dolls so Thistle can stick pins in them," I said.

"Will that work?" Landon looked interested.

"No," I shook my head. "It's more like psychological warfare."

"I don't think Tillie is going to fall for that," Landon said.

"She doesn't need to fall for it," Thistle said. "We just need to distract her for a little while."

"And that will distract her?" Marcus asked.

"You'd be surprised at how easily distracted she is," I said.

"Why don't you just steal the recliner and get rid of it?" Landon asked.

I raised my eyebrows as I looked to Thistle. That wasn't a bad idea. She smacked her head in realization. "We can hold the recliner ransom."

"How are we going to get it out of there?" Clove asked.

"You're going to distract her while Marcus and Landon carry out the chair," I said.

"How did we get involved in this?" Landon asked.

"It was your idea," I reminded him.

"Yeah, but that doesn't mean I want her going after me," he said.

"The chair is too heavy for Thistle and me to carry. We need you. You can get it out of there in a few minutes."

"We won't tell her you were involved," Thistle promised.

Marcus still looked doubtful. "I don't want to get on her bad side. She likes me. She always makes sure I get an extra slice of pie."

"She likes you?" Landon looked impressed.

"I weed her gardens in the summer."

"Which garden?" Landon was suspicious. It was a well-known fact that Twila and Aunt Tillie maintained a small pot garden in the summer. They didn't think anyone knew but, the truth was, everyone in town knew. Even a few high school kids had tried to find it. Instead they found themselves with a poison oak rash in a rather uncomfortable place thanks to a cloaking spell around the infamous pot field. We're not talking dirt weed here.

Marcus looked uncomfortable. "Her vegetable garden."

Landon didn't look like he believed him.

Thistle suddenly burst into a fit of hysterical laughter. "Our family is crazy."

Landon tipped his head back and drained the rest of his martini. "That's putting it mildly. Your family is certifiable. I can't believe some of you – especially your Aunt Tillie – haven't been locked away."

I know I should have been insulted, but the truth hurts sometimes.

SEVENTEEN

"*B*ay!"

It took me a second to get my bearings – and when I did, I found that I wished the blissful darkness that had previously cocooned me was still in place. When the early morning light filtered in and collided with my sleep crusted eyes, followed closely by the drum that was beating inside of my head, I had to fight the urge to scream. That would just hurt more.

"Who is yelling?"

I rolled over when I heard the voice and just about bolted out of my own bed when I saw Landon lying beside me. What the hell?

Last night's events started running through my mind. There had been a cold excursion to a burned-out inn, warm pizza and chocolate martinis. I rubbed my head ruefully. Lots and lots of chocolate martinis.

I slid a sideways glance at Landon. His dark hair was sprawled out on the pillow next to me. Thankfully, he wasn't naked. I quickly glanced under the covers and breathed a sigh of relief. I was still dressed, too.

I felt Landon shift next to me and watch me warily. "Don't worry, I didn't take advantage of you."

"I was just checking," I rasped. Man, I needed some water – and half a bottle of aspirin. A pot of coffee wouldn't hurt either.

"You really thought I would do that?"

"I couldn't remember," I admitted. "I didn't exactly expect to find you here. Not that it's not a nice surprise," I added hurriedly.

"You said I shouldn't leave because it was snowing. You don't remember that?"

"Not really," I replied. "The last thing I really remember was plotting to steal Aunt Tillie's chair."

"You still think that's a good idea?" Landon raised his eyebrow but the effort must have been taxing to him because he immediately raised his hand to his forehead and started rubbing it absentmindedly.

"I don't know," I admitted. "All I can think about right now is a bottle of water and a handful of aspirin."

"Let's throw some dry toast on that, too," Landon said. "We need to eat something and I want something bland enough that my stomach won't rebel."

I couldn't help but laugh – which caused another shooting pain to course through my head. "Your stomach rebel a lot?"

"Only around you, apparently."

I struggled to my feet, lurching forward two steps until I regained my equilibrium. "This is why you don't drink on work nights," I lamented.

"I don't think drinking that much is ever a good idea," Landon muttered.

"That's not what you said the last time Aunt Tillie got her wine out," I reminded him.

"Yeah? Well you didn't see me the next morning. I was thinking the exact same thing then as I am now."

"Then why did you drink last night?"

"I can't remember," Landon groaned. "It seemed like a good idea at the time."

"It always does," I agreed.

I watched as he struggled to get out of bed. He was wearing the same white T-shirt he had worn under his flannel shirt the night before. He had stripped out of his blue jeans, but he was wearing a pair of boxer shorts that actually made me smile. Landon saw me looking at his shorts and rubbed the stubble on his chin ruefully. "This isn't doing much for my street cred, is it?"

"No," I shook my head. "I think you look tough. Even if you are wearing *Teenage Mutant Ninja Turtle* underwear."

"I'd come up with a suitable lie for wearing them if my head didn't hurt so much."

"You can think of one over coffee," I said, moving toward the bedroom door. I paused, though, when my hand hit the doorknob. "Did you hear someone calling my name a few minutes ago?"

"What do you mean?"

"That's what woke me up. Someone was yelling my name."

Landon thought about it. "It was probably just Thistle or Clove. They're probably hung-over, too."

"I know Clove will be."

"Didn't she pass out on the living room floor?"

"Yeah, I seem to remember something like that," I acknowledged. I threw off the feeling of dread that had washed over me when I had reached for the doorknob the first time and instead pushed it open and walked into the living room. I immediately wanted to go back to bed.

"Well, well, well. Isn't this a pretty picture?"

I swallowed hard when I met Thistle's glazed-over gaze on the couch. Marcus was sitting next to her in a random state of undress. On either side of them were my mom and Twila, while Aunt Tillie was sitting in the big chair in the corner.

"What are you doing here?"

"Checking up on you after the storm last night," Aunt Tillie said.

"What storm?" I asked in a wobbly voice.

"We got like a foot of snow or something," Thistle gritted out. She looked like she wanted to murder someone. I was guessing Aunt Tillie was on the top of that list.

"We got six inches of snow," my mom corrected her. "It was mixed with ice, though, so it was more dangerous."

"Huh." I sank into one of the kitchen chairs that were placed around our small dinette set in the little room between the dining room and kitchen. We never used the table. It had essentially become a stopgap for magazines, old copies of The Whistler and random tabloids that we liked to thumb through.

"You don't usually check on us for snow," I said, looking around the room for Clove and Marnie.

"Marnie was convinced that we needed to come down here for some reason. She thought that there might be trouble," Aunt Tillie said.

Aunt Marnie wasn't clairvoyant, but she did have a sense for uncovering trouble. She was always the one that busted us for drinking in a field when we were teenagers. It was beyond annoying.

"We have a phone," I reminded Aunt Tillie.

"That's what I suggested," Aunt Tillie said. "I knew you weren't in any real trouble." Aunt Tillie looked Landon up and down, pausing to stare at his colorful boxer shorts a little longer than necessary. "Not any trouble that you didn't want to be in, that is."

I rolled my eyes at Aunt Tillie. "Nothing happened." I don't know why I felt the need to explain myself. I wasn't a child anymore. Aunt Tillie just brought it out in me sometimes.

"Really? Because it looks like you had an overnight visitor," my mom answered shrilly.

"Who?" I feigned ignorance.

My mom's mouth dropped open in surprise. "Landon."

"So?" I was starting to feel belligerent. My head was really pounding.

"What will people in town think?" My mom looked scandalized. "You don't let gentlemen callers spend the night."

"Who cares? Marcus spends the night here all the time."

Thistle shot me a murderous look.

"He does?" Twila looked down at her daughter with a disapproving frown.

"Thanks for that," Thistle said dryly.

I shrugged. I wasn't exactly at my intellectual best. "Where is Clove?" I changed the subject.

"In the bedroom with Marnie," Aunt Tillie chortled.

"Marnie thinks she needs rehab," Thistle interjected.

"Why?" I found myself looking toward the coffeemaker longingly. Landon followed my gaze and walked over to the countertop contraption and started filling it up wordlessly. He didn't seem too bothered by our morning guests. Of course, he could just be using his cop training to remain calm in a tense situation.

"She thinks we drink too much," Thistle said with a laugh.

"That's why she thinks Clove needs rehab?"

"Well, you're all making unsafe choices," Twila said carefully. "You have strange men staying in the house overnight. You could get the herpes."

"They're not strange men," I grumbled. "Landon is a federal officer and you've known Marcus since he was a little kid. Neither one of them has herpes." At least I didn't think.

"That doesn't mean that it's okay to have a … ." Twila looked around nervously and then lowered her voice. "That doesn't mean it's okay to have an *orgy*."

"Do you even know what an orgy is?" This wasn't the first time she'd been convinced we were having wild sexual parties at the guesthouse.

Aunt Tillie looked at Twila with interest. She wanted to hear the answer, too.

"It's people having sex in the same house," Twila said obstinately.

"No, it's not," I shook my head irritably. "An orgy is when a lot of people get together and have sex with each other. Everyone. Like as a group."

Twila looked confused. "I don't understand what you're saying."

"She's saying that two guys spending the night with their girlfriends is not an orgy." Clove appeared in the doorway of her bedroom. Her face was tired and blotchy and her eyes were mired with an emotion I couldn't quite read. I think it might have been fury.

I wanted to correct her notion that Landon was my boyfriend, but this didn't exactly seem like the appropriate time.

"So, are you going to rehab?" I asked, trying to stifle the mad desire to laugh.

"You're not funny," Clove muttered. She smiled at Landon, though, as he handed her a cup of freshly brewed coffee.

"I don't think having parties like this, at your age, is a very good reflection on us," Marnie said, appearing in the door behind Clove.

"We didn't have a party," Thistle argued. "We had pizza and chocolate martinis. And what age? We're in our twenties; we're not dead."

"Too many chocolate martinis," Marcus whined from his spot next to Thistle. I couldn't help but notice he was clad in only boxer shorts and a T-shirt, too. Clove, Thistle and I were all still dressed exactly alike from our adventure the night before.

"You got that right, brother," Landon agreed, sliding into the chair next to mine and pushing a cup of coffee toward me.

"That's not exactly a raging kegger," I agreed, sipping the coffee gratefully.

"I don't know what that is," my mom said dubiously. "But if that's some sort of drug reference, it's not funny."

"The fact that you're accusing us of having a problem when you're the ones with a pot field is just ridiculous," Thistle barked out.

Twila's face went completely ashen as she looked at Landon guiltily. "She's making that up."

"I've seen the pot field," Landon said dryly. "I saw it when I went looking for you guys out in your little field a few months ago."

Twila looked like she was going to pass out. "It's not mine. It's Aunt Tillie's," she pointed to her aunt nervously.

"I have glaucoma," Aunt Tillie said calmly. "It's medicinal."

"Chief Terry knows about it, too," Landon said. "I don't really care about it, as long as you're not selling it. You're not selling it, are you?"

Aunt Tillie mustered up an outraged glare. "Of course not. How could you think that an old woman would do something like that?"

"Don't you brew illegal wine in the basement, too?" Landon kept his eyes level as he sipped from his coffee. I was impressed that he had managed to turn the tables on Aunt Tillie so effectively.

"That's a lie," Aunt Tillie sniffed. "I may make a few bottles of wine, but it's certainly not illegal. I need it for my bad joints. That's not a crime."

"It is if you're selling it," Landon said blithely.

"Well, I'm *not* selling it," Aunt Tillie said evasively.

"If I ask the locals about it, are they going to say the same thing?" Landon was playing a game, and he looked like he was enjoying it.

Aunt Tillie met Landon's gaze without blinking. "Of course."

Landon glanced over to me. "Is that true?"

"The townspeople are scared of her," I said dismissively. "They're not going to roll over on her."

"Plus, her wine is really popular," Thistle offered. "They don't want to piss off their supplier."

"That is neither here nor there," Aunt Tillie said hurriedly. "You can't prove that I'm doing anything illegal."

"I don't care about proving it," Landon said carefully. "I just thought I would throw out some random accusations and see what sticks. That seems to be the theme of the morning."

Twila, Marnie, and my mom all looked appropriately abashed by Landon's statement. Aunt Tillie, though, she didn't look the least built guilty.

"You should watch your tone," Aunt Tillie warned Landon.

"You should mind your own business," Landon shot back.

I sucked in a deep breath, waiting for Aunt Tillie to freak out. Instead, she remained calmly sitting in her chair. "I like him," she said finally, turning her gaze to me. "He's not nearly as wishy-washy as I originally thought."

"He's good," Clove said finally, laughing despite herself.

"Bay's the expert now," Thistle said slyly.

I shot her an angry look. "Don't go there."

"What are you going to do?" Thistle taunted me.

"There's big snow banks out there," I reminded her. "I'm going to bury you in one with yellow snow and leave you there."

"Your empty threats have no power over me," Thistle replied airily. "They'll just put you in yellow snow rehab."

Landon chuckled as he took another sip of coffee.

"Every single one of you should be involuntarily committed," he said. "At least Aunt Tillie likes me now, though. I feel privileged."

"You won't when she starts calling you for favors."

Landon didn't look too perturbed – at first. He thought about what I said for a second and then turned to me, alarm written all over his handsome face. "What kind of favors?"

"You don't think she takes care of that pot field herself, do you?"

EIGHTEEN

*T*hings settled down – at least by my family's standards – relatively quickly after that. Marnie and Twila set about making a quick breakfast for us, while my mom started tidying up the living room.

"You don't have to do that," I protested.

"Well, you're not going to do it before you have to leave for work," my mom said primly.

"So, we'll do it when we get back."

"You shouldn't leave a dirty house. Men don't like that," my mom glanced at Landon pointedly.

"He helped make the mess."

"That's not the point."

"I need a shower," I muttered.

When I walked back into the living room after getting cleaned up and dressed, I found that everyone was eating breakfast without me. "Thanks for waiting," I grumbled.

"It's your own fault," Aunt Tillie said. I noticed she was sitting next to Landon – something that was making him decidedly uncomfortable.

He got up when he saw me and moved past me toward my

bedroom. "I'm going to shower and then Marcus and I are going to try and clear some of this snow out of here so we can get into work."

"That's not necessary," Aunt Tillie said.

"It's not?" Landon looked surprised.

"No," she shook her head. "Once he's done using the snow blower up at the inn, Trevor is going to come down here and clean up the front porch."

"Trevor's coming?" Clove was on her feet almost instantaneously. She scurried into her bedroom and slammed the door shut behind her.

"There's not going to be any hot water left by the time I get to shower," Thistle grumbled.

"What about the roads?" Landon asked. "Have the county plows been through yet?"

"The county only does the main roads," I informed him. "We're responsible for the road to the inn and the guesthouse."

"Are those roads clear?" Landon asked. "Do you guys have a service?"

"No," I shook my head. "We have Aunt Tillie."

Landon looked confused. He bent his head down and whispered in my ear. "Are you telling me she casts spells to get rid of snow?"

"No," I laughed. "But that's a good idea."

"Then how does she get rid of the snow?"

"She has a plow," I said simply.

"She has a plow?"

"She has a plow," I repeated.

"Does she even have a driver's license?" Landon shifted his gaze in Aunt Tillie's direction.

I shrugged. I had no idea.

"Do you think she should be driving, let alone pushing around a foot of snow? You know, with her glaucoma and all," he said sarcastically.

I glanced over at Aunt Tillie. "I don't know. Why don't you ask her?"

Landon obviously didn't think that was a good idea. "I'm going to forget we had this conversation."

"I think that's probably best," I agreed.

WHEN WE GOT to town about an hour later, Landon offered to drop me off at the paper and pick me up later.

"You're coming home with me again tonight?"

Landon looked uncomfortable with the question. "I hadn't decided yet," he said. "You know, we're supposed to be getting a really big blizzard in two days."

"Are you allergic to snow?"

"No, but I'm probably going to have to find a place to stay over here, especially if this case is still ongoing."

"You only live an hour away," I reminded him.

"I know," he said. "But an hour and two feet of snow actually ends up being five hours and no guarantee that I can get over here. Plus, if that snow is blowing, it's just dangerous to be on the roads."

"Are you fishing for me to invite you to stay with us?"

"No," Landon said innocently. "I was just wondering if you knew of somewhere nice I could stay if I get stuck here. I mean, you don't want me to die on dangerous roads, do you?"

I smiled knowingly at Landon. "Why don't we take it a day at a time," I said. "The weather forecasters say that the blizzard is still almost two days off. You should be fine to spend the night at your own place tonight."

Part of me wanted to invite him to stay with us. The other part of me, though, the part that remembered being woken up by a family of embarrassed witches, wanted to maintain at least the illusion of taking things slow.

Landon rolled his tongue into his cheek and considered my statement. "You're probably right. I need to pack some things."

"Like your *My Little Pony* boxer shorts?" I teased.

"That shows what you know," Landon scoffed. "They don't make *My Little Pony* boxer shorts."

"I bet they do," I countered. "What else do the Bronies sleep in?"

"What's a Brony?" Landon knitted his eyebrows in confusion.

"A grown man that is obsessed with *My Little Pony*."

"You're making that up."

"Don't you watch the news?"

Landon eyed me dubiously. "I'm going to look this up. If you're making it up, like I think you are, then you're going to owe me a back rub the night of the blizzard."

"You're being awful presumptuous."

"I have a reason to be," Landon said.

I bet.

"So, where do you want me to drop you off?" Landon changed the subject.

"I'll just go to the police station with you," I said. "I want to talk to Chief Terry about the case."

"Then what?"

"Then I'll go home with Thistle and Clove," I shrugged.

"You don't have to go to the paper?"

"Probably not," I said. "We're a weekly, I've already got the edition ready for this week and – if we get the blizzard we're supposed to – that will put off production until Monday."

"That's not how a real newspaper works," Landon argued.

"That is how The Whistler works," I corrected him. "There's no sense printing during a blizzard if no one is going to buy it."

"And your advertisers are okay with that?"

"They're businessmen," I said. "They understand that printing on a Monday when people will actually see the paper instead of a Friday when they won't makes good business sense."

"I guess so," Landon said dubiously. "It still seems like a really weird way to run a business."

"Hey, do I tell you how to be a cop?"

"I'm not a cop."

"Whatever."

CHIEF TERRY DIDN'T LOOK SURPRISED to see Landon and me together. In fact, he seemed more irritated than anything else.

"What's up?"

"Your Aunt Marnie says that Clove needs rehab."

Great. "She called you and told you that?"

"She called to tell me that it was Polish night out at the inn if I wanted to come to dinner. You know how I love Polish sausage."

"That's what she said," I replied without realizing what I was saying. It was an ongoing dirty joke with Thistle, Clove, and I -- and it just slipped out.

"What?" Chief Terry looked confused, while Landon was shaking with silent laughter.

"Nothing," I waved off his question. There really was no explanation that didn't make me look like a teenage girl.

"So, do you think Clove needs rehab?" Chief Terry asked me pointedly.

"I think we had too many chocolate martinis last night and that our moms are a bunch of alarmists," I replied. I didn't add that I thought it was beyond hypocritical that these same women were known to imbibe whole bottles of wine and dance under the full moon whenever the whim hit.

"That's possible," Chief Terry conceded. "They all have weird freak-out moments."

"It works out well for you," I said. "When they freak out, they cook."

"Yeah, I can't complain about that," Chief Terry agreed.

"So, what's going on with the Hobbes?" Landon asked wearily.

Chief Terry shifted his full attention to Landon for the first time. "Isn't that what you were wearing yesterday?"

"Yeah."

"Didn't you go home last night?" Chief Terry looked like he was growing in his chair. It was like he was the Hulk or something.

"I had too many chocolate martinis, too," Landon replied.

"So you stayed the night at the inn?" Chief Terry asked hopefully.

"No, I spent the night at the guesthouse." Landon seemed to be enjoying himself.

"You know I think of those girls as my daughters, right?" Chief Terry said brusquely.

"I figured," Landon replied.

"That means I still picture them in their Girl Scout uniforms selling cookies."

"That sounds hot," Landon said, sliding a sly smile in my direction. "Do you still have the uniform?"

Chief Terry cleared his throat angrily. "Don't do that!"

"She's an adult," Landon protested.

"I don't care," Chief Terry said. "If I even think you're doing anything untoward … ."

"Untoward?"

"You know what I mean."

"So what have you learned about the case," I interjected earnestly. I desperately wanted a shift in the topic of conversation.

Chief Terry shot one more warning look in Landon's direction and then turned back to me. "Not a lot."

"Anything?" I asked hopefully.

"We know that someone used a credit card in Lillian Hobbes' name in Traverse City four days ago," Chief Terry started.

"Someone? You don't think it was her?"

"We're not sure," Chief Terry said. "It was used at a restaurant at one of those waterfront restaurants on the bay."

"So no cameras?"

"No cameras," Chief Terry confirmed. "We're having some agents pick up the slip to see if the signature matches one from Lillian Hobbes that they have on file in Canada."

"How long will that take?"

"I have no idea," Chief Terry said wearily. "Canada may be a nice place to visit, but when it comes to law enforcement, they're not adverse to taking their own sweet time."

"Is that all?"

"No," Chief Terry shook his head. "Another credit card, this one belonging to Byron Hobbes, was used to put down a room reservation at the Bayfront Inn."

"Is that in Traverse City, too?"

"No, Suttons Bay," Chief Terry said.

"Still, that's not that far away."

"No, it isn't."

"Did you check to see if they ever checked in?" Landon asked.

"I'm not new," Chief Terry growled. "I know how to run an investigation. To answer your question, though, no one ever checked into the room."

"So they were on their way to Suttons Bay?" I asked.

"That's what it looks like."

"And their family hasn't heard from them?"

"No."

"We're checking to see if there are any mechanical problems on the boat that would cause it to stall right now," Chief Terry said. "I don't expect to hear from Mike, though, until later this afternoon."

"Mike Derry?"

"Yeah," Chief Terry nodded. "He knows more about boats than anyone else I know. He agreed to look it over. Things are slow for them right now, too."

"So that's all we know?" Landon looked frustrated. "It's not much."

Chief Terry glanced at me uncomfortably before speaking. "There is one more thing."

"What?" I asked curiously.

"As part of the investigation, we ran the registry at the Bayfront to see if there were any red flags with the guests," he said. "It's standard procedure, even if they didn't ever make it there in case they were meeting someone."

"And you found something?" I asked.

"All of the guests were pretty much cleared," Chief Terry said. "Most of them were just couples visiting the area for Christmas. They all had ties to the area or were on vacation. No one with a record or anything."

"And?" Landon prodded.

"There was one guest that caught my attention," Chief Terry averted his gaze from mine.

"Who?"

"Ted Proctor."

Landon looked confused for a second and then realization dawned on his face. He turned to me cautiously.

"Uncle Teddy?"

"Yeah," Chief Terry swallowed hard.

Well, that wasn't good.

NINETEEN

I headed across the street to Hypnotic when I was done at Chief Terry's office. Landon had offered to go with me – I think he was worried that Thistle would freak out when I told her about the Ted situation – but I declined.

"She'll be fine," I said. "She's not even sure how she feels about him. Plus, it could just be a coincidence. It's not like it's proof of anything."

I found myself stalling outside of Hypnotic, though. Despite my words, I wasn't a big believer in coincidence. I couldn't figure out why Uncle Teddy would be involved in something like this. I hadn't told Landon or Chief Terry about what we had seen out at the Dragonfly – or that Thistle had initially thought that one of the voices belonged to her father. She had admitted she wasn't sure afterwards, I reminded myself.

I probably should have told them, I chastised myself. Of course, that would be admitting we broke into the inn and searched it – which would put us on a slippery slope, too.

I blew out a frustrated sighed and walked into Hypnotic. Maybe I just wouldn't tell Thistle this most recent development at all? That seemed like a viable option – at least until we knew more.

I found Thistle and Clove working in the store – even though they didn't have any customers. That wasn't exactly surprising. The snow would keep any tourists away.

"What's up?" Thistle asked. I noticed she was wearing an old pair of track pants.

"Your jeans still don't fit?"

"Nope."

"Did you ask Aunt Tillie about it?"

"I'm not going to give her any more power," Thistle said. "I've decided to pretend that she doesn't exist."

"You mean you're going to ignore her?" Clove asked.

"Yup. If she asks me a question, I'm going to pretend I didn't hear it. If she tries to pick a fight I'm going to pretend she didn't say a thing."

"Do you think you can do that?" I asked dubiously.

"I'm going to at least try," Thistle said honestly.

"If you can pull it off, it will probably drive her crazy," I said.

"It would be more effective if you and Clove did it, too," Thistle hedged.

Clove's eyes widened unhappily. "I don't know."

"I'll think about it," I said. "If it looks like you're having fun, maybe I'll give it a try." Driving Aunt Tillie off a cliff had entertainment value – even if it was usually a really short trip.

"This is not about fun," Thistle said seriously. "This is about teaching Aunt Tillie a lesson."

"She might be too old to teach a lesson to," I pointed out.

"You're never too old to learn," Thistle mimicked her mother.

"Okay, she's probably too stubborn to learn a lesson," I conceded.

"That may be," Thistle said stiffly. "That doesn't mean I'm giving up, though."

"Well, I'll have a nice speech ready for your funeral," I said.

Thistle rolled her eyes and went back to the ordering she had previously been distracted with.

"So, what are you guys doing?" I asked finally. I was a little bored.

"We're just putting a few orders in and going home," Clove said.

"There's no reason to stay. It's not like we're going to have any customers."

"Plus the town is going on lockdown tomorrow," Thistle said.

"It is?" I hadn't heard that.

"It's supposed to be a bad one," Thistle replied. "That means, come sundown tomorrow, this place will be a ghost town."

"Great choice of words," I grumbled.

"Sorry."

"We should probably hit the store on the way home," Clove said pragmatically. "We need to stock up. We don't want to be stuck eating every meal at the inn for two days."

"Two days?" Thistle looked unhappy.

"Yeah," I said. "The night of the blizzard and the whole day after are going to be hell. The only way to get around on the roads is going to be Aunt Tillie's plow."

"And the snowmobiles," Clove reminded me.

I smiled, despite myself. I did love the snowmobiles.

"We'll stop at the store on the way home," Thistle agreed. "We need to stock up."

"Landon might be staying over," I said haltingly.

"Tonight?" Clove asked.

"No, he's going home to get clothes and stuff tonight," I said. "Tomorrow night and the night after, though."

"Well, that will be fun. Orgies all around," Thistle said bitterly.

"What about Marcus?" I ignored the orgies comment.

"He'll probably spend the night, too," Thistle conceded. "He'd rather be stuck with us – no matter how crazy our family is – than be stuck at home with his mom and dad for two days."

"I bet Trevor will be around," I teased Clove.

"He will," she avoided eye contact. "My mom offered him a room for the next few days because the weather is supposed to be so bad."

"Well, that will be convenient," I said.

"He's having dinner at the inn tonight," Clove said happily.

"I thought we were getting supplies so we could eat at home," Thistle whined.

"It's Polish night," I interjected.

"How do you know?" Thistle asked suspiciously.

"Marnie called Chief Terry."

"Did he have anything new on the case?" Clove asked.

I swallowed hard and then told them what I knew – everything except the part about Uncle Teddy being registered at the same hotel. I didn't see how it could help at this point. And, if it was just a coincidence, it could do a lot more harm than good where Thistle was concerned.

"Well, that's a bummer," Thistle said. "I don't suppose they'll find out much more before the storm hits either."

"No, they definitely can't be out in that type of snow on the water," I agreed.

"Okay," Thistle finally agreed. "We'll go to the inn tonight. I want to ignore Aunt Tillie and see if it drives her crazy anyway."

"If that doesn't work, we could all repeat everything she says like we did when we were little," I suggested.

Thistle smiled to herself. "That was pretty funny."

"Not one more word!" I imitated with a bemused smile.

"We'll still stop at the store," Clove interrupted. She didn't like to talk about Aunt Tillie -- just in case she really could hear us from miles away like she claimed.

"Yeah," Thistle agreed. She turned to me. "Are they making pierogies?"

"Don't they always? And Polish sausage, too."

"Oooh, I love Polish sausage," Clove gushed.

"That's what she said," Thistle and I sang out in unison.

Sometimes it's okay to be immature.

TWENTY

$\mathcal{W}$hen we got to the inn for dinner that night, Thistle was excited about her plan to unhinge Aunt Tillie and Clove was all dolled up for dinner with Trevor. I didn't want to burst her bubble, but I figured one dinner with our family might be enough to send Trevor running for the hills – even if those hills were buried under a mountain of snow.

We entered through the private family residence, dropping our coats in the living room before wandering into the kitchen. The smell of sauerkraut assaulted my olfactory senses the minute I walked into the room.

"That smells awesome," I admitted.

"It should," Marnie said as she stirred. "We've been making it from the same family recipe for as long as I can remember."

Thistle looked over her mom's shoulder as she dished Polish sausage up on a plate. "Those look good, too."

"You guys haven't made Polish food in a while," I said.

"It's comfort food," my mom said. "It's best on really cold nights."

"It's definitely going to be cold over the next few days," I agreed, sneaking a pierogi off of the plate my mom was readying and popping it into my mouth.

My mom smacked me playfully. "Those are for the guests. It's unsanitary to pick food off of a community plate with your fingers."

"Then maybe you shouldn't be such a good cook," I tried to charm her.

She pulled the plate away from my wandering hands and narrowed her eyes at me. "That doesn't work on me anymore. You're not ten and I'm not stupid."

It was worth a try.

"Where is Aunt Tillie?" Thistle was looking at the empty recliner.

"She's in her room getting dressed," my mom said.

Thistle looked at the chair again and raised her eyebrows. I shook my head. Now wasn't the time to steal the chair. If we did it in front of our mothers, they would fall like dominoes when Aunt Tillie went on the rampage. They wouldn't mean to, but they would roll over on us to save themselves from her wrath in a heartbeat.

"So, where is Landon tonight?" My mom asked pointedly.

"He went back home," I said easily. "He has to pack stuff. He thinks he's going to be stuck over here when the blizzard hits tomorrow night."

"And just where will he be staying?" My mom asked, hands on hips.

"I don't know yet," I said honestly. "I figured he could get a room here or just stay with us at the guesthouse. It depends on whether or not I'll be up for another orgy so soon or not."

"That's not funny, fresh mouth," my mom swatted me with a wooden spoon.

"What's for dessert?" I asked curiously.

"Chocolate cake," my mom said.

"That's not really Polish. You usually commit to one theme and see it through."

"Your Aunt Tillie wanted chocolate cake," my mom said primly.

Translation: Whatever Aunt Tillie wants, she gets. It's easier than arguing with her.

"Besides," my mom continued. "You love chocolate cake."

"She loves all desserts," Thistle scoffed.

"I'm not the one who can't fit into her pants," I reminded Thistle.

"You can't fit into your pants?" Twila looked Thistle up and down. "Is that why you're dressed for the gym? You're going to work out after dinner?'

"I'm not fat," Thistle protested. "My pants don't fit because Aunt Tillie is evil."

Marnie crossed herself and looked to the kitchen door quickly. I think she was worried Aunt Tillie would overhear the conversation.

My mom decided to change the subject. "How is work?"

"It's fine," I said. "Edith is convinced that Brian is up to something, though."

"Like what?" My mom and aunts had taken to Brian Kelly – like they did most people. Aunt Tillie, though, she hadn't trusted him the minute she had laid eyes on him.

"I don't know," I admitted truthfully. "I think he might be trying to sell the paper."

"Why would he do that?" my mom asked.

"To make money? I don't know," I shrugged.

"Why does Edith think this?"

"She says he's been making a series of secretive phone calls," I explained. "Something about keeping it secret from me. I thought, at first, it was about him doing business with Uncle Teddy. Now I think it's more, though."

"Would you be okay if he sold the paper?" My mom asked, concern etched on her timeless face.

"I don't know," I shrugged. "I know that William left Brian the paper with the stipulation that I be kept on as editor. Whether that is still in effect if the paper gets sold, though, I have no idea."

"I knew he was a lout." Aunt Tillie made a dramatic entrance into the kitchen.

"I don't know that he is really trying to sell the paper," I cautioned Aunt Tillie. The woman loved to torture us, but she fought like a mountain lion when someone else meant to do us harm. "It's just one theory."

"He still knew about Ted being in town and hid it from us," she said angrily. "And after everything we've done for him."

"What have you done for him?" Twila asked curiously. "Besides threaten to put a scorpion in his bed?"

"When did she do that?" I asked, trying to fight the mad grin that was trying to flit across my features.

"When he suggested that we get rid of the brochure rack in the front foyer and replace it with Whistler sales racks," Marnie said.

I had been telling them to do that for years, but I didn't remind them of that fact. "Well, no harm no foul. I mean, it's not like she could really get a scorpion."

My mom and Marnie exchanged guilty looks.

"Where did you get a scorpion?" I asked wearily.

"I ordered it off the Internet," Aunt Tillie sniffed. "His name was Fred."

"They sell scorpions on the Internet?" Clove looked horrified.

"They sell everything on the Internet," I acknowledged. "It's more than just good porn these days."

"That is not funny," my mom smacked me with the wooden spoon again.

"What happened to Fred?"

"He ran away," Aunt Tillie said evasively. "I think he's on a nice farm in the hills now."

"We can't find him," my mom said. "We were going to give him to Mrs. Korr for her pet shop, but when we went to get him he had mysteriously disappeared."

"He's not still in the house, is he?" Clove looked around fearfully.

"We're not sure," Marnie admitted.

"What if he gets into someone's room?"

"Fred is not interested in getting in anyone's room," Aunt Tillie explained. "Fred is a good guy. He's just misunderstood."

"He's also deadly," my mom reminded her.

"Only if you piss him off."

That was true of just about anyone.

We helped carry the food into the kitchen. I couldn't help but notice that Clove conveniently put her plate down in front of Trevor so she would have an excuse to sit next to him. He was a hard guy to read, but his eyes did seem to light up when he saw her. That was a start.

I took a seat next to Aunt Tillie. I wanted to make sure I could control her – or at least attempt to – should she go after Brian. Besides that, I wasn't keen on sitting next to him, which left the only open seat next to Aunt Tillie.

"This smells wonderful," the elderly couple at the end of the table said.

"I'm sorry," I said politely. "I didn't get your name when we were here earlier in the week."

"I'm Lenore Baker," she said in a friendly tone. "And this is my husband, Tom."

"And how has the antiquing been going?"

"We haven't found anything yet," Lenore admitted. "We've just been having fun exploring the town, quite frankly. We're a little worried about the storm, though."

I could understand that. Still, she seemed a little nervous. Maybe she wasn't too keen on snow?

"Where are you from?"

"Grand Rapids," Tom said hurriedly.

"How long are you here for?"

"Through the weekend, at least." He kept his eyes fixed on me, making sure not to make eye contact with anyone else at the table.

"Well, you'll probably be stuck here after tomorrow night for sure," I said. I was trying to be helpful. They were old, after all.

"Well," Lenore said warmly. "If we have to be stuck here, I can't think of a better place to be snowed in. Or more friendly people," she beamed at my mom and aunts.

She obviously hadn't spent a lot of time with Aunt Tillie.

"What are we going to do about this week's edition?" Brian asked.

"I've got it mostly ready. I'm going to do a small write-up on the blizzard tomorrow," I said. "I already called the printer and said that, odds are, we'll be printing Monday instead of Friday."

Brian nodded in agreement. "It's just a waste to print on Friday if this storm hits. No one will get their paper. We can't ask George to deliver in two feet of snow."

George was The Whistler's one and only delivery person. That generally consisted of dropping off big piles of papers at the various businesses in town, but he went out of his way to take newspapers to the older housebound seniors in the area, as well.

"Well, you won't have to worry about that for very long, will you?" Aunt Tillie asked Brian darkly.

I swung out to kick her under the table and missed. She really was quicker than I gave her credit for sometimes.

"What do you mean?" Brian asked curiously.

"Aren't you trying to sell the paper?"

Crap. I should have embraced Thistle's ignore Aunt Tillie mantra.

For his part, Brian looked both surprised and uncomfortable. "No," he said. "I'm not trying to sell the paper. Where would you get that idea?"

I expected Aunt Tillie to throw me under the bus. She never does what you expect, though.

"Mrs. Little said you were considering it," she lied smoothly.

"Mrs. Little? From the unicorn store? How would she know anything about me and the paper?"

"You like to brag about yourself," Aunt Tillie said evenly. "I figured you were just bragging about it to her."

"Well, Mrs. Little is mistaken," Brian said carefully.

"Are you calling her a liar?" Aunt Tillie looked outraged. It was an impressive feat since the whole story was made up.

"Of course not," Brian held his hands up in a placating manner. "I'm just thinking that she heard an errant rumor or something."

"Dude," one of the snowboarding hipsters seated on the other side of the table finally spoke around a mouthful of food. "I wouldn't mess with her."

Brian looked at the kid and dismissed him immediately. "You don't know what you're talking about."

"Tillie knows things," the kid said. "She can see the future."

I slid a suspicious glance in Aunt Tillie's direction. "Has she been reading your fortune for you?"

"Sludge saw me reading my tarot cards," Aunt Tillie said. "He wanted to know what I saw."

Aunt Tillie couldn't really read tarot cards. She only got them out when she wanted to make a little extra money from unsuspecting tourists.

"And what did your future hold, Sludge?" I asked curiously.

"It wasn't very good," he said honestly. "She said I was going to make the run of all runs on the Devil's Snare after the blizzard. Unfortunately, I would fall to my death from the chairlift afterwards."

Nice.

"She took the curse off of me, though," Sludge said brightly. "Now I won't die after the run."

"And how much did that cost you?" I asked dryly.

"Only fifty bucks," Sludge said. "I figured my life was well worth fifty bucks."

I turned to Aunt Tillie incredulously. "You don't think that's a little underhanded?" I whispered under my breath.

"The boy named himself Sludge," Aunt Tillie said dismissively. "He deserves what he gets."

Marnie decided to change the subject – a move I was grateful for. "So, how are you liking the area, Trevor?"

Twelve sets of eyes shifted their focus to Trevor. He didn't look thrilled with the sudden attention. "It's nice," he said. "The people are nice."

"That's good," Marnie said.

"What exactly did Mrs. Little tell you?" Brian piped up from down at the other end of the table.

Aunt Tillie turned her attention back to him. "She said you were trying to sell the newspaper and get out of town."

She was sticking to the lie.

"I don't understand why someone would spread a rumor like that," Brian looked genuinely concerned.

"It's probably because you're running around with scoundrels," Aunt Tillie explained breezily.

"Scoundrels?"

"Ted Proctor," Aunt Tillie replied.

Thistle looked like she was about ready to jump up from her chair and stab Aunt Tillie with her fork. I put my hand on her arm to still her, shaking my head in warning. That would just give Aunt Tillie what she wanted.

"Ted Proctor is a businessman," Brian said firmly. "I understand he has a ... dubious past with your family. That doesn't make him a bad businessman, though."

"There's nothing good about that man," Aunt Tillie replied.

"That's enough," Thistle hissed. "He's my father."

"That's not your fault, dear," Aunt Tillie said blithely. "Thankfully, you got most of our genes and your mother changed your last name when you were little."

Thistle looked surprised. "What do you mean? Was my last name Proctor at one time?"

"Of course," Aunt Tillie said. "Your father wanted you to have his name."

"Until you scared him off?"

So much for ignoring her. I figured that plan was dead in the water before she even launched it.

"I didn't scare him off," Aunt Tillie seethed. "He left on his own. That's what cowards do."

Thistle jumped to her feet. I was afraid she was going to attack Aunt Tillie – or at least scream at her in front of the guests – but she stormed out to the kitchen instead.

"You really are unbelievable," I sighed.

"Sometimes the truth, whether you want to hear it or not, is hard to hear," Aunt Tillie said honestly. "Thistle has some hard truths in her future."

I couldn't disagree with that, especially knowing that Uncle Teddy was starting to look like he really was up to something nefarious. Still, though, I was loyal to Thistle.

"You could at least let her face those truths wearing real pants," I grumbled.

Aunt Tillie considered my statement. "I'll think about it."

TWENTY-ONE

The next morning, we all got up early and headed to town as soon as possible. There's something about the air when a blizzard is about to hit. Even when you're outside, things feel like they're closing in on you. That's exactly how Hemlock Cove felt today.

"It's definitely coming," Clove said, lifting her head to sniff the air with her ski-slope nose.

"Yeah, you can feel it," Thistle agreed.

"I'm going to go down to the paper and make sure everything is set there and then I'll come back and help you get the wood shutters closed," I said.

"Okay," Thistle agreed. "It's always such a pain."

"It's better than the windows breaking," I reminded her.

"That's definitely true," Thistle agreed.

"At least your jeans fit again," I reminded her, glancing down at her well-worn blue jeans.

"Yeah, but she just swapped out curses," Thistle said bitterly.

"What do you mean?"

Thistle pointed to her lip. "I'm getting a cold sore."

"That could just be a coincidence."

Thistle looked at me like I had just sprouted wings. "Do you really believe that?"

"No," I shook my head. "We'll stop at the store and pick up some medicine on our way home. They have that one-dose stuff now that is supposed to work practically overnight."

"I'm going to go rub my lip all over her favorite recliner," Thistle promised angrily.

"Well, just tell me before you go," I replied easily. "I'm going to want to take a picture."

I left Clove and Thistle to their blizzard preparations and headed toward The Whistler. I considered stopping in to see Chief Terry first, but figured I might as well get everything set with this week's edition first.

Once I was at the paper, Edith met me at the door. "We're getting a blizzard."

"I heard."

"I don't like snow."

"Well, then why did you live in Northern Lower Michigan?"

"This is where I grew up."

"Oh."

"I always had this reoccurring nightmare about being buried alive in an avalanche," Edith said.

"We don't have mountains here," I reminded her. "We can't have an avalanche."

"That's not the point," Edith said stiffly.

"Also, you're a ghost. You don't breathe."

Edith sighed tiredly. "I expect you'll be away from the paper for a couple of days then"

"Probably," I agreed. "I'm just here to finish up a couple of things and then we're going home. We're still not sure when the storm is supposed to hit – or when it's supposed to get really bad."

"So, I'll be here all alone?"

"You can come out to the inn, if you want." I immediately regretted extending the invitation. Aunt Tillie was going to curse me with a cold sore to match Thistle's if Edith made an appearance out at The Overlook.

"Spend time with your Aunt Tillie? On purpose? Pffft."

Well, that was good to know.

"Is Brian here yet?"

"No," Edith shook her head.

"Aunt Tillie confronted him about selling the paper last night," I explained.

"Did he admit it?"

"No, he denied it."

"Do you believe him?"

"I honestly don't know."

"Well, at least now he knows that we're on to him," Edith said.

"If that's what he's really doing," I agreed.

"You don't think that's what he's doing?"

"I just don't know."

I spent about two hours finishing things up at the paper. I repeated my invitation to visit the inn to Edith before I left, locking the door behind me. Brian hadn't made an appearance, and I didn't know if he was going to.

I headed back toward Hypnotic, stopping at the police station first. The secretary's desk was empty, so I walked directly to Chief Terry's office.

"You missed dinner last night," I said by way of greeting.

"I know, I had a lot of stuff to check on with the storm coming," Chief Terry replied. "Your moms sent a big plate over for me, though. They're wonderful women."

He didn't have to live in close proximity to them.

"What kinds of things?"

"I like to check on the seniors before a big storm and make sure they're okay," Chief Terry said. "I offered them transportation if they wanted to stay with a family member or something."

"You're a pretty good guy," I said fondly.

"It's no big deal," Chief Terry said gruffly, his face turning red.

"So, anything new on the boat?"

"The forensic team found fingerprints below deck and on top," he said. "We're running them now, but that could take a long time."

"Well, at least that's something," I said.

"That's not all the forensic team found," Chief Terry said grimly.

Uh-oh.

"The dogs alerted on a scent."

"Cadaver dogs?"

"No, narcotic-sniffing dogs."

"You're kidding."

"Nope."

"What was an elderly couple doing with drugs?"

"That is the question," Chief Terry agreed. "Of course, we don't know if they put the drugs on there or if something happened to them and someone else used the boat to transport drugs. All we know is that were a few empty crates on the boat and we think they had drugs in them."

"You mean they could have been killed for their boat," I deduced aloud.

"Pretty much," Chief Terry agreed.

"So what's next?"

"Next? We batten down the hatches and survive the blizzard. That's all we can do at this point."

TWENTY-TWO

"*I* think we should go back out to the Dragonfly." I made the bold announcement when I walked into Hypnotic – before I got a chance to talk myself out of it.

"I knew it!" Clove exploded.

"I figured," Thistle nodded, barely looking up from her task. "If we're going to go, we need to do it now."

Clove's eyebrows nearly shot off of her forehead. "It's going to start snowing soon." She's got a tendency to whine – which has a tendency to irritate Thistle and I.

"That's why we have to go now," Thistle said calmly. "No one should be out there because the blizzard is coming and we still have a few hours before the blizzard hits. What better time will we have?"

"How about never?" Clove griped.

"Would you rather go now or in the dark again?" Thistle asked pragmatically.

Clove bit her lower lip. "Fine," she slammed the ledger book she was balancing down on the counter angrily. "But if I die, I'm haunting you forever."

"Why would you die?"

"That coffin is probably empty now," she exclaimed. "They need someone to put in it."

"What coffin?" I asked.

"There was no coffin," Thistle said irritably.

"Then what did the killers drag out of the Dragonfly?" Clove asked sagely.

"What killers?" Thistle was losing her cool.

"The ones we saw at the Dragonfly," Clove replied.

"Who did they kill?" I asked curiously. Clove's mind was a mystery sometimes.

"The people from the boat," Clove responded testily.

"The people from the boat on the channel? How did you get there?"

"Who else was in the coffin?" Clove was exasperated.

"What coffin?" Thistle and I both exploded at the same time.

"The one from the inn," Clove shot back angrily, glaring at us like we were the crazy ones.

"I'm going to kill you," Thistle seethed.

IT TOOK us another forty-five minutes to make sure Hypnotic was locked up tight. Then we all crowded into Thistle's car and headed back out toward the Dragonfly. The air had turned bitterly cold in the intervening hours since we'd gotten to town and the wind was starting to pick up. Thankfully, the snow hadn't hit yet.

"Do you think we should stop back at home long enough to change our clothes?" Thistle asked.

"No," I shook my head. "That will look really strange if someone sees us."

"People already think we're strange," Thistle reminded me.

"Yeah," I agreed. "Not that strange, though. Let's just go and get it done."

When we got out to the Dragonfly, Thistle pulled off to the side of the road and parked where she had before. In the daylight, the car was fairly obvious, but there was no getting around that.

"What if someone sees us?" Clove asked.

"Then we'll either run or play like we're dumb girls who got lost," Thistle said grimly.

We entered the inn the same way we had before. We had left the front door unlocked when we left that night, but I wasn't surprised to find it locked again. Thistle used the same spell to tumble the lock and we closed the door behind us as we entered.

In the light of day, the front foyer looked even creepier than it had in the dark. There was a layer of dust on every surface, marred only by the footprints that tracked through it. There were also cobwebs in almost every corner.

"This would make my mom break out in hives," I lamented.

"It's actually a nice space," Clove said after a minute. "It needs a lot of work, though."

"Don't forget that whole missing wall in the back either," Thistle reminded her.

"There's that, too."

We wandered back through the dining room, making sure to look everywhere this time as we went. We didn't want to miss anything this time. That room was empty too, though.

When we got to the kitchen, Thistle immediately headed for the larder and looked inside. "Someone has been here," she said.

"How do you know?" I walked up behind her.

She pointed to a crate on the ground. "Should we open it?"

I exchanged a wary look with her. "Do you want to?"

"That's what we're here for, isn't it?"

I walked back out into the kitchen, hoping to find something to jimmy the lid from the crate. Unfortunately, there wasn't a lot of anything in the kitchen. I walked back to the larder. "We should have brought something with us."

Thistle was trying to pry the lid up with her fingers, grunting from the effort. "We could try a spell," she said finally.

"What kind of spell?" I asked dubiously.

"An opening spell?" Thistle asked hopefully.

"Like on the front door?"

Thistle shrugged and ran her hand over the crate, muttering the spell as she traced the edges. We all looked at it expectantly, but nothing happened. Thistle tugged on the top of the crate again for good measure, but it remained firmly shut.

"We could do a reverse glamour, to see what is inside," Clove suggested helpfully.

"There's a truth inside, let us see, let us see," Thistle chanted, touching the crate for good effort. "There's a truth inside, let us see, let us see."

Nothing.

"We could kick it," I offered.

Thistle cocked her head and considered it. She stood up and thumped her heavy boot against the crate, slamming it into the wall angrily. Still nothing.

"Well, we can't get it open," Clove said nervously. "Let's go home."

"We could call Chief Terry," I said finally.

"Not until we know what is in the crate," Thistle said firmly.

"We can't open it without him," I replied.

"Are you afraid there's drugs in there?" Clove asked fearfully.

"I'm afraid that if there's not drugs in here, and we call the police, then it's going to be really hard to explain to my dad," Thistle admitted.

She had a point.

"We can come back after the blizzard," I said finally.

"What if it's gone by then?" Thistle asked.

"Then we'll just keep checking." I didn't want to push Thistle too far. With the cold sore and all, she was liable to crack.

Clove nodded her silent assent. She just wanted to get out of here. We left the crate where we found it and headed back out of the Dragonfly, making sure to lock the front door when we left this time.

"Well, this was a waste of time," Clove announced when we were out in the open air. She looked relieved to be out in the open – even with the impending storm heading our way.

I glanced up at the sky, watching as the snowflakes started to fall on us lightly. The storm wasn't quite here – at least not yet. It was getting closer, though.

"We had to look," Thistle said wearily. "It would have just driven us nuts when we're cooped up during the storm if we hadn't."

"It wouldn't have driven me nuts," Clove countered.

"Fine, " Thistle said irritably. "It would have driven the two of us nuts. You would have been fine."

"I didn't mean anything by it," Clove protested.

"Oh, just shut up."

We were walking back toward the car when we heard the unmistakable sound of a car driving up the road. Crap. I grabbed Clove's arm instinctively and started dragging her into the woods.

"What are you doing," she slapped at my hand.

"We have to hide."

"We'll just say we're lost."

"I don't want them to see us," Thistle said. "Especially if it's my dad. She's right; we have to hide."

Thistle helped me drag Clove into the woods and we crouched behind a clump of trees to hide ourselves. We didn't have a clear view of the Dragonfly from our locale, but I didn't want to move in case that drew attention to us.

The car, a dark SUV, pulled up in front of the inn – pulling right up to the front porch. I could hear three people getting out of the SUV and heading toward the inn. Unfortunately, because of the trees, I couldn't see any of them, though.

"This is going to be one hell of a storm," one of the men said.

"That's why we had to do this now. We're not going to be able to get back out here for a couple of days. This is going to be one of the last roads they plow."

"How is everything else going?"

"Right on schedule."

"So, we're moving forward?" The third voice piped in. It sounded vaguely familiar, but I couldn't figure out why. I would have to think on that later.

"Things should be fine," the second voice said. "As long as we keep the Winchester women out of this, things should be fine. They're the only ones that could stop us now."

"What if they find out?"

"Then we'll have to find a way to keep them quiet."

"And what way would that be?"

"Whatever way we can think of."

TWENTY-THREE

Once all three men had disappeared into the inn, we made a break for it. We kept along the tree line until we were out of sight and then raced to Thistle's car. Once inside, Thistle fumbled with the keys before she managed to slip them into the ignition. She spun out on the road in an effort to drive away quickly.

"It's not going to do us any good if you get stuck in the ditch," I said grimly.

"I know."

Once we were safely away, we took a few minutes to catch our breath. "They're going to kill us next," Clove finally blurted out.

"That's not what they said," Thistle corrected her. "They said they had to keep us quiet."

"And what do you think that means?" Clove was close to hyperventilating at this point.

"We don't know that they're going to kill us," Thistle shot back.

"Did you recognize anyone?" I asked in a low voice.

"No," Thistle shook her head. "I was looking for anything that would tip me off that it was him, but I can't be sure."

"I can't be sure either," I agreed. I didn't mention that one of the voices had seemed familiar to me. I would have to think on that some more.

"So, are we heading back home?" Thistle asked finally.

"Let's stop at the store in town first," I suggested. "We need to get the cold sore medicine and this is going to be our last chance."

"It's snowing," Clove said.

"It's Michigan," Thistle shot back.

When we got to town, the entire main drag was empty. We all rushed into the small pharmacy to grab a few things and then we were back out to the car within fifteen minutes. The store owner, a nice old man named Mr. Hunter, warned us about the roads.

"You girls take your time getting home," he said. "This one looks like it's going to be a doozy. I wouldn't leave again tonight."

"That's the plan," Thistle said. "This was our last stop."

"You be careful," he cautioned us one more time.

The snow was really starting to come down now. We all raced toward Thistle's car, Clove taking a big spill in the middle of the road because it was so slick as we went.

Thistle bent over at the waist and started laughing. "Why is it always you?"

"Just help me up," Clove grumbled.

I reached down to grab her hand, pulling her toward me. I happened to glance toward the docks as I did. I couldn't be sure, but it looked like there were two figures walking around the abandoned boat.

Thistle walked up next to me and followed my gaze. "What is it?"

"Do you see people down there?"

Thistle scrunched up her face as she tried to see through the snow. "Kind of. I can't be sure, though."

I started walking toward the docks purposefully.

"Where are you going?" Clove whined. "If we don't leave now, we're not going to be able to get home. We've had two inches of accumulation in less than an hour."

"It will just take a minute."

Thistle shrugged at Clove and then followed me. She wasn't about to let me disappear in a blizzard.

It took a lot longer than it normally would to walk to the docks. When we finally got there, I found that it was completely deserted.

"There's no one here," Clove said.

"Someone was here," I argued.

"Maybe it was Chief Terry, making sure that the boat was secure for the storm," Thistle suggested.

"Then where did he go?" I countered. "We would have seen him walking back to the station."

"Maybe it was one of his officers?" Clove was desperate to get out of this storm.

Thistle turned to me seriously. "We can't do anything about it now. We really do need to get out of this storm."

I blew out a frustrated sigh. I knew she was right. Unfortunately for us, when we got back to the main drag of town the village's plow had already been through – and Thistle's car was practically buried.

"See!" Clove's voice was frustratingly high. "We're stuck here now."

"We're not stuck here," Thistle argued. "If we have to leave the car, we will."

"And walk back to the inn? That's ten miles."

"Not walk," Thistle shot back. "We'll call Aunt Tillie and she can pick us up in the plow."

No one really wanted that. "Let's at least try to get the car out first."

After a fruitless five minutes, that left us all freezing – and ready to kill one another – Thistle pulled out her cellphone and called the inn. "We're stuck," she said to whoever answered the phone.

"Yes, I know we should have been back home an hour ago," Thistle said irritably. "That doesn't change the fact that we're still stuck downtown."

Thistle listened for a second and then sighed. "Tell her we're in front of the store."

Thistle disconnected and shoved her phone back in her pocket. "We're never going to hear the end of this."

We all looked up when we heard the sound of a vehicle. I was relieved when I saw that it was Landon. He pulled up to us and climbed out of his SUV, leaving it running as he did so.

"You stuck?"

"No, we just like standing here in the snow," Thistle said sarcastically.

Landon raised his eyebrows at her. "Nice attitude. I could just leave you here, if you want."

"Go ahead," Thistle challenged him. "Aunt Tillie is on her way."

"You're in a mood," I grumbled and turned to Landon. "I think it's a lost cause."

"I've got a tow rope in the back. I could try to pull you out."

"You could get stuck in the process," I replied.

"Then I guess we'll all be riding back with Aunt Tillie," he sighed. "Let me at least give it a shot."

The three of us moved up on the sidewalk to watch Landon work. Once he had everything secured like he wanted, he looked to us expectantly. "One of you has to be in the car to help."

"It's Thistle's car," I said.

Thistle blew a giant raspberry with her tongue and then hiked back through the snow and climbed into the car.

Once Landon was inside of his truck, he turned to her. "You ready?"

"This isn't going to work," she complained.

"Not with that attitude," Landon agreed.

He started to accelerate his truck in an effort to pull Thistle's car out of the snow bank, but his tires were having trouble finding traction. After a few minutes of not moving, Thistle turned to me. "Men are idiots," she mouthed from the car.

I nodded in agreement. We were going to have to use shovels to get that car out, and that wasn't going to be an option for days.

Landon gave one more hard tug with his truck. Instead of pulling Thistle's car out, though, it had the opposite effect. The rope actually tugged his truck backwards and he was suddenly spiraled into the snowdrift right alongside Thistle. He didn't look happy.

He got back out of his SUV and untied the towrope. "That's not going to work."

I crossed my arms over my chest and watched him. "I'm fairly certain we told you that."

"Get in and I'll drive you to the inn," he said irritably.

I cast a dubious look at his truck, now stuck in its own patch of snowplow drift, and shook my head. "You're stuck, too."

"No, I'm not."

"Yes, you are."

"No, I'm not."

Landon climbed back in his truck in an effort to prove he wasn't stuck. One look at his face, though, as his tires spun helplessly beneath his vehicle and I knew I had been right.

Landon jumped back out of the truck and glared in my direction. "I'm blaming you for this."

Thistle was climbing back out of her car. "It's not her fault. She told you that it wouldn't work. You had to be pigheaded, though. Men always know what's best, right?"

"Are you always such a pain?"

"Most of the time," Thistle replied airily. "You'll get used to it."

Landon put his hands on his hips defiantly. "When is your Aunt Tillie getting here?"

I pointed down the street. "Here she comes now."

Landon turned and I couldn't stifle my laughter when I saw his mouth drop open at the sight of Aunt Tillie and her truck. The Ford pickup was big, indescribably big. It was two-toned, blue and gray, and it had an industrial-sized plow on the front of it. Aunt Tillie was so small, she could barely see over the steering wheel as she drove toward us. She skidded to a stop when she saw us and rolled down the window irritably.

"You act like you've never been in a blizzard before," she griped. "I'm so embarrassed that it's my nieces that got snowed in. How will I live this down at the senior center?"

"You're banned from the senior center," Thistle shot back.

"I'm not banned," Aunt Tillie said primly. "I'm just on a time out."

"That's better?" Landon looked at me.

"It's all semantics with Aunt Tillie," I smiled.

Everyone gathered their belongings from their vehicles and then headed for the truck. Clove and Thistle climbed in the back and settled on the very small and uncomfortable pull-down seats there. Luckily it wasn't a long ride back to the inn. I climbed up into the front seat and scooted along until I was in the middle spot. Then I turned to Landon expectantly. "Are you coming?"

"Maybe I should drive," he glanced at Aunt Tillie nervously.

"This is my truck," she barked out.

"Do you even have a driver's license?"

"Do you want me to leave you here?" Aunt Tillie countered.

Landon looked like he was actually considering it and then he blew out a sigh and climbed into the truck next to me. "Are you sure you can get us there in one piece?"

"Son, I've been driving longer than you've been alive."

"That's not what I asked."

"Is he going to be like this all night?" Aunt Tillie turned to me. "If he is, that's going to put me in a bad mood."

"He's just grumpy because we told him he would get stuck if he tried to pull us out and he didn't believe us," I said. "I think it's a man thing."

"Oh, you mean he's being a stubborn fool," Aunt Tillie said knowingly.

I saw Landon's jaw clench angrily, but he remained silent.

Things probably would have been all right if Aunt Tillie hadn't kept chattering on. "When you think about it, it's kind of like I'm your hero," she said to Landon pointedly. "I'm a super hero."

"Here she comes to save the day," Thistle and Clove sang out from the backseat happily.

Landon dropped his forehead into his hands tiredly.

"Mighty Aunt Tillie is on the way," I joined in with my cousins to finish the song. Aunt Tillie was a pain, but I was enjoying watching her make Landon squirm.

It was going to be a long two days – for Landon especially.

TWENTY-FOUR

The ride back to the inn was harrowing – for Landon, at least. His knuckles were white from gripping the door handle, and his face was weary from the effort it took for him to remain quiet during the drive. When we finally got up to the inn, he jumped out of the truck and raced around to the other side of the truck to help Aunt Tillie climb down from the cab.

"You're a vehicular menace," he announced when she was safely on the ground and looking up at him defiantly.

"You got here in one piece," she argued, smacking him on the arm. "Stop whining like a baby. You're worse than the three of them combined. It's kind of embarrassing for a law enforcement officer, isn't it?"

Landon turned to me, frustration etched on his handsome face. "How do you live with her?"

I shrugged. "You get used to it."

When we all got inside the inn, we found Twila fretting by the front door. "I thought you were all dead."

Thistle rolled her eyes. "How does us getting stuck in a snow drift equate to us all being dead?"

"Your Aunt Tillie was driving," Landon supplied.

"The roads are terrible," Twila ignored Landon, although she did flash him a warm smile. "You could have been buried in a drift for days and had to resort to cannibalism before someone found you."

Thistle glanced at Clove. "Sometimes I think she should have been your mother. She's an alarmist, just like you."

"I'm not an alarmist," Clove countered.

"It's a coffin," Thistle mimicked Clove.

I stepped on Thistle's foot to silence her. Luckily, Landon wasn't looking in our direction and didn't see the gesture. "What's a coffin?" He asked distractedly.

"It's just a joke from when we were kids," I lied.

Thistle looked appropriately chastised. She hadn't realized what she was saying until it was out of her mouth. Thankfully for all of us, that was a family affliction that popped up at regular intervals so we didn't hold it against each other.

"Dinner will be ready in a few minutes," Marnie said from behind the counter. "I'm figuring you guys should probably stay up here with us tonight."

That didn't sound like any fun at all.

"Aunt Tillie can just give us a ride down to the guesthouse," I argued.

"I'm done driving for the day," Aunt Tillie announced. "You'll be fine here."

"How many rooms do you even have open?"

"There's one open room that you girls can share," Marnie said. "And Landon can bunk with Brian."

"Over my dead body," Landon countered.

"That might be a fun game to play," Aunt Tillie glared at him over her shoulder as she flounced out of the foyer.

Landon slid a mutinous look in my direction. "I'm not sleeping with Brian."

"We don't have a lot of choice," I said. "Maybe you can bunk with Trevor."

"The handyman?"

I nodded.

"I'd rather bunk with the three of you."

Twila rounded on him. "You will not. That's not proper etiquette. What would people say?"

"How would people know?" Landon countered.

"I'd know," Twila said.

"We could have another orgy," Thistle offered helpfully.

"You shut your mouth," Twila warned her.

"I'm starving," Clove wandered out of the foyer and into the dining room. "What's for dinner?"

"Meat loaf, mashed potatoes, corn, fresh vegetable soup and bread," Twila said, her face lighting up. My family is very food oriented, what can I say?

"What's for dessert?"

Landon glared at me. "This room situation is not settled yet," he said. "We can talk about food in a minute."

"You can sleep on one of the couches instead, if you want," I offered.

"Red velvet cake, Bay," Twila ignored Landon. "Your favorite."

Yum. It was my favorite.

Once everyone was settled around the dinner table and filling their plates with warm goodness, the conversation started.

"It's good to see that you girls made it here safely," Lenore Baker said. "I know your mothers were worried something awful."

"We weren't in any real danger," Thistle said. "We would have been fine if Landon didn't try to tow us out, even though we told him it wouldn't work."

Landon pursed his lips angrily. "Yes, I'm to blame for trying to help."

"We're all glad you tried to help," my mom interjected.

Landon smiled at her thankfully.

"It's just that sometimes it's better to just do what women tell you," my mom continued. "Especially the women in this family. We're all extremely intuitive."

Landon looked like he was about ready to shove his fork into his own eye socket to end the pain. Sludge, who was sitting on the other side of him, leaned over and patted him on the back. "These women are amazing, bro. They know things."

"And what do they know?" Landon eyed Sludge suspiciously.

"They can see the future," he said.

"Really? Then you would think they would have foreseen getting plowed in at the store. What were you guys even doing there?" Landon rounded on me. "I saw you leave an hour before that and I thought you were going home then."

"We forgot we needed something at the pharmacy," I said evasively.

"What? What could be so important that you would need to be out in that storm?" Landon was using his irritation as a weapon now.

"Thistle has a cold sore," Clove said helpfully.

Thistle shot her a dirty look. "Not for long," she grunted out, shifting her angry eyes to Aunt Tillie.

For her part, Aunt Tillie looked appropriately innocent. Anyone that didn't know her would think she was a sweet old lady enjoying her mashed potatoes. Until she opened her mouth, that is. "At least your pants fit again."

"There is that," Clove said hurriedly. She was desperate to avoid another family fight. Her need to play peacemaker, though, backfired on her.

"You should be taking Thistle's side," Aunt Tillie said.

"What?" Clove looked confused.

"You should remain loyal to your cousin," Aunt Tillie said. "You shouldn't be siding with me, no matter how scared you are that I'll retaliate. That's what family does."

You never know what's going to set Aunt Tillie off. This was just further proof.

I turned to Landon. "Aren't you glad you decided to stay in town for the blizzard?"

"This isn't exactly what I had in mind."

"What did you have in mind?"

"You and me, a warm fire," Landon shrugged. "Trust me, your mom and aunt didn't play into the fantasy."

I glanced up and saw that my mom was watching us with a disapproving look on her face. "Well," she said stiffly. "It looks like things have worked out for the best then, doesn't it?"

Landon looked taken aback. "I guess so," he swallowed hard. "I thought she liked me," he whispered.

"She does," I laughed. "When you're not making dirty comments, that is."

"How was that dirty?"

"I think the visions of naked sugar fairies dancing in your head tipped her off." I was only teasing, but Landon looked frightened.

"She can read my mind?"

"No," I shook my head. "It was written all over your face."

Landon had gone white. When he glanced back up at my mom, she was still giving him a dirty look.

"I guess I'm sleeping on the couch tonight," he said finally.

"I think that would be a good idea," my mom agreed.

Thistle and Clove were exchanging conspiratorial looks across the table. I knew what they were thinking: Just because he went to bed on the couch, that didn't mean he would stay there.

TWENTY-FIVE

*A*fter dinner, everyone had hot chocolate in front of the fire and listened to Twila tell ghost stories. Unfortunately, Twila's ghost stories were essentially episodes of *General Hospital* wrapped around ghosts. When she got to the part about the evil Greek ghosts trying to freeze the world, I was done.

My mom had brought out three warm blankets and two fluffy pillows for Landon. He had opted for the big couch in the library, since it was off the main drag of the house and secluded.

After that, everyone retired to their individual rooms. I thought about sticking around with Landon for a while, but my mom was watching me like a hawk. Instead, I waved a half-hearted goodnight to him and followed Thistle and Clove upstairs.

Once we were safely on the other side of the door, Thistle sighed heavily. "This day has really sucked."

I picked up the flannel sleeping pants and T-shirts lying on the bed – all belonging to our mothers – and nodded in agreement. "It couldn't have gone much worse."

Clove pulled one of the T-shirts over her head – the one that said "Witches do it the wicked way" and shook her head. "This sucks."

I threw myself on one of the double beds lazily.

"What are you thinking?" Thistle asked. "Other than wondering what Landon looks like naked, I mean."

"I wasn't thinking about that," I said irritably.

"Right." Thistle didn't look convinced.

"I was thinking about the Bakers," I said finally.

"The Bakers?" Thistle looked grossed out. "That's a weird fantasy."

"Not like that," I lobbed a pillow at her. "I was just thinking that it was weird that they decided to stay, even though they knew a blizzard was coming."

"The snowboarding hipsters stayed, too," Clove said.

"Yeah, but they want the snow," I said. "They want to go out to the resort and play in it. The Bakers are an old retired couple."

Thistle regarded me curiously. "So, wait, what are you thinking?"

"We still don't have a picture of the couple from the boat," I said. "And the Bakers showed up right before the boat showed up."

"So, you think the Bakers are really the Canadian couple from the boat?" Thistle didn't look convinced.

"I think it's a possibility," I said finally.

"I think you're suspicious by nature," Clove interjected. "I think you see a conspiracy around every corner."

"Says the woman that sees coffins around every corner," Thistle scoffed.

"I'm just saying that the Bakers seem like a nice and normal couple," Clove said.

"I'm not saying they're not," I said finally. "I'm just saying I want to make sure."

"We could just go and check the ledger book," Thistle suggested. "They should have a copy of their credit card down there."

"Wouldn't they have noticed if the credit card didn't match the names when they checked in?" Clove argued.

"Not if Twila checked them in," I said. "Or Aunt Tillie."

"Aunt Tillie doesn't check in guests," Clove said.

"She does sometimes, when she's bored," Thistle said. "Come on," she moved toward the door. "It will just take a minute. Besides, Bay isn't going to be able to sleep unless we look."

Clove sighed and got to her feet. "Fine, but if we get in trouble, I'm blaming you."

"You always do."

"That's a mean thing to say," Clove sniffed.

"I'm not the one that said it," Thistle replied. "Aunt Tillie did."

"I'm starting to see what you mean when you say that she's an evil old lady," Clove said.

"Oh, *now* when she yells at *you*, she's evil," Thistle said sarcastically. "When she's cursing me left and right, though? She's just misunderstood."

I shushed them both as we opened the door. "Can we finish this argument later?"

Clove and Thistle wordlessly filed in behind me. I saw Thistle reach out and pinch Clove, though, when she thought I wasn't looking. Clove smacked her hand and then yanked her hair. I stepped in between them. "When we're back in the room," I reminded them.

"Fine," Thistle grumbled.

The hallway was silent as we made our way down it. Once we got to the stairs, Thistle paused. "Remember, the third step squeaks."

We had found that out the hard way when we were sneaking out as teenagers. Aunt Tillie hadn't thought we were so funny that night. She'd taken to locking us in our rooms for an entire week with a spell. Thistle had tried to get around the spell by climbing out the window, but since it was the second story, that had ended with a broken leg. We were a lot more careful after that.

When we got to the main floor, Thistle listened at the kitchen door for a minute and then shook her head. "I can hear Aunt Tillie snoring in her chair," she whispered.

We all tiptoed to the front foyer, although I did cast a glance into the library to see if Landon was sleeping. I couldn't hear anything, but his back was turned to us and he wasn't moving. That was probably good. I didn't want to explain what we were doing.

Once we got to the foyer, Clove moved to turn on the light – but Thistle stopped her. "They'll see the light," she argued. "It might wake Landon up."

"So? What does he care?"

"Do you want to explain to him what we're doing?" I asked.

"I don't care," Clove shrugged. "It was your idea."

"Well, I don't want to explain that we're looking for dirt on an old couple," I grumbled.

"Because now you realize you're crazy," Clove said knowingly.

"Let's just look at the records and be done with it," Thistle sniped.

We followed her behind the desk and watched as she lit the oil lamp on the counter with a snap of her fingers. Thistle reached under the counter and pulled out the big ledger. She flipped a few pages and then turned to me. "They're in room six."

I pulled out the expandable file folder that my mom and aunts used for current guests and found the folder for room six. I pulled out the papers from inside and studied them under the dim light for a second. Thistle glanced over my shoulder. "Thomas Baker of Grand Rapids, Michigan," she read. "Looks like you were wrong."

"I guess so," I agreed. "At least we know."

"I already knew," Clove said disdainfully.

"You know everything," Thistle said haughtily.

"What are you three doing?"

We all jumped when we saw Landon standing in the doorway. He was a mix of sleep and confusion.

"Nothing," I said hurriedly.

"Nothing? You're sneaking around and looking at inn records in the middle of the night for nothing?"

"Bay thought the old couple was suspicious," Clove said quickly. "We were just making sure all their financial records were right."

Thistle elbowed Clove hard.

"I am the snitch," Clove sighed. "I'm always the snitch."

Landon looked confused. "You thought the old couple was suspicious?"

"Not suspicious," I corrected him. "I just thought it was weird that they showed up right before the Canadian couple disappeared."

Realization dawned on Landon's face. "You thought they were the Canadian couple?"

I shrugged.

"What did the records say?" Landon looked interested, despite himself.

"Tom and Lenore Baker from Grand Rapids," I sighed. "Just like they said."

"It wasn't a bad idea," Landon said gently. "Now we know."

"Now you know what?"

All four of us froze at the sound of Aunt Tillie's voice.

"I thought you said she was sleeping," I hissed.

"She was snoring," Thistle countered.

"I can hear the sounds of evil-doers in my sleep," Aunt Tillie said. "Now, what are you all doing?"

There was no way I was going to tell her that we were sneaking around being suspicious of her guests. Thistle obviously read my mind because she clamped her hand over Clove's wrist to keep her quiet.

"I was just sneaking around to see Landon," I said finally.

Landon looked surprised, but he didn't contradict me.

"And you brought Clove and Thistle with you?"

"They thought I needed a chaperone," I said sheepishly.

"They're probably right," Aunt Tillie said. I couldn't meet her searching gaze out of guilt. "You always were the easy one."

"The easy one?" I protested. "That's unfair."

"Weren't you the one suspended for making out with the quarterback in the nurse's office when you were in high school?"

I had forgotten about that.

"Weren't you also the one that I caught in the Miller's barn with their youngest boy when you were fifteen?"

"That's not fair," I countered. "I really did go in there to look at the kittens."

"Only Bobby Miller got to see the ... full cat," Thistle said with a laugh.

Landon smirked in my direction. "Are you saying you were the town slut?"

Aunt Tillie rounded on him angrily. "She's not a slut," she argued.

"She was just sexually curious. It got her into a lot of trouble when she was younger. I had hoped she'd grown out of it."

"I have," I said lamely.

"Obviously not."

Aunt Tillie turned to the three of us. "Do you need me to walk you back to your room?"

"That won't be necessary," I said stiffly as we moved past her and started climbing the steps that led back to our room.

"See, you got us in trouble," Clove hissed.

I could hear Landon laughing behind us. "What are you laughing at? Do you need me to walk you back to your couch?"

"No, ma'am."

Once we were back in our room, I changed into the proffered pajamas and then tiptoed back to the door.

"Where are you going?" Thistle asked.

"I just want to say goodnight to Landon," I said innocently.

I opened the door and then pulled back in surprise. Aunt Tillie was sitting in a wood chair in the hallway – and she had a shot gun on her lap. "What the hell?"

"I'm saving you from yourself," she said tiredly. "Now go to bed."

I shut the door behind me and turned to Thistle and Clove. "I'm an adult, for crying out loud."

"Not to her."

I climbed into one of the beds and pulled the covers over my head irritably. I could feel Clove slide in next to me. "This is not how I saw this night going," I said finally.

"I don't think anyone saw the night going this way," Thistle grumbled from the other bed. "Don't you think I'd rather be cuddled up with Marcus and a good book?"

"A book?" Clove scoffed.

"A book, a marathon of *The Walking Dead*, I'd be fine with either."

"Go to sleep," I muttered. "The sooner we go to sleep the sooner we can get up and go back home."

Clove giggled. "You go to sleep first. You're the one keeping us up."

"If you don't all go to sleep right now I'm going to separate you,"

Aunt Tillie yelled from the hallway. "I'll make you go sleep with your mothers."

"See," Clove whispered. "You two always get me in trouble."

"And you always tell on us," Thistle shot back.

"I said, go to sleep!"

"Yes, Aunt Tillie," we all sang in unison and then dissolved into giggles. It was like we were teenagers again.

TWENTY-SIX

"Wake up!"

Aunt Tillie's face swam into view, inches from my own. "Gah!" I rolled away from her instinctively and fell off the left side of the bed I had, just seconds before, been slumbering in.

From my spot on the floor, I glanced up at the other bed to see Thistle wearily rubbing the sleep from her eyes as she regarded Aunt Tillie suspiciously. "What is your deal?"

"It's 7:30 a.m., it's time to get up," Aunt Tillie said primly. "You're sleeping your lives away."

"It's a snow day," Clove grumbled from the other side of the bed I had just been sleeping in. "You don't have to get up early on a snow day."

Aunt Tillie walked around the bed and yanked the covers off Clove irritably. "I said, get up."

"Why are you being so mean?" Clove whined.

"That's what keeps her alive," Thistle grumbled. "She's nourished by the pain she inflicts on others."

"It's like *The Addams Family* motto," I grumbled.

"What is?" Clove asked in confusion. None of us are exactly sharp in the morning.

"Sic gorgiamus allos subjectatos nunc," I enunciated slowly, trying to pull the memory from my brain.

Thistle giggled from her own bed. "I forgot," she said. "We were obsessed with that for a few months when we were in middle school. We were convinced that Aunt Tillie was the real life inspiration for *The Addams Family*."

Aunt Tillie narrowed her eyes at Thistle. "What does it mean?"

"Look it up," Thistle replied harshly.

Aunt Tillie swung around, hands on hips, and pursed her lips at me. "What does that mean?"

I didn't try to hide my smirk. Thistle, Clove, and I had gone through a phase as kids where we talked in Latin so Aunt Tillie wouldn't be able to know what we were talking about. Unfortunately, we were as lazy as we were ingenious – we'd given up learning actual Latin after two weeks and started speaking pig Latin instead. It wasn't quite as effective.

Aunt Tillie smacked the top of my head. "What does it mean?"

"It's nothing bad," I groaned and climbed to my feet. "Why are you always so suspicious?"

"If it was nothing bad, you would tell me what it means," Aunt Tillie countered.

"We will gladly feast on those that try to subdue us," I bit out in aggravation.

"What does that mean?" Aunt Tillie's face was starting to redden. I couldn't decide if it was the wine she'd been sipping in the hall before she fell asleep last night or the morning exertion of trying to wrangle the three of us into a wakeful state that was getting to her. I had a feeling it was a combination of the both.

"That's *The Addams Family* motto," I said blithely. "We will gladly feast on those that try to subdue us."

Aunt Tillie rolled the words through her mind for a second and then smiled. "I like it."

"I don't doubt it," I replied.

"Get ready for breakfast," Aunt Tillie turned on her heel. "Your mothers have gone all out because we're housebound."

"How much snow did we get?" Clove asked.

"More than a foot and less than two feet," Aunt Tillie said.

"Are you going to plow?"

"Eventually," Aunt Tillie said. "I have to be able to get out to the plow before that can happen." Aunt Tillie paused at the door. "I have the boys working on clearing the snow."

"That's good," I said distractedly. "Wait a second, what guys?"

Aunt Tillie didn't answer. Instead, she just left the bedroom, leaving the door ajar behind her as she did.

I turned to Thistle, worry etched on my brow. "What guys?"

"What guys do you think? Landon, Brian and Trevor for sure," she said, pulling on her jeans tiredly. She looked relieved when they easily buttoned. "I'm sure Sludge and that other hipster are probably helping, too."

"What is that kid's name? The other kid?"

"I don't know," Thistle shrugged. "I'm just going to start calling him Toxic Waste."

"That sounds like fun," I said.

We all dressed quickly, with Thistle and I foregoing makeup while Clove applied enough to make it look like she hadn't just woken up. "What?"

"Nothing," Thistle said.

"I know what you're thinking," Clove shot back. "You think I'm putting makeup on for Trevor."

"You're not putting it on for us," I said.

"I wish you guys would stop being mean to me," Clove said.

"We're not being mean to you," Thistle challenged.

"You get more and more like Aunt Tillie every day," Clove taunted.

"You take that back," Thistle said, reaching for Clove.

Clove sidestepped her easily and flopped over the corner of the bed and lunged out the bedroom door. Thistle raced after her. "You take it back!"

I followed them downstairs, following the sound of Thistle's raised voice and Clove's hysterical giggles as she tried to evade her. When I made it to the main foyer, I found Thistle on top of Clove poking her in the chest.

"Take it back."

"No."

"Take it back."

"Ow! Stop doing that!"

"Take it back!"

I watched the scene with mild interest. Clove was probably stronger than Thistle, but Thistle was definitely meaner than Clove. Thistle would undoubtedly win. That, of course, would prove that she actually was like Aunt Tillie – but I wisely stopped myself from saying those thoughts aloud.

"What's going on?"

Landon moved in behind me. I noticed his face was flushed from physical exertion and cold. He pulled his hands out of the work gloves he had been wearing and pressed them to the exposed flesh of my neck. I jumped in surprise.

"It's cold out there," he said. "Looks like things are a little hotter in here."

I noticed that Landon was looking at me and not at my wrestling cousins on the floor. "You're feeling flirty this morning."

"Yeah," Landon guilelessly agreed. "It was a long night on an uncomfortable couch."

"You could have slept upstairs," I reminded him.

"I tried," Landon said. "Your Aunt Tillie was guarding your room with a shotgun."

"That's not what I meant," I said.

"Yeah, but that was the only way I wasn't going to sleep alone," Landon replied.

"It would have been pretty crowded," I said ruefully. "You, me, and Clove."

"I could live with that," Landon teased.

I smacked Landon playfully and he caught my hand and brought it to his lips suggestively. "You don't think that sounds like fun?"

"Not really," I replied slyly. "Clove snores."

Landon shook his head, but he didn't let go of my hand. I couldn't deny the little rush of warmth that shot through me at the gesture. Unfortunately, I didn't get to enjoy the moment.

"What are you two doing?" My mom rushed into the room and pulled Thistle off of Clove effortlessly. She may look small, but this isn't the first tussle she's had to break up. "Why are you two fighting?"

"She said I'm like Aunt Tillie," Thistle huffed.

"So?"

"So?" Thistle looked flabbergasted. "That's the meanest thing she's ever said to me."

"Oh, please," my mom shrugged off Thistle's faux argument. "She once told you that we found you in a cabbage patch and took you home because we needed a new family pet."

"I still haven't been proven wrong on that," Clove said from her spot on the floor.

Landon reached down and helped Clove to her feet. I saw her eyeing Thistle mischievously. "Arf," she barked shrilly. "You're still my favorite pet."

Thistle launched herself at Clove again and the duo was wrangling on the floor for a second time in two seconds flat. My mom didn't even try to break them up this time. "When they're done, tell them we need help with breakfast in the kitchen."

My mom paused as she was leaving the room. "That goes for you, too," she said.

"I got it," I shot back grimly.

Landon's mouth tipped at the corners as he tried to hide a small smile. "Your family is a trip," he said, pulling the gloves back on.

"They're definitely something," I agreed. "Are you enjoying shoveling snow?"

"Trevor is a great worker," Landon said. "Brian seems to think he's only out there in a supervisory position."

"That doesn't surprise me," I said. "He's a tool."

"There's no arguing with that."

Landon shot me one more smile before he stepped around Clove and Thistle and headed back outside. For their part, my cousins were starting to tire of their spat. "Just take it back," Thistle was panting as she tried to keep Clove pinned to the ground.

"I shall not tell a lie," Clove sang out.

"We need to go help with breakfast," I reminded them.

"Suck up," Clove shot back. She was clearly feeling a rush of adrenaline from her aerobic antics of the past few minutes.

"You're a suck up," Thistle agreed.

"I'm not the suck up," I argued. "Clove is the suck up."

"I'm not the one whining about helping with breakfast," Clove said.

Thistle shifted slightly to give me room to sit next to her on top of Clove. With the weight of both of us, any bravado Clove was feeling evacuated her body with a whoosh. "I can't breathe."

"Then admit you were wrong and I'll let you up," Thistle said sagely.

"I plead no contest," Clove gasped out finally.

"No contest?"

"She means that she's not fighting the charges," I snickered. "She's not admitting her guilt, though, either."

"I don't know if that's good enough," Thistle mused.

I plopped down a little harder. "It's definitely not good enough for me."

Any further torture of Clove was postponed, though, when we heard raised voices outside of the inn.

"What the hell?" Thistle and I climbed off of Clove. She was on her feet in seconds next to us.

"What's going on?"

"It sounds like someone is fighting outside," I said thoughtfully. "Maybe Landon snapped and beat the crap out of Brian."

"We can only hope," Thistle said, opening the door to the winter wonderland outside curiously.

None of us were prepared for what we found, though. Brian was on the ground and the figure that was attempting to hold him there wasn't Landon. It was Trevor. "Listen, you little worm, I'm sick of hearing your voice."

I was surprised. I had never heard Trevor as much as raise his voice in a stressful situation. And, when you spend time with the Winchester women, there is nothing but stressful situations. I swung around looking for Landon. He was leaning against the outside of the inn and watching the scuffle with a small smile on his face. "Aren't you going to do something about this?"

"I am," Landon shrugged. "I'm enjoying it."

"What did he do?"

"He won't shut up," Landon said.

"I'm delegating," Brian whimpered from the ground.

"Delegating is not helping," Trevor said angrily.

"Some of us are worker bees and some of us are the queen," Brian said pragmatically from his spot on the ground.

"Are you saying you're the queen in this situation?" Landon asked.

"No," Brian sputtered. "I don't know what I'm saying. Will someone get him off me? Please?"

Landon seemed to consider the question for a second and then pushed himself away from the building. "Let him up, Trevor," he sighed.

"Not unless he promises to shut his thin-lipped little mouth," Trevor grumbled.

"Is it just me, or is Trevor really hot when he's angry," Clove whispered.

"It's just you," Thistle and I said in unison.

Landon had moved over and started to pull Trevor off of Brian. I was surprised that Trevor seemed to be fighting Landon's efforts. We were all so enthralled by the tableau playing out in front of us that we didn't notice that another figure had joined the fray.

"Should I try to help?"

We all turned in surprise when we finally registered the new arrival.

"Dad," Thistle said quietly. "What are you doing here?"

TWENTY-SEVEN

"I thought I should come out and make sure everyone was okay," Ted said uncomfortably, shifting his gaze from Landon, Trevor and Brian to the three of us. "It looks like it was a tough night."

"The night was fine," Trevor grumbled. "It's the morning that has sucked."

"You're only saying the night was fine because you weren't being hunted by a militant little Nazi with a shotgun," Landon countered.

"You have a Nazi staying here?" Ted looked confused.

"Aunt Tillie," Thistle said dismissively. "She was guarding the hallway last night. With a shot gun."

"From what?"

"She wanted to make sure that Landon didn't ravish Bay," Thistle said. "And that Clove didn't inadvertently hurt herself when she was trying to flirt with Trevor."

Clove looked scandalized and I noticed that Trevor's already cold-flushed face had reddened even more under everyone's sudden scrutiny. For his part, Landon didn't look fazed by Thistle's admission.

Ted allowed himself a small smile at Thistle's explanation. "That brings back memories."

"Of what?" I asked suspiciously.

"Your Aunt Tillie used to patrol the grounds of the house when your moms were teenagers," he laughed. "I bet she still uses the same shotgun – filled with buckshot."

"Buckshot?" Landon asked curiously.

"Yeah, she doesn't really want to kill anyone," Ted laughed. "Maiming them is perfectly okay with her, though."

Landon raised his eyebrows in my direction dubiously. "I don't think she's too worried about killing someone, if the situation warrants it, that is."

Ted brushed off Landon's statement. "Those rumors about bodies being buried on the property aren't true. I asked Twila when we started dating."

"What rumors about bodies?" Landon asked.

"It's just an old wives' tale," I brushed the question off. "Aunt Tillie used to tell area kids that she killed and buried other little kids on the property when they trespassed."

"Let me guess, she didn't want them stumbling on her pot field?" Landon sighed.

"She has a pot field?" Trevor looked suddenly interested.

"Not in winter," Brian scoffed. I noticed he was still spread eagle on the ground, even though Trevor had finally climbed off of him. "Pot doesn't grow in the middle of winter."

"Thanks, professor," Landon barked, shooting a dangerous glare in Brian's direction. "I never would have figured that out on my own."

"Well, you are the federal investigator," Brian replied stiffly.

Ted took in the situation on the front porch again and then turned back to Thistle. "I guess I should probably go," he shifted back and forth uncomfortably. "I just wanted to make sure you were okay."

"Since when?"

Everyone on the front porch turned to see Marnie standing in the open front door frame. I had no idea how long she had been there.

"Marnie," Ted said, lowering his gaze. "I just wanted to make sure everyone was okay," he repeated.

"Did you think we suddenly forgot how to make it through a blizzard? That the knowledge suddenly fell out of our heads?"

"No," Ted said. "I was just … ."

"Do you think that women can't take care of themselves?" Marnie pressed.

"No," Ted said hurriedly. "I just … ."

"You just wanted to make sure everyone was okay," Marnie supplied. "As you can see, we're all fine." Marnie glanced down at Brian, who was still on the ground in the snow, and shook her head. "Well, most of us are fine."

"Okay then," Ted started to move away.

"Why don't you have breakfast with us," Marnie offered gruffly.

My head snapped up in surprise at the invitation. One thing you can say about the Winchester women, they never do what you expect of them.

"You want me to have breakfast?" Ted looked understandably confused.

"I don't want you to," Marnie clarified. "You just came a long way, through a lot of snow, and you look hungry."

Marnie didn't wait for his answer. She turned on her heel and walked back into the inn, leaving us to continue our hijinks outside. I glanced over at Ted, but he still didn't look convinced. "I don't know," he hedged.

"It will be fine," Thistle brushed off his concerns. "Aunt Tillie has other things on her mind."

Ted smiled at Thistle warmly. "Like Bay and Landon?"

"And Trevor and Clove," Thistle added evilly.

Clove stuck her tongue out in Thistle's general direction. She was looking anywhere but in Trevor's direction. He didn't seem overtly bothered by the innuendo. If he was embarrassed, he wasn't showing it. That was good news for Clove. Maybe he was already getting used to our family.

Everyone traipsed back into the inn, the men discarding their heavy winter garments on the front bench and snow-covered boots underneath it. Then everyone filed into the dining room. My mom

177

was standing at the end of the table clucking angrily. "I thought you were going to come and help with breakfast."

"We got distracted," I explained.

"Like I haven't heard that before," my mom chided.

Once everyone was seated and filling their plates with blueberry pancakes, eggs, bacon and hash browns, the conversation turned to the storm.

"It wasn't as bad as it could have been," Landon said. "The roads will probably be rough, but not impassable."

"Especially when you have a plow," Aunt Tillie supplied.

Landon narrowed his eyes at Aunt Tillie. "Maybe you should leave the plowing for the professionals."

"Maybe you should mind your own business," Aunt Tillie countered. "Maybe you should ... ."

I put my hand on Landon's arm to silence him, shaking my head imperceptibly. "It's not worth it," I said under my breath.

"Yes," Aunt Tillie said brightly. "I will only devour those that try to subdue me."

Thistle shot me a dark look. "Aren't you glad you told her what it meant?"

"What what meant?" my mom asked suspiciously.

"*The Addams Family* motto," Landon interjected surprisingly.

"You know it?" He never ceased to amaze me.

"I loved that show."

"We think the family motto fits Aunt Tillie," I laughed. "It wasn't meant as a compliment, but she took it as one."

Landon looked Aunt Tillie up and down dubiously. "It suits her."

"Thank you," Aunt Tillie said happily.

"I don't think he meant it as a compliment either," Marnie said.

"I'm fine with that."

I glanced down the table and noticed the two hipsters weren't present. "Where is Sludge and ... and his friend?"

"They went snowboarding at the crack of dawn," Twila said. "And his name is Wreck."

"How did they get there?"

"We loaned them two snowmobiles."

"You just loaned them snowmobiles? That doesn't sound like something Aunt Tillie would do."

"I like them," Aunt Tillie said. "They know how to respect their elders."

"You mean fear them," Thistle said bitterly.

"Are we going to have a thing this morning?" Aunt Tillie asked.

"Define 'thing.'"

"You've always been surly in the morning," she said finally.

"I'm not being surly," Thistle practically exploded.

"So that wasn't you holding Clove down on the carpet in the foyer?"

"How do you even know that? You weren't there."

"I know all and see all," Aunt Tillie said ominously. "Sometimes, I know things even before they happen. That's why I was standing guard in the hallway last night."

"What do you mean?" My mom asked.

"I was making sure that Landon didn't take advantage of Bay," Aunt Tillie said simply.

Landon's face colored, even though he managed to remain calm under the sudden consternation of my mother and aunts. "I don't know what she's talking about."

"They were all trying to play musical beds last night," Aunt Tillie said.

"What?" My mom's eyes went wide. "In my house? With guests present?"

"We were not trying to play musical beds last night," I said hurriedly.

"And it's not like Bay's virtue is intact," Thistle laughed. "It hasn't been since high school."

Twila swatted Thistle angrily. "You stay out of this."

Landon slid me a sideways glance and then turned back to my mom. "See, she's a pro."

I think he was hoping my mom would laugh, but she didn't. "That's not funny," she snapped.

"I wasn't trying to sneak into her bedroom last night," Landon tried a different tactic. "I was looking for the bathroom."

Aunt Tillie snorted. "He only tried once, Winnie," she explained. "That was after I found the girls sneaking around downstairs."

"What were you doing downstairs?" My mom asked, turning her irritation in my direction.

I glanced down at the end of the table, where Lenore and Tom Baker were happily enjoying their breakfast and the morning show, and quickly made a decision. "We were trying to get a snack. We forgot Aunt Tillie was sleeping in the kitchen."

It was a weak lie, but I was hoping it would work. Thistle saw what I was trying to do and swooped in quickly. "You guys are the reason she's sleeping in the kitchen, after all," she interjected quickly. "Trying to take an old lady's favorite recliner from her? You should be ashamed of yourselves."

I bit the side of my lip to keep from laughing out loud.

"Since when are you on her side?" Marnie charged.

"I just don't think it's right," Thistle continued. "And that's on top of taking away her wine closet."

Aunt Tillie's eyes lit up. "See! Even they know it's wrong for you to be persecuting me this way!"

"Who is persecuting you?" My mom countered. "We just think that chair is old and gross."

"And we have nowhere else to put the new furnace," Twila added, shooting Thistle a murderous look.

At least they'd forgotten the previous line of questioning.

"You just get off on being mean to me," Aunt Tillie said petulantly. "You've always gotten a charge about being mean to me."

"That's not true," my mom protested. "You know we love you. We've always loved you."

"And we've put up with a lot more than anyone else would have, where you're concerned," Marnie added under her breath.

"Then why won't you let her keep her wine closet?" Thistle pressed.

My mom swung on her angrily. "You guys are just trying to distract us from what you were doing last night. That's why you're doing this."

"I don't know what you're talking about," Thistle said innocently.

My mom narrowed her eyes into dangerous slits. "What were the three of you doing last night? I want to know right now." I could hear my mom stomp her foot under the table. "You better just tell us now. I won't let it go. You know that."

Oh, boy, did I know that. My mom had an elephant's memory. She never forgot. Ever. Despite that, though, I wrinkled up my nose defiantly. "We were looking for a bottle of wine," I admitted finally – even though it was a false admission. "We were bored and wanted something to drink. We thought that would make the night go quicker, you know, if we were passed out from Aunt Tillie's special brew."

"So you were going to take some of my wine without asking?" Aunt Tillie screeched. "See what little miscreants you three raised?"

"How is this our fault?" Marnie looked like she was about to blow a gasket.

"You're the ones that raised them to think it was fine to fornicate with men they're not married to," Aunt Tillie swung back to me. "And steal my wine."

I turned to Thistle. "You always push it too far. Why do you always push it too far?"

"It's a gift," she shrugged and slammed a huge bite of pancakes into her mouth so she didn't have to talk anymore.

Landon was shaking with silent laughter at my side.

"What are you laughing at?"

"Never a dull moment, I swear," he choked out. "You should all be committed."

After the morning we had all just survived, I couldn't really argue with him.

TWENTY-EIGHT

*T*he second half of breakfast pretty much mirrored the first half of breakfast – meaning it was an uncomfortable free-for-all.

Aunt Tillie wasn't letting go of her anger (manufactured or otherwise) regarding the recliner or her wine closet: "You'll all feel guilty when this drives me to an early grave!"

My mom wasn't letting go of her suspicions: "I want to know what the three of you were doing creeping around the inn in the middle of the night!"

Thistle was uncomfortable in the presence of both her mother and her father, so she was pointing fingers at everyone else: "It's Bay's fault! She couldn't have done it without Clove, either!"

Clove was busily trying to flirt with Trevor – and deny she was interested in him at the same time: "I wish you would leave me out of this stuff!"

Landon was enjoying breakfast and trying to tune everyone else out: "Will someone pass me the maple syrup? Is this fresh? Nice."

Trevor seemed uncomfortable with the whole situation: "Maybe I should go back out and start clearing the snow?"

Twila was trying to pretend that having Ted at the breakfast table wasn't throwing her for a loop: "So, Ted, it's so nice that you're in town for business – and to visit Thistle, of course. When are you leaving?"

Marnie was still angry with Thistle for turning the conversation around on her: "You guys think you're so smart, but you're not. Remember, everything you even consider doing, we've already done, and we've done it better."

Brian wanted to get away from the noise – and the manual labor – and head to work: "So, do you think the roads will be passable or not?"

The Bakers were just enjoying the entertainment value: "It reminds me of being home," Lenore Baker sighed.

Ted looked like he wanted to be anywhere else but here: "I should probably be going. Breakfast was great, though."

And me? I just wanted the dull roar of the morning's festivities to fade away. "Can everyone just shut up?"

Everyone at the table froze in the middle of their own personal freak outs and regarded me – and the massive one I was about to embark on -- carefully.

"What's your deal?" Aunt Tillie asked finally.

"Excuse me? I have a headache, and you all are making it worse."

"You're the one yelling," my mom pointed out.

"I had to yell to make myself heard over all of you," I grumbled, getting to my feet irritably. I headed toward the kitchen. I could hear Aunt Tillie making apologies for me to the Bakers as I left the room.

"She's always been a little high strung," she said.

I attacked the mound of dishes in the sink with gusto, an attempt to wash away this morning's stressful highs and lows. It wasn't exactly working. I heard someone clear their throat behind me and I was surprised when I turned and found Ted standing there instead of Landon.

I raised my eyebrows questioningly. "Do you need something?"

"Your Aunt Tillie sent me in for another pot of coffee." Ted looked uncomfortable at the prospect of being alone with me. I figured it had something to do with the fact that I had just screamed at everyone in the other room.

I punched the buttons on the automatic coffee maker – a little more harshly than I had initially intended. Ted backed away from my jabbing fingers.

"It will take a few minutes," I said finally.

"Yeah, I figured."

I eyed Ted for a second, wondering briefly if I should take advantage of the fact that I had him alone. What the hell, right? I might as well make the morning a complete disaster. "How's your business going, Ted?"

Ted seemed surprised by the question. "It's good."

"Yeah, you're buying up property all over the area," I agreed. I was trying to catch him off guard.

Ted met my gaze evenly. "I'm working for a business consortium. They've got their eye on quite a few properties in the area."

"A business consortium is interested in property in this area?"

"That surprises you?" Ted was playing the situation coolly, but I could tell my questions had him teetering on the edge of some unseen precipice.

"Surprises me? I don't know if that's the term I would use. I guess it would be more apt to say that it confuses me."

"Meaning?"

"It's just that the property you've bought, it doesn't make a lot of sense for a business consortium," I continued. "What, exactly, are they going to build out at the Hollow Creek, for example? That's not zoned for business. The only thing you could build out there is a house."

"I see you've been checking up on me," Ted pursed his lips in response. He was hard to read. I couldn't decide if he was angry or nervous.

"Of course I checked up on you, Ted," I plowed on. "You came to town in the dead of night, you told my boss to lie to me about what you were doing, and then you asked me to lie to Thistle about seeing you. You can see why I would be a little curious."

"I told you, I didn't want you to lie to Thistle," Ted replied. "I just wanted the chance to be the one to talk to her first. I don't see what that has to do with you checking up on my business dealings. It's really none of your business. I guess you're more like your mother than you let on. Everyone's business is your business, huh?"

I ignored the jab – even though I wanted to poke his eyes out for it. I was nothing like my mother. "I'm really more interested in the Dragonfly," I said. "I mean, half that inn is burned out. The property is in a weird location, on a dirt road and all, and your business consortium is going to have to put a lot of money into that property."

"That's their business," Ted said grimly.

"Your business consortium?"

"Yes."

"Have you been out to the property?" I have no idea why I push things like this sometimes – I just can't stop myself.

Ted stilled at the question and turned to me suspiciously. "Have you?"

"I haven't been out there in years," I lied smoothly. "I was just wondering if you had been out there. You know, how closely you've been working with your consortium?"

"I have seen the property," Ted said finally. "I have not spent any time out there, so to speak."

"So, your business consortium is going to open a new bed and breakfast, I'm assuming."

"I have no idea what their plans are once they've acquired the property."

"From you," I interjected.

"What?" Ted looked confused.

"Well, you technically own the property. So they would have to acquire it from you."

"That's just business stuff," Ted waved off the comment like I was a pesky child asking about the meaning of life, or some equally deep question that I couldn't possibly understand the answer to. "There are certain tax incentives and deed documents that have to be explored. It's not a big deal."

"Of course," I said stiffly. *Pardon me for me being interested in some-*

thing I couldn't possibly understand. "You never answered, though. What do they plan to do with the piece of property out at the Hollow Creek?"

Ted stiffened. "I really have no idea. Why do you care?"

"I'm a reporter; it's my job to care," I said blithely.

"You're a reporter for a weekly," Ted scoffed. "I don't think that qualifies you as Lois Lane."

"Why are you skirting the question?"

I looked up in surprise when I saw Aunt Tillie slink into the room. It didn't surprise me that she had been listening at the door. The only thing that surprised me was that she had held her tongue as long as she had.

"Tillie," Ted's demeanor changed from irritated to fearful. "I didn't know you were there."

"I was just checking to see what was taking so long with the coffee," Aunt Tillie said. "I figured, given your track record and all, that maybe you had just run out and abandoned it."

I couldn't help but smirk. I was annoyed with Aunt Tillie – like any other day – but when she turned her considerably evil talents to messing with someone else it was always an entertaining event.

"I'm getting sick of your jabs," Ted swung on Aunt Tillie suddenly, his face red with rage. "You have your version of events, and it's pretty far removed from the truth."

I was stunned with the change in Ted's demeanor. He was actually trying to tower over Aunt Tillie – which wasn't hard, given her slight frame – and he was trying to intimidate her. For her part, Aunt Tillie didn't look all that worried. Bigger men had tried to terrify her into submission – that usually ended up with them crying and begging for mercy.

"Ted," Aunt Tillie said calmly. "I don't blame you for everything that happened when your marriage to Twila fell apart."

My mouth dropped open in surprise. Was she actually placating Ted?

"I do, however, blame you for being a spineless worm that walked out on his daughter in his haste to extricate himself from a marriage that wasn't working – and was never going to work."

So much for placating him. I took a leery step toward Aunt Tillie. I didn't think Ted would be stupid enough to physically attack her, especially given the fact that there was an FBI agent in the next room, but I couldn't be a hundred percent sure.

"You're right," Ted said miserably.

"What?" I turned to him in surprise.

"She's right," Ted's eyes were suddenly swimming in unshed tears. "What kind of father runs away from his own child?"

"A deadbeat one," I said honestly.

Ted met my gaze, surprised by my honesty. "I know that you and Thistle are close … ."

"They're sisters," Aunt Tillie said prissily.

"If you don't like me, if you keep pushing me, Bay, then she won't like me and she'll pull back."

I realized what Ted was asking – but I wasn't sure it was something I could give. "It has nothing to do with liking you Ted. I think you're up to something," I said honestly. "Thistle is a grown up," I continued. "She can make her own decisions."

"Does she think I'm up to something, too?" Ted asked.

Aunt Tillie shifted her gaze to mine, waiting to hear the answer. She looked just as interested as Ted. My mind shifted to not one but two different excursions into the Dragonfly under the cover of snow and dark. "We all think you're up to something," I said reluctantly. "And until you own up to what you're really doing out at the Hollow Creek and at the Dragonfly, I don't see that changing any time soon."

Ted swallowed hard. He looked like he wanted to say something else, but instead he just nodded. "I guess I've earned that."

"I guess you have."

Aunt Tillie and I watched Ted start to leave the kitchen, both of us with heavy hearts and minds. I didn't think our hearts were heavy with the same thing, though, until Aunt Tillie spoke.

"I don't think you're a bad man, Ted," she said finally.

Ted turned to her, hope lighting up his brown eyes.

"You hurt that girl, though, you make her shed one single solitary tear – even one – and I'll castrate you and tie you to a fence post and let the vultures eat you."

Ted's face went ashen in the face of Aunt Tillie's colorful threat. Once he left the room, I turned to Aunt Tillie. "There aren't any vultures in the area," I said. "It was an intriguing threat, though. Visual. One you can't help but picture."

"You think I can't conjure up vultures?" Aunt Tillie raised an eyebrow and then sashayed out of the kitchen.

Cripes, that woman was definitely scary. It was a good thing she was on our side – most of the time, anyway.

TWENTY-NINE

"*I* think you should let me drive."

"I think you should mind your own business."

"I think you should let me drive," Landon repeated. He was standing next to Aunt Tillie's aged plow truck – blocking her from the driver's side door that she was trying to utilize.

"And I told you that you should mind your own business." For her part, Aunt Tillie looked like an enraged – but appropriately layered against the cold – hobbit with a purpose. And that purpose? To clear the country road between the inn and town from about a foot and a half of snow.

Landon, who often vacillated between amused and annoyed when dealing with Aunt Tillie, was firmly in the annoyed category at the present moment. He also wasn't giving up any ground. "Do you have a driver's license?"

"Of course."

"Show it to me."

"No," Aunt Tillie balked. "I have a right to privacy, and that's invading my privacy."

"How is that invading your privacy?"

"There's stuff on there that I don't want anyone to see," Aunt Tillie said stubbornly.

"Like?"

"Like my weight."

"I won't look at your weight."

"Now that I've told you that I don't want you to look at it, that's the first thing you'll look at," Aunt Tillie said knowingly.

Landon rubbed his chin ruefully. I couldn't help but notice that he hadn't shaved that morning – and morning stubble made him look even sexier than usual. I internalized the sigh that threatened to escape. Now was not the time for flights of fancy with Landon and his scruffy face.

"I think you should let me drive," Landon tried a different tack. "I'm a man and it will hurt my ego if you don't let me drive."

Aunt Tillie narrowed her eyes at him distrustfully. "I have my doubts about you being a man. Men are better liars."

Landon grabbed his heart in faux pain. "You wound me." His eyes were deadly serious, though, despite the mirth in his words.

"I'm driving."

"No, I'm driving," he corrected her.

"Bay, will you tell your boyfriend that this is my truck and I'm the one driving?" Aunt Tillie turned to me expectantly.

"Yeah, Bay," Thistle sang out from behind me. "Tell Landon how it's going to be. Lay down the law."

I shot Thistle a dirty look and, if I'm being truthful, the finger, too. Then I turned back to Aunt Tillie. "Landon isn't my boyfriend," I said.

Landon glared in my direction. "That's what you're arguing with? The fact that she called me your boyfriend?"

"What should I be arguing with?" I asked stubbornly.

"How about the fact that she shouldn't be driving? How about that?"

"She's fine," I waved off his concerns. "She's not going to die behind the wheel of her plow."

"That's not what I'm talking about," Landon seethed. "I'm talking about her hitting someone else."

"I would never do that," Aunt Tillie looked scandalized.

"She hasn't had any accidents in years," I said.

Landon didn't look convinced. "Just let me drive."

"No," Aunt Tillie put her hands on her hips stubbornly. "And if you say it one more time, I won't give you a ride into town."

"That may be a blessing," Landon said under his breath.

"You want to stay here and spend time with my mom?" I asked him pointedly.

Landon seemed to consider the suggestion for a second. His shudder, though, told me that he was dismissing it outright. "Fine."

Thistle and Clove climbed into the back of the truck again, leaving me to slide over to the center seat. Landon begrudgingly climbed into the passenger side seat of the truck and fastened himself in. Aunt Tillie was a lot more smug when she climbed into the truck and settled herself behind the wheel. "Everyone ready for an adventure?"

Landon didn't look happy with the levity of her words or the condescending nature of her stare. I had to bite my lip to keep from laughing out loud, though, when I felt his hand grip my knee. His knuckles were white from the effort he was exerting to keep from jerking the wheel out of Aunt Tillie's hands.

Here's the thing, Aunt Tillie really is a poor driver. She's so short she has trouble seeing over the steering wheel – especially in a big truck like the one we were in now. She had long ago taken to stacking kitchen chair cushions underneath her so she could see out of the windshield. That was only one problem taken care of, though. The other was the fact that she had a lead foot. It was bad enough on dry roads in the summer. On wet ones in the winter, though, it was kind of like being in a runaway roller-coaster with snow banks.

Each time we ricocheted off one snow bank Landon gritted his teeth. Every time we careened into another, he muttered under his breath. It took us about an hour to get to town. And, by the time that we did, I had heard pretty much every swear word ever invented – and even a few I had never heard before. Landon looked relieved when we came around the corner and found that Hemlock Cove itself had already been plowed out. Not only that, whomever had done it had pulled his vehicle and Thistle's car out of the snow drifts and left them in the parking lot of the police station.

"You're probably going to have to pay a fine," I glanced at Thistle in the rearview mirror.

"It won't be the first time," she sighed.

"Since it's my fault we got caught downtown, I'll pay for it," I offered.

"We'll split it," Clove said congenially. "Even though I told you that I didn't want to go on that little adventure."

Thistle kicked Clove viciously, causing her to yelp out. She shot a pointed look in Landon's direction and then raised her finger to her lips in a shushing gesture. The exchange wasn't lost on Landon. "Why would you get a ticket?"

"It's a snow emergency," I said breezily. "You can't leave vehicles on city streets overnight in a snow emergency." I had no doubt that Landon knew I was lying. I tried to pretend that I didn't notice his grip on my knee tightening, though.

"Why was it your fault that you were downtown so late yesterday?" Landon asked the question like it wasn't important, but I could tell that he was thinking the exact opposite. "Were you doing girl things?"

"Yeah, we were buying tampons," Thistle shot back pointedly. "And douche. We were buying tampons and douche." She was trying to make Landon uncomfortable, that much was obvious, but I was the one feeling the blush creeping over my cheeks. I glanced at Landon and noticed the color rushing to his face, as well.

"You know what's funny about that?"

"What?" Thistle said innocently.

"I don't believe you," he said. "I know women."

"How many women have you known?" Aunt Tillie interjected. I glanced over at her. She had no idea why she was helping; she just knew that she didn't like Landon's tone. I let her have her malevolent fun, though. I didn't think that admitting we were breaking and entering when we should have been ducking and covering was going to make him all that happy with me.

"What does that have to do with anything?" Landon asked irritably.

"I'm just curious. The sexual exploits of a man's past tell you a lot about a man's future."

Landon's face looked blank for a second. "Are you trying to confuse me?"

"That depends," Aunt Tillie placed her tongue in her cheek. "Are you confused or are you evading me?"

"Evading you? Why would I be evading you?"

"Because you don't want to tell me how many women you've slept with."

"How many men have you slept with," Landon challenged her.

"One."

"One?" Landon turned to me for confirmation.

"Don't look at me," I said. "I have no idea."

"How many have you been with again, dear?" Aunt Tillie turned to Landon.

Landon snorted in disgust. "I'm not answering that."

Aunt Tillie turned to me. "That means he's been with a lot. Maybe he's like that Kareem Abdul Chamberlain."

"Who?" I furrowed my eyebrows.

"That basketball player that slept with a hundred women," Aunt Tillie supplied.

"I haven't slept with a hundred women," Landon challenged.

"Maybe he's still a virgin," Thistle piped up from the backseat.

Aunt Tillie nodded sagely. "That could be it."

"I'm not a virgin either," Landon growled.

"So why won't you tell us how many women you've slept with?" Clove piped up from the backseat, joining the fun.

Landon slid a dangerous look in my direction. "You and I are spending our next date alone."

"This was a date?" I was surprised.

"I certainly didn't sleep on your mother's couch for my health," Landon said.

Aunt Tillie parked in front of the police station. I saw Chief Terry wander out curiously. His face broke into a wide smile when he saw Landon in the passenger seat of Aunt Tillie's ride. Once we were all out of the truck, Chief Terry couldn't rein in his amusement any longer. "You spent the night out at the inn?"

"On the couch," Landon said stiffly.

"I made sure of it." Aunt Tillie had rolled down her window and was enjoying Landon's discomfort in front of Chief Terry.

"How did you make sure of it?" Chief Terry asked, although I think he already knew the answer.

"My shotgun," Aunt Tillie shrugged.

"That will do it."

I glanced around a second, realizing that what had started out as a caravan from the inn had turned into a solo trek at some point. "Where did Trevor and Ted go?"

Thistle glanced up and down the street. "I have no idea."

"Do you think they got stuck?" Clove looked appalled – and ready to run to Trevor's rescue. I imagine she had a fuzzy image in her head that involved hot chocolate, a roaring fire and absolutely no clothes.

"I think we would have noticed that," I said.

"Not the way your Aunt Tillie drives," Landon grumbled.

Chief Terry snickered. "If I understand you correctly, you're saying you had more people with you when you left the inn?"

"We did."

"And you lost them somewhere?"

"Yeah."

Chief Terry looked thoughtful. "Ted was one of them?"

"He stopped by the inn for breakfast to make sure everyone was okay," Thistle said defensively.

"I didn't say anything," Chief Terry held up his hands in surrender.

"I think he's jealous," I teased. "He's worried Twila will pay less attention to him and more attention to Ted."

Chief Terry shot me a dirty look. "At least Aunt Tillie isn't guarding Twila's virtue with a shotgun."

"Whatever," I huffed. I decided to change the subject. "So, where do we think Ted and Trevor went?"

"I guess we better find out," Landon sighed.

I watched as he moved around to the driver's side of the plow truck, opened the door, and then forcefully moved Aunt Tillie from the driver's seat to the center seat. "I'm driving this time."

"All you had to do was ask," Aunt Tillie sniffed. "You don't have to be a Neanderthal."

Thistle, Clove, and I watched the exchange in surprise. Aunt Tillie can run hot and cold without any indication of what temperature she's leaning toward at any given moment.

"What are you waiting for?" Aunt Tillie eyed Landon curiously.

"My girlfriend to get in the car," he said grimly. "I'm not finished with the conversation we were having and I thought I could kill two birds with one stone."

"Oh," Aunt Tillie said knowingly. "You're going to tell her how many women you've slept with."

"No," Landon said. "I'm going to find out what she and her cousins were doing last night when they should have been taking cover."

"Oh, *that* conversation."

"Yes, *that* conversation."

Landon turned to me. "Get in the truck, Bay."

Crap.

THIRTY

*L*andon seemed to have no trouble turning Aunt Tillie's monster truck around. Once it was pointed in the right direction, he gunned the engine and headed back out of town.

"He's a good driver," Aunt Tillie said.

Landon ignored her. "What were Thistle and Clove talking about?"

The question was pointed. I wasn't sure what to do. Our previous problems had stemmed from the fact that I couldn't tell the truth because of my family. Currently, we were facing the problem of me not being able to tell the truth because I didn't want to go to jail. Okay, my family might be playing a part in this deception as well.

Aunt Tillie watched me struggle internally and then blew out a frustrated sigh. "You might as well tell him."

"You just want me to tell him because that means you'll find out, too."

"That's an ugly thing to say to your elder," Aunt Tillie pouted.

"I'm sorry," I said.

"I accept your apology," Aunt Tillie said. "Now, why don't you tell both of us what you and your delinquent cousins have been hiding?"

I pursed my lips ruefully. "We haven't been hiding anything," I said carefully.

"Lies," Aunt Tillie said. "I can always tell when you're hiding something, and the three of you have been acting like you're up to something for several days."

I wanted to kick her.

"We haven't been hiding anything," I repeated.

"Then what were you and Ted talking about in the kitchen?"

Landon kept his eyes on the road, content for the moment to let Aunt Tillie grill me.

"I looked into his financials," I admitted. "I thought it was weird that he came to town, fronting some business consortium, and tried to initially hide from us."

"And what did you find out?" Aunt Tillie asked.

I explained about the three pieces of property. Landon and Aunt Tillie listened but didn't speak. When I was done, Aunt Tillie looked irritated. "He's bringing competition into town."

"What do you mean?"

"Why else would he buy the Dragonfly?"

"You think that's why he was trying to be all stealthy?" Something about that scenario didn't quite fit.

"Why else?"

"Then what does he want with the property out at the Hollow Creek?" I asked.

"I don't know," Aunt Tillie said thoughtfully. "If they wanted to have that rezoned, they would have to go before the city and we would have heard something about that if it happened."

"Are you sure?" Landon finally spoke.

"It's a small town," I said.

"Do you know everything that goes on in town?"

"Pretty much," I shrugged.

"What did Ted say to you when you questioned him about it?" Landon had his immovable cop face on. His eyes were glued to the road ahead of us, but he was still listening to everything I had to say.

"He just said he was buying up the property for a business consortium. That's all he would say."

"But you don't believe him?"

"No."

"What else?"

"What else what?"

"What else?" Landon pressed. "What were you, Clove and Thistle doing right before you got stuck yesterday?"

There was no way I was going to answer that. "We were running errands," I said evasively. "Checking a few things out."

"What things?"

"Just things," I said.

Aunt Tillie sensed my sudden distress. "What were you really doing sneaking around the inn last night?"

I glanced at her a second and then blew out a weary sigh. She was giving me an out here – but it was one that benefitted her. I didn't have a lot of choice in the matter. "We were looking at the financial information for the Bakers."

"The Bakers?" Aunt Tillie looked surprised. "Why?"

"Because I thought their arrival – at the same time a boat was found abandoned in the channel – was a little bit suspicious," I admitted. "Anyone else in their right mind would have packed up and left before the blizzard hit."

Aunt Tillie mulled through the puzzle. "You have a point," she said finally.

"It happens on occasion."

"You're smarter than you look sometimes," Aunt Tillie agreed.

Landon gritted his teeth and shook his head. I could tell he wanted to press me on my movements yesterday afternoon, but he was letting it slide – for the moment, at least.

"So what did you find out?" Aunt Tillie asked.

"It's clean, as far as I can tell."

"Why didn't you just tell me what you were doing last night?"

"Because I didn't want you to freak out on us for going through your clients' personal information."

"I wouldn't have freaked out about that."

"Since when?"

"Your mothers would have freaked out," Aunt Tillie corrected me. "I would have joined you in the investigation."

I considered the statement. She had a point. She had never been one for respecting a person's right for privacy – except when it came to her own.

"You still think there's something off about the Bakers, don't you?" Landon asked the question quietly, but with determination.

"I don't know," I shrugged. "Something just feels off."

"I'll do a little more digging into them," Landon said finally.

"You will?" This sounded like a trap.

"I will," Landon agreed.

I blew out a relieved sigh.

"If you tell me what you were doing yesterday afternoon."

Crap on toast.

"I already told you, we were just running errands."

"I don't believe you."

"I don't know what you want me to say," I said helplessly.

Landon slowed down the truck. I thought, for a second, he was going to jump out of the vehicle and run away screaming into the snow about women and lies. I saw that he was scanning the fork in the road instead. "Someone went in that direction," he said finally. "Where does that go?"

"Nowhere," Aunt Tillie said. "There's nothing out there. It's a dirt road."

"Are there any houses out there?" Landon asked.

"A few," Aunt Tillie said. "Those are survivalists, though. They wouldn't be out driving around this early after a blizzard."

"What else is out there?" Landon pressed.

"Just the Dragonfly," Aunt Tillie said. She swung on me suddenly, surprise smoothing the wrinkles around her ancient and suspicious eyes. "Ted!"

"Why would he want to go out to this inn in the middle of a snow-storm?" Landon asked pragmatically. "The way you make it sound, it's a dump."

199

"Maybe he's keeping something out there," Aunt Tillie said. "Like drugs."

I felt my heart clench in my chest.

"Or bodies," Aunt Tillie continued, not dissuaded by the warning glances I kept shooting in her direction. "Maybe he killed the people on the boat and hid their bodies there."

"Why would he kill the people on the boat?" Landon asked.

"Why would he buy an inn just to hide bodies at it?" I chimed in.

"Maybe he's a Devil worshipper," Aunt Tillie stiffened her chin.

"Maybe he's a witch," Landon grumbled.

"There's no devil in the craft," Aunt Tillie corrected him.

"Sorry," he muttered. He looked like he was debating on whether or not he should follow whatever vehicle had traversed the snowy road.

"You're not mean," Aunt Tillie said. "You're just uneducated. I get that."

Landon shot her a dirty look.

"Bay will teach you. You'll teach each other a few things, I would gather," Aunt Tillie continued.

I felt my face redden. Landon didn't look like he was in the mood for Aunt Tillie advice. "If that's the truth, then why did you sleep outside their room with a shotgun last night?"

"I would prefer it if you taught each other things away from the roof I sleep under," Aunt Tillie said stiffly.

"Fair enough," Landon agreed. "We're going back to town," he said finally. "I want to talk to Chief Terry and make sure you're safe in town."

"I don't need your protection," I corrected him.

"Yeah? Well, you're going to get it," Landon said. "Especially since you still seem to be reluctant to tell me what it was you were doing yesterday afternoon."

"Are you calling her a liar?" Aunt Tillie swung on Landon angrily.

"Yes."

Aunt Tillie shrugged. "Fair enough."

"Aunt Tillie," I chastised her.

"I can tell you're lying, honey. So can he," Aunt Tillie countered. "I just don't think he realizes you're not lying to protect yourself."

Landon seemed to consider Aunt Tillie's statement for a second. Realization dawned across his face. "You're protecting Thistle."

"How do you figure?" I asked warily.

"You suspect Ted is up to something. Ted has disappeared. You disappeared yesterday afternoon. All of this ties together somehow. I'm just not exactly sure how."

"Well done, officer," Aunt Tillie said.

"I'm an agent," Landon said.

"Don't get a big head," Aunt Tillie said. "You've started to grow on me – but that can change."

It took us about fifteen minutes to get back to town. Aunt Tillie used that time to explain to Landon why he should never call me a liar to my face and – instead – just learn to trick me into telling him the truth. She had tips, in case he was interested. When we got back to town, Landon grudgingly let Aunt Tillie climb back in the driver's seat of her truck and head back toward the inn. She promised she would go straight there and not stop anyplace else.

"Drive slowly," he admonished her.

"I've been driving for longer than you've been alive," she reminded him.

"That doesn't mean I want you to die," Landon said.

"You'd miss me," Aunt Tillie scoffed sarcastically.

"No, Bay would," he corrected her. "I don't want to see her sad."

Aunt Tillie started to roll up her window. "I might miss you a little," he conceded.

Aunt Tillie beamed at him for a second and then quickly wiped the smile off her face. "There's no accounting for taste."

Once she was gone, Landon turned to me. I couldn't decide if he was angry or tired – or maybe a little of both. "We're going to talk about whatever you're hiding later. By a fire. When it's just the two of us."

"That sounds a little presumptuous," I said.

"I don't care," Landon replied. "After last night, you owe me."

I ignored the statement. "What are you going to do now?"

"I'm going to go talk to Chief Terry and then the two of us are going to go check out those tracks."

"I could go with you," I offered.

"No," Landon shook his head. "You can stay here in town. In fact, I want you to stay at Hypnotic with your cousins. Don't go to the paper. Don't go to the cop shop. You stay in that store."

"Why?"

"Just do as I ask, for a change," Landon sighed.

"Are you punishing me?" I narrowed my eyes in his direction.

Landon grabbed the lapels of my coat and pulled me toward him. He planted his lips on mine for a second and then pulled away somewhat reluctantly. "Trust me," he said. "When I punish you, you'll know it."

Despite myself, I felt a little thrill rush through me as I crossed the street – accidentally tripping over the curb as I stepped up onto the sidewalk in front of Hypnotic – and opened the door to the store. When I turned around, I found that Landon was still watching me. That gave me a little thrill, too.

Crap! I was definitely getting in deep now.

THIRTY-ONE

Clove and Thistle were waiting for me when I entered Hypnotic.

"Well?" Thistle was sitting on the couch, looking dejected. I wasn't a hundred percent sure why.

"Well what?"

"Well, where did they go?"

"Aunt Tillie and Landon? Aunt Tillie went home and Landon went to talk to Chief Terry."

"No, not Aunt Tillie and Landon," Thistle replied irritably. "Trevor and my dad."

"I don't know," I answered truthfully. "There was at least one set of tracks breaking off from the main road on the route back."

"What road?" Thistle asked blandly.

"Maple."

Thistle grimaced. "Back out to the Dragonfly. Why would he go there?"

"I may have let on that we knew about the property he bought," I said sheepishly.

"Why would you do that?"

"I don't know," I admitted. "It seemed like a good idea at the time."

"Do you still think that?" Clove asked.

"Probably not."

"So, now what? Did you tell Landon about us breaking into the Dragonfly?" Thistle asked.

"Are you crazy? I don't want him to arrest me."

"He wouldn't arrest you," Clove scoffed. "He already knows we're hiding something."

"He doesn't know that we're hiding something illegal."

"It's barely illegal," Thistle said. "The inn has a wall missing from it, for crying out loud. We could have just wandered in."

"Do you think he'll believe that? And we didn't just wander in," I reminded her. "We used the front door – and we used magic to open it."

"He probably won't believe that," Thistle conceded. "He won't arrest you, though. I'm sure about that."

I started to pace without even realizing what I was doing. Clove and Thistle watched me for a few minutes in silence, leaving me alone with my rather cluttered brain. Finally I stopped and looked back to them. "Something isn't right about all of this."

"Just one thing?" Clove asked drolly.

"Wasn't Brian behind us, too?"

Thistle looked surprised. "What? Brian Kelly? Yeah, I guess he was at the back of the caravan, now that I think of it."

"Where did he go?"

"That's a good question," Thistle agreed. "You think they're all doing it together?"

"There are three of them," I said simply.

Clove looked aghast. "Are you insinuating that Brian, Uncle Teddy and Trevor are working together?"

"Maybe," I shrugged.

"Don't you think you would have recognized Brian's voice?" Clove was desperate. "I'm absolutely positive I didn't hear Trevor out there."

"It could just be a coincidence that they all disappeared," I admitted. "It wouldn't be the first time we've jumped to the wrong conclusion."

"It wouldn't be the first time this week," Clove grumbled.

"I'm not saying it's them," I said hurriedly. "I just think the fact that all three of them disappeared at the same time is a little strange."

"Maybe they just didn't want to follow Aunt Tillie," Clove said. "She drives like a crazy person."

"That's a possibility," I agreed, although my heart wasn't really in it.

"The question is," Thistle interjected. "What would they all be doing out there?"

"Maybe they're opening up a new inn," Clove said. She was getting desperate now. "Maybe they don't want anyone to know because they're afraid Aunt Tillie will curse them if she finds out that they're competition."

"She hasn't cursed any other inn owners," Thistle pointed out. "This area can actually sustain another inn without anyone losing any business. As it is now, people have to stay in some of the surrounding towns."

"Well, maybe they're all planning a surprise for us?" Clove's voice was becoming uncomfortably shrill.

"Killing us would be a surprise," Thistle said blandly.

"That's not funny," Clove whimpered.

"It wasn't trying to be funny."

"You think your dad is planning your death? That's so … ."

"I don't think he's planning my death," Thistle sighed. "I just think he's up to something."

"And I think Brian is involved," I added.

"What about Trevor?" Clove's lower lip started to quiver.

"I have no idea where Trevor fits into this," I said. "I actually can't think of a rational way for him to fit into this."

"But you think Brian is up to something?" Clove seemed a little less upset by my admission.

"I know Brian is up to something," I said forcefully. "I've had Edith spying on him."

"What has she told you?" Thistle asked.

"I haven't talked to her in a few days."

"No time like the present," Thistle suggested.

"Landon said we should stay here," I hedged.

"Is Landon the boss of you?" Thistle poked me in the ribs.

"Not last time I checked," I agreed. "He'll be mad if we leave, though."

"What he doesn't know won't hurt him," Thistle said, jumping to her feet. "We can go down to the paper, talk to Edith, and be back before anyone even knows we're gone."

I sighed. I had already decided to do just that. Blaming it on Thistle might save me a tongue lashing later, though. "Let's go."

It took us longer than normal to get down to The Whistler – mostly because we had to walk on the main street because the sidewalks were still clogged. I was hopeful that Landon and Chief Terry were already out investigating, because if they looked out the window of the cop shop – there was no way they could miss us.

When we got to the paper, I headed to my office first. Clove and Thistle were right behind me. They were both curious if they would be able to see Edith. We had found out, in recent months, that Clove and Thistle could eventually hear ghosts if they were close to me. They hadn't been able to see one yet, but they were both anxiously looking forward to the possibility of it happening. Thankfully, I didn't have to go looking for Edith. She was waiting for me in my office.

"Where have you been?" She asked irritably.

"We had a blizzard."

Edith glanced out of my office window. "It doesn't look that bad."

"That's easy for a ghost to say," Thistle grumbled.

"She can hear me?"

"Sometimes," I said. "We actually came down to talk to you, Edith."

Edith couldn't hide the smile that flitted across her face. "Why?"

"It's that task I gave you a few days ago," I said.

"Spying on Brian?" Edith's smile began to falter. "You came here to pump me for information?"

"Well, no," I lied. "I came here because I missed you. I was just hoping that you might have some information, too."

Thistle hid her snort in her sleeve, trying to cover it up with a fake sneeze.

"Oh," Edith still looked doubtful. "Well, I do have some news on that front."

"Oh, yeah?" I tried to temper my interest. I didn't want to tip Edith over from uncertainty into a righteous snit.

"Before he left yesterday, I heard him on the phone again," Edith said.

"Who was he on the phone with?"

Edith looked at Thistle dubiously. "Maybe we should do this in private?"

Thistle couldn't see Edith, but she recognized the tone in her voice. "It was my dad, wasn't it?"

"Yes," Edith said.

"What were they saying?" I prodded Edith.

"They were saying the deal was essentially done and that they only had to keep you in the dark for another week," Edith said.

"Me personally?"

"Actually, they said the Winchesters," Edith corrected herself. "He said that the Winchesters had no idea what was going on and that they had essentially done what they set out to do. He went on to say that you were all too distracted with your crazy Aunt Tillie."

"He called Aunt Tillie crazy?" Thistle asked.

"No, I might have added that part myself," Edith admitted stiffly.

"I thought Brian was trying to sell the paper," I admitted ruefully.

"He can't do that," Edith said sharply.

"Why?"

"It was in William's will," Edith said. "He can't sell the paper. If he doesn't want to run it anymore, he has to turn it over to you."

"I didn't know that," I said. "Why didn't you tell me that?"

"I don't know," Edith shrugged. "I thought you knew – and I had forgotten until just now."

"How would I know that?"

"You're a witch," Edith said simply. "I thought you could cast a truth spell on him or something."

Technically, I could do that. I generally tried to avoid any spells, though, that took over someone's free will. Karma has a funny sense of humor.

"Well, if I had known that, I would have been more suspicious of Brian earlier," I said finally.

"Haven't you always been suspicious of him?" Clove chided me.

"Well, obviously I had a reason."

"So Brian has been having meetings with my dad," Thistle said thoughtfully. "And whatever they're doing involves the Dragonfly and making sure we don't find out what's going on?"

Edith nodded, even though Clove and Thistle couldn't see her.

"It's got to be drugs," Thistle said. "What else could it be? What else could they have in those crates?"

"What crates?" Edith asked.

"We don't know that it is drugs," I said, ignoring Edith's question. "It could be anything."

"Anything? Or anything that's illegal and they're desperate that we don't find out?"

"They could just be opening an inn," I said lamely.

"Really? Are you channeling Clove or something?" Thistle shot back snottily.

"Hey, I'm just standing here listening to the two of you and you decide to attack me?" Clove looked hurt.

"Oh, just get over it," Thistle grumbled.

"Is she always this mean to you?" Edith asked.

"Always," Clove nodded.

"That's terrible," Edith clucked.

"Tell me about it," Clove agreed.

"You know what we have to do," Thistle said suddenly.

Clove snapped her head in Thistle's direction. "No, we don't have to do anything."

"I know," I blew out a sigh.

"No, we don't have to do anything," Clove repeated.

"How are we going to get out there?" Thistle asked.

"We're not going anywhere," Clove crossed her arms across her chest obstinately. "It's cold and we just had a blizzard."

"We could take your car," I suggested.

"It probably won't make it down Maple if the snow hasn't been cleared yet."

She had a point. "We could go back out to the inn and get the snowmobiles?"

"Then we would have to explain what we were doing," Thistle shot me down.

"See, there's no way out there," Clove said primly.

I considered the conundrum for a second and then turned to Thistle grimly. "We could snowshoe."

Thistle's eyes lit up. "That's a great idea."

"Where are you snowshoeing?" Edith asked Clove.

"To Hell," she replied angrily. "To Hell."

THIRTY-TWO

"*I* want it noted, for the record, that I thought this was a bad idea from the start."

"We know, Clove," Thistle grunted. "You've told us the exact same thing for the last five minutes. We get it. You don't want to go back out to the Dragonfly."

"You don't have to go," I said mildly. "Thistle and I can go by ourselves."

Clove rolled her eyes and stomped her foot impatiently. "Oh, yeah, right. Like that's going to happen."

"Bay is right," Thistle said knowingly. "You stay here. We'll go by ourselves."

"That's great," Clove said petulantly. "I'll stay here and if you guys die then I'll be wracked with guilt for the rest of my life."

"At least you'll be alive," Thistle pointed out.

"And if you do survive," Clove continued. "I'll forever be reminded that I was the one that missed the adventure."

Thistle smirked in my direction. "So, I guess you're coming?"

"I guess so," Clove sighed. "I still think snowshoeing out there is a mistake. It's too far."

"Not if we cut across property instead of going around it," Thistle replied shortly.

Clove turned to me for help. "You can't think that this is a good idea. That's got to be a five-mile hike, even cutting across every piece of property between here and there."

"It's more like two miles," I laughed.

"One way," Clove pointed out.

"That's still only four miles total," Thistle said. "We've done more than that for exercise."

"Not since we were teenagers."

She had a point. Working out wasn't something any of us liked to do.

Thistle thought about what Clove was saying for a second and then shook her head. "We don't have a lot of options."

"We could tell Landon what we know," Clove said suddenly. "We could let the police do the investigating, for a change."

"I don't know," I hedged.

"I do," Thistle charged. "I don't want to accuse my dad of doing something illegal without proof."

Clove sighed dramatically. "Fine. But if we die, I'm going to haunt you forever."

"Duly noted," Thistle said.

"I think we should at least leave a note for Landon at the store," I said finally.

Thistle regarded me seriously. "I think that's probably one of your better ideas."

Clove nodded energetically. I think she was hoping that we would run into Landon on the street and have our plans thwarted, but that was a chance I was willing to take.

"Just in case," I said.

When we got back to Hypnotic, I was surprised to find Aunt Tillie sitting on the couch in the middle of the store. "What are you doing here?"

"Waiting for you," Aunt Tillie said simply.

"How did you get in here?" Thistle asked. "I locked the door."

"That won't keep Aunt Tillie out," I laughed. "You know that."

"I knew that the three of you were up to something," Aunt Tillie said airily. "Let's just say I had a feeling that you would need me."

"You can't come," Thistle said. "We're snowshoeing out to ... somewhere."

"The Dragonfly," Aunt Tillie said. "Bay told me."

Thistle swung on me. "You told her?"

"Not everything," I hissed. "She was in the truck with Landon and me. I didn't tell her everything."

"I know you guys have been out there," Aunt Tillie said.

"Who told you that?" I narrowed my eyes.

"You just did."

"Well, you can't come. You can't walk that far."

"Walk? Who's walking," Aunt Tillie scoffed. "I have my plow."

Clove turned to me and raised her eyebrows, her interest was suddenly piqued. "That's definitely better than walking."

"I don't know," Thistle shook her head. "You can't miss that truck. It's too obvious."

Aunt Tillie shot Thistle an angry look. "You're just saying that because you want to leave me behind."

"We do want to leave you behind," I agreed. "That doesn't mean that taking your truck is a good idea."

"Fine," Aunt Tillie agreed. "If we can't take the truck, then we'll go back to the inn and take the snowmobiles."

"We thought about that," I explained. "However, then we would have to explain to our mothers where we were going and what we were doing."

"And no one wants that," Thistle said.

"You have a point," Aunt Tillie nodded sagely. "Doesn't Marcus have snowmobiles?"

Thistle froze at the suggestion. "Why didn't I think of that?"

"We're not at our best when our sleep cycle is interrupted," I suggested helpfully. "Still, though, that's such a better idea."

"How many do they have?" Clove asked.

"We only need two," I said. "We'll double up."

"I'm not taking Aunt Tillie," Thistle said hurriedly.

Aunt Tillie glowered at Thistle. "You should be so lucky."

"I'll take Aunt Tillie," I sighed.

"Now you want to take her?" Thistle looked incredulous.

"Uncle Teddy and Brian are both terrified of her," I reminded Thistle.

"Brian?" Aunt Tillie looked confused. "What does Brian have to do with this?"

I told her what we had found out – everything we had found out. I even told her about breaking into the Dragonfly, hearing three mysterious voices, and then returning to the Dragonfly a second time. When I was done, Aunt Tillie looked like she was going to spontaneously combust.

"Let me get this straight," she seethed. "You broke into the Dragonfly twice, you almost got interrupted twice, you had Edith spy on Brian and now you want to go out to the Dragonfly for a third time because someone clearly went out to the inn after leaving the Overlook this morning?"

"That's about it," Thistle said wryly.

"Good job," Aunt Tillie said.

"Good job?" I was surprised by her accolades.

"You know where you screwed up?" Aunt Tillie asked.

"I do," Clove raised her hand enthusiastically.

"Clove?" Aunt Tillie turned to her, like she was asking a question of her favorite pupil in a classroom. "Tell your cousins where they went wrong."

"We should have taken you with us from the beginning," Clove said smugly.

"That's exactly right," Aunt Tillie nodded.

Thistle and I exchanged dubious glances. Clove always was the suck-up. "Fine," Thistle grumbled. "We should have told you from the beginning. Are you happy now?"

"I'm not unhappy," Aunt Tillie said.

"Let's go," I sighed. "The longer we drag this out, the worse it's going to be for everyone."

"I agree," Aunt Tillie jumped to her feet. "Let's go crack the case."

Thistle grabbed my arm as we started to file in behind Aunt Tillie. "I have a bad feeling about this."

"It's Aunt Tillie," I said. "I always have a bad feeling when she's involved."

"I heard that," Aunt Tillie called out from the front door of the store.

"Of course you did," Thistle grumbled. "You hear all and see all."

"And don't you forget it."

At the door, I remembered that we had actually come to the store to leave a note for Landon. I quickly scrawled one out on a sheet of paper and propped it up against the cash register before leaving the building. A surge of guilt coursed through me, but I quickly tamped it down. Landon had told me to stay put, but he wasn't the boss of me, I reminded myself.

When I joined everyone, I fell into line behind Aunt Tillie and plodded down the street with her. It was too late to turn back now. Aunt Tillie was going regardless, and we couldn't let her go alone. The truth was, Thistle wasn't the only one that had to know what was going on out at the Dragonfly. I had to know, too. It would plague me; haunt my dreams, if I tried to ignore it.

Once we got to the stable, Marcus greeted us with a warm smile – and a curious eyebrow. "What's going on?" He dropped a kiss on Thistle's waiting mouth, but he didn't make a move toward Aunt Tillie. She was generally friendly with him, but he was terrified of her.

"We need to borrow two snowmobiles," Thistle said apologetically.

"Why?"

"What does it matter," Aunt Tillie replied irritably.

Marcus took an involuntary step back. "Of course. I'll gas two of them up."

"That would be great," Thistle put a hand on his arm.

"Where are you going?" Marcus asked nervously.

"We're going to the Dragonfly," Thistle said.

"That old burned out inn?"

"Yeah."

"Why?"

"What are you, the snowmobile police?" Aunt Tillie barked.

"Oh, leave him alone," Thistle argued. "He's doing us a favor."

Aunt Tillie turned to me for support.

"You're being mean," I agreed.

"Well, he's not moving fast enough," Aunt Tillie said. "I'm not getting any younger."

"All physical evidence to the contrary," I laughed.

"What?"

"Nothing."

"I'm not sure what you're talking about," Aunt Tillie said. "I do think I've been insulted, though."

"It's not an insult," I sighed heavily.

"I'll decide that later," Aunt Tillie said. "After we crack the case."

"Great." I had definitely spent too much time with Aunt Tillie today. In an effort to get just a minute of quiet time, I wandered away from the group and back outside. The day didn't look like it was going to be over any time soon.

Marcus was busy gassing up the snowmobiles and I could hear Aunt Tillie griping about how long it was taking him. I let my eyes wander over the town, taking in the almost untouched winter wonderland laid out in front of me. Hemlock Cove may be small, but it had a beauty that couldn't be denied.

I was enthralled with that beauty for a few minutes, just breathing in the cold air and enjoying my hometown, when a hint of movement caught my attention. I turned and stared toward the docks, squinting to try and clarify what I was seeing.

"What is that?" Thistle had slid up beside me.

"There's someone on the docks," I said.

"By that abandoned boat," Thistle said. "I see him, too."

Thistle turned to me slowly, realization dawning on her face. "Why would someone be on that boat the day after a blizzard?"

"Let's go find out."

THIRTY-THREE

"Are you sure you want to do this?"

I was surprised by Thistle's sudden reticence. She was usually the first one through a door in a crisis. I regarded her speculatively. "You don't want to go see who is over there?"

"I don't know," Thistle admitted.

"You're worried it's your dad," I said sagely.

"Maybe," Thistle worried her bottom lip with her teeth.

"We don't know that whatever is happening out at the Dragonfly has anything to do with the Hobbes going missing from their boat," I reminded her.

"We don't know that it doesn't either," Thistle replied. "I think you think that the two cases are entwined."

"Why do you say that?"

"Because Hemlock Cove is a small town," Thistle said. "It would be more surprising if we had two crimes going on at once and they had nothing to do with each other."

She had a point. "We don't know that anything illegal is going on out at the Dragonfly."

Thistle shot me a harsh look. "I'm not Clove," she said. "I don't need things white-washed for me."

"We don't even know that your dad was one of the people out at the Dragonfly."

"We don't know that he wasn't either."

I blew out a sigh. "I need to know who is over on that boat."

Thistle glanced behind us. Aunt Tillie was still verbally lambasting Marcus – and she was doing it out of our sight line. "We should go now. We'll never be able to sneak up on whoever it is if she's with us."

I nodded my silent assent. Thistle and I detached from the shadows that had been hiding us under the eaves of the stables and started down the street. There really was no way to hide our approach, but I was hoping we could at least pretend we were going to the newspaper as a momentary diversion.

The closer we got to the docks, the more my heart started to race. You know when you have that feeling where you're sure that your life is about to change – although you can't pinpoint why you have that feeling? That's how I was feeling now.

When we got to the docks, we tacitly agreed to go single file – pressing close to the fence on the far side of the walkway. Thistle gestured to the footprints on the walkway silently. There were three different sets. It was impossible to tell – for us at least – if they belonged to men or women. They just looked like boot prints in more than a foot of snow to us. It was the number of prints, though, that was troubling. It kept coming down to three. Three people at the Dragonfly. Three cars disappearing from the caravan into town. Three sets of footprints.

We followed the tracks right to the boat. Unfortunately – or maybe fortunately – the deck of the boat was empty. I glanced at Thistle. The set of her jaw was grim, but determined all the same. She climbed onto the boat first, slipping a little on the smooth deck. I followed her and we both glanced around nervously.

"Do you think we should go inside?" Thistle whispered.

"I think that's where the footprints lead."

"Actually," Thistle furrowed her brow. "Only two sets of footprints lead to the boat. The others broke off at the dock and then headed down the trail that leads to the library."

I followed the line of her finger as she pointed and nodded. I didn't know if that was a good thing or a bad thing.

"Let's just do it," I said finally. "It's not like we're unarmed. We can conjure something if we have to – even if it's just a glamour to get away."

"Too bad we can't conjure Aunt Tillie's shotgun."

I grunted in agreement and stepped in front of Thistle to take the lead. If someone was sitting below deck with a gun, I wanted him to shoot me first. Kind of. Okay, I didn't really want that, I just wouldn't be able to live with myself if it happened the other way around.

I descended the steps into the below-deck cabin, taking as much care as possible to be quiet, and found myself in a small living area with a couch, an easy chair and a small bookshelf. It was empty other than the furniture.

Thistle blew out a sigh of relief that seemed to echo in the silence of the cabin. I slapped her shoulder to silence her, but that was even louder in the ominous quiet. Thistle smacked me back before she realized how loud we were being.

"Shhh!" We both shushed each other at the same time.

"You're not going to sneak up on anyone if these are your spying skills."

Thistle and I both froze at the sound of the new individual entering the room. My heart stuttered as I recognized the voice – even though it wasn't one that exactly filled me with fear. Finally, I swiveled my upper body and looked at the doorway that separated the living room of the cabin from the hallway that led to – what I assumed – was the bedrooms and bathroom.

"Mr. Baker," Thistle said in surprise before I could initiate my own vocal chords.

"Actually, it's Byron Hobbes."

"I knew it!" Oh, look, I found my voice. "I told you," I swung on Thistle. "Didn't I tell you?"

"You were right," Thistle grumbled. "You want a cookie?"

"Maybe later," I said. "What are you doing here, Mr. Hobbes?"

"Seeing if the boat is seaworthy or not," he admitted. "We're ready to get out of here. It's a nice place, don't get me wrong, but I wouldn't want to live here. Too much snow."

"Don't you live in Canada?" Thistle asked.

"Yeah, but when you get snow up there it's not as big a deal," Byron shrugged. "Here, you get a foot of snow and it shuts everything down for three days. That's not normal."

"Who are you talking to, Byron?" Mrs. Baker – or Lillian Hobbes, I guess – wandered up behind her husband. She didn't look surprised to see us.

"Thistle, Bay, what a nice surprise."

"You don't seem all that upset to see us," Thistle said.

"It was just a matter of time before someone put it together," Lillian said. "We were hopeful that we might be able to get out of town before the police realized that the Bakers only existed on paper – but we were doubtful that would be feasible."

"Why did you abandon the boat in the middle of the channel?" I asked.

"We wanted a new life," Lillian said. "We wanted to just disappear, letting everyone think we were dead, and then just find a new place to live out our golden years."

"We were going to go someplace warmer," Byron said. "The blizzard kind of messed us up, though."

"Why would you want to disappear?" Thistle asked. "What about your family?"

"You haven't met our family," Lillian said. "They're all lazy losers."

"Not a one of them has a job," Byron agreed. "Our kids sponged off us their entire lives. It was our fault, I know that, but they don't have a work ethic. We got sick of taking care of them.

"Then, when they had kids," he continued. "They taught their offspring that work was a dirty word and all they needed to do to get money was ask us for it."

"I don't understand," I admitted. "Why didn't you just cut them off?"

"You can't just cut off family," Byron said. "Trust me, I've tried. The tears, I tell you."

"The crying, the wailing," Lillian supplied. "And that was our son."

"So you were going to fake your death? I don't get it," Thistle said honestly.

"Our family isn't exactly normal," Byron admitted.

"Whose is?" Thistle said bitterly.

"Oh, honey," Lillian grabbed Thistle's hand compassionately. "You have no idea how lucky you are."

"Have you met my Aunt Tillie?"

"A woman that loves you with her whole heart."

"And the devil horns she keeps hidden under that curly cap she calls hair," Thistle supplied.

"She has a few quirks," Lillian acknowledged. "But you live in a family that loves each other. It's not about the money. It's about the ... magic."

Thistle shared an uncomfortable gaze with me before turning back to Byron. "I still don't understand why you just can't cut your kids off. Give them a date where they have to get a job and stand firm."

Byron sighed and sat down on the couch. "You see, we're rich people."

"I noticed," I replied, glancing around the boat appreciatively.

"The thing is, we didn't exactly make our money the old-fashioned way."

"I don't know what that means," Thistle said.

"Well, you see," Byron hedged. "We own a string of laundry facilities."

"Like Laundromats?"

"Yes," Byron nodded.

"What's wrong with that?" I asked.

"It was a good living," Lillian supplied. "It just wasn't going to make us rich."

"Not filthy rich," Byron agreed. "And we wanted to be filthy rich."

I had no idea where they were going with this.

"So," Byron continued. "When a local businessman approached us with an opportunity that would allow us to bring in five times the money we were making on a monthly basis, well, we jumped at it."

"And how did you do that?" Thistle asked suspiciously.

"We took on a series of investors that would give us a sum of money," Lillian said quickly. "We would then give those same investors – under a different name, of course – most of that money back. We would keep a portion of the money ourselves for our trouble."

"I still don't get it," Thistle looked befuddled.

"They're money launderers," I supplied.

"Oh," Thistle said. "Oh!"

Byron shrugged apologetically. "It's a living."

"It's a crime," I countered.

"They don't exactly look like criminals," Thistle said.

"We're not criminals," Lillian corrected Thistle. "We're the people that help criminals."

"Well, that makes it better," I said sarcastically.

"I still don't understand why that stops you from cutting your kids off?" Thistle said.

"Well," Lillian shifted her gaze to her husband. "You see, our daughter happened to marry one of the individuals we worked with."

"Your daughter married a mobster?"

"Yes," Byron nodded.

"And he threatened you?"

"Alex? No," Byron laughed. "Alex never threatened us."

"Then I still don't understand," Thistle pressed.

"Our daughter and Alex's son is a different story," Lillian said.

"He threatened you?"

"Not exactly," Lillian said. "It's more like he used some of our property, this boat for example, as a way to get involved with his father's business."

Realization finally dinged in my foggy brain. "He used your boat to run drugs between Canada and the U.S."

Lillian pursed her lips and nodded. "We didn't know," she said hurriedly. "Not until we got on the boat to leave."

"We knew that he was hiding stuff in our house," Byron said. "We found bags of powder and pills hidden in our basement."

"What did you do?"

"We told him, if he did anything like that again, that we would call the police," Byron replied.

"And how did he take that?" I asked.

"Not well," Byron said. "He said if we even thought of calling the police, he would kill us."

"Your grandson threatened to kill you?" I asked incredulously. "Why didn't you tell his father?"

"Well, you see, we found out he wasn't running drugs for his father," Lillian said. "He was running drugs for one of his father's rivals. If we told Alex, there's a good chance that our grandson would have been killed."

It was like a soap opera, for crying out loud.

"So you decided to take yourselves out of the equation," Thistle said sympathetically.

"Pretty much," Byron agreed.

"So what went wrong?" I asked.

"When we took out the boat, our plan was to abandon it in the water and then pick up a new life in a new state," Lillian said. "We had a bag of fake blood to leave on the deck and we had made arrangements for another boat to pick us up in the channel and a vehicle waiting for us in town. We figured we would be long gone before anyone found out we were even missing."

Thistle and I both waited for Lillian to finish the story.

"We found something on the boat, though."

"Drugs," I supplied.

"Drugs," Lillian nodded. "Apparently, our grandson had left his latest delivery on our boat and he wasn't exactly happy about us taking our boat. We knew he would be following us, but we didn't realize how close he was."

"He's here, isn't he?"

"He is," Byron said. "He's staying at your inn, in fact."

Thistle's eyebrows nearly shot off her head. "It's Sludge, isn't it?"

"No," Byron shook his head quickly. "Those boys are innocent. They're just here for the snow."

"That leaves Brian," Thistle said dubiously. "We know who his family is."

"You're forgetting someone," I said.

"Who?"

"Trevor."

Tears flooded Lillian's eyes. "Yes, Trevor is our grandson."

"Why didn't you just give him the boat and continue on with your plan?" Thistle asked.

"He doesn't just want the boat," Lillian said. "He wants what was on the boat. He's been following us around for days and demanding that we return his property."

"The drugs," I said. "Where are the drugs? Did he take them from you?"

"No," Byron said. "We hid them."

"At the Dragonfly?" Thistle looked really confused right now. I didn't blame her.

"What's the Dragonfly?" Now Lillian looked confused.

"It's a burned out inn down Maple Road," Thistle said.

"I don't know about anything about another inn," Lillian said. "Besides, Trevor doesn't have the drugs. He doesn't have any idea where we hid the drugs."

"Where did you hide the drugs?" I asked the question, even though I didn't want to hear the answer I knew in my heart was coming.

"In the basement of your mothers' inn," Byron admitted. "In the room your Aunt Tillie has been brewing her special wine."

Crap, crap, crap!

THIRTY-FOUR

"*L*et me get this straight," Thistle pursed her lips dangerously. "You're running from your murderous thug grandson and you stole his drugs and hid them in my mom's inn?"

Lillian looked uncomfortable. "Well, we didn't know what else to do."

"How about going to the police?"

"We didn't want to go to jail ourselves."

"Sonofabitch," I swore. "We have to get back out to the inn."

"Why?" Thistle looked confused.

"Because I think that's where Trevor went."

Thistle and I both swung to leave the cabin of the yacht and froze when we saw Aunt Tillie on the bottom step. The set of her jaw was grim, and she looked like she wanted to kill someone. My guess was that Byron and Lillian were at the top of that list – right next to their delinquent grandson.

"How much did you hear?"

"Most of it," Clove supplied from her spot behind Aunt Tillie.

"We have to get back out to the inn," I said to Aunt Tillie, forcefully shaking her out of her murderous reverie. "I think Trevor is out at the inn now looking for his drugs and if our moms get in the way … ."

"He'll kill them," Aunt Tillie said. She was succinct in her determination, but she wasn't moving. I was starting to wonder if she was in shock.

"So we need to get going," Thistle took a step forward.

Aunt Tillie ignored her. She was staring down Lillian and Byron like they were flies and she was the swatter. "How dare you," she finally gritted out. "How dare you bring drugs into my home."

Lillian and Byron looked properly abashed, while Thistle and I exchanged wary glances behind Aunt Tillie's back. That was pretty rich from a woman that cultivated her own pot field on a yearly basis.

"We didn't know what else to do," Lillian shrugged helplessly.

"So you were just going to run again and leave us with the cleanup?"

Now that was a pretty good question.

"We figured, once he knew we were gone, that Trevor would follow us again. We just needed a head start."

"You just thought he'd abandon his box of drugs?" Clove didn't look like she believed the statement.

"We didn't know," Lillian admitted. "And it's a big bag, not a box."

"Cripes, we can't stay here any longer," I said irritably. "We have to get back out to the inn."

"You should call Landon," Thistle said quietly. "Maybe he and Chief Terry can get out there faster than us."

I paused at the suggestion and turned to Aunt Tillie, a question in my eyes. "What do you think?"

Aunt Tillie finally turned to me, seeing me for the first time since she'd entered the boat's cabin. "Call them," she said finally. "We're going out there, too. Thistle, go get my plow truck."

"Wait," I grabbed Thistle's arm. "If Trevor is there, he'll see – and hear – that truck coming from a mile away."

"So?" Thistle looked confused. "Isn't that what we want?"

"Not if it's going to set him on edge," Aunt Tillie said sagely. "He's already teetering. We saw that this morning when he jumped on Brian."

"You weren't even outside," I pointed out.

"How many times do I have to tell you? I see all and know all."

"Whatever," Thistle grumbled. "She's right, though, we can't send him over the edge."

"How do we know what they're telling us is true?" Clove piped in. "Maybe they're the drug dealers?" She still didn't want to give up hope on Trevor, that much was obvious.

"They're money launderers," I said firmly. "They're not drug dealers."

"We don't have time to deal with your crap right now," Thistle interjected angrily. "We have to get out to the inn. We're going to take the snowmobiles."

I turned to her in surprise. "We are?"

"We can sneak up to the back of the inn that way," Thistle said. "They're already gassed up."

I tilted my head to the side, considering. "Okay," I agreed. "Let's go. I'll call Landon and Chief Terry on our way back to the stables."

We started to climb the steps. When we got to the deck above, Aunt Tillie paused.

"What are you doing?" Clove turned around to watch Aunt Tillie.

"I'm not letting them escape, that's for sure," Aunt Tillie said, placing her hand on the deck. I could hear her muttering under her breath. I was sure it was a spell, but I couldn't hear what she was saying. Suddenly, a light pulsed under Aunt Tillie's hands and coursed over the yacht quickly and then diminished.

"What was that?" Thistle asked suspiciously.

"Just a little bit of insurance," Aunt Tillie said primly, holding out her hand expectantly so Thistle could help her climb down safely from the boat deck to the dock.

Clove and I followed. When we were all standing together, I turned to Aunt Tillie. "What's going to happen to them if they try to leave?"

"Nothing good," Aunt Tillie huffed. "Let's just leave it at that, for now."

"Are they trapped on the boat?" I was still unsure we should leave the older couple to their own devices. I had visions of returning to the boat later and finding them gone – even if they couldn't take the boat.

"They're not leaving and the boat is staying here," Aunt Tillie said angrily. "I know what I'm doing."

"No one said you didn't," Clove said calmly.

"She just did," Aunt Tillie gestured in my direction.

"I did not."

"You did, too."

"Whatever, let's go." Arguing with Aunt Tillie has all the appeal of beating your head against a wall – and the outcome is never as good.

We raced back toward the stable – and by raced, I mean walked briskly. Aunt Tillie is spry for a woman in her eighties, but she has limitations. I used the time to call Landon's cellphone. Unfortunately, it went straight to voicemail. I left him a message, telling him as much as I could, and then disconnected.

"I think we're on our own," I said.

"Good," Aunt Tillie said. "There will be fewer witnesses."

Thistle and I exchanged worried glances. That wasn't a good sign.

Marcus had the snowmobiles gassed up and waiting. Thistle climbed onto one of them, with Clove sliding in behind her wordlessly. Unfortunately for me, Aunt Tillie had already slid into the driver's seat of the other snowmobile.

"I'm driving," I told her hurriedly.

"I'm already settled," Aunt Tillie argued. "I'll drive."

"Just slide back."

"You just sit behind me."

"I said I'm driving."

"I'm driving."

"You don't see all that well when you're on a road," I reminded her. "We're going to be riding through a lot of trees. We need to get out there fast."

"Fine," Aunt Tillie huffed, sliding back reluctantly. "I won't forget this, though."

"Fine," I muttered through gritted teeth. "You can punish me later."

"I will, don't you worry."

We set a brisk pace to get back out to The Overlook. I let Thistle lead while I contemplated what we would find when we got out there. I could only hope that Trevor was still trying to hide his real identity, which meant he was searching the inn under the guise of being a handyman. If he was becoming too desperate, though, I didn't doubt he would kill anyone that got in his way.

It took us almost a half an hour to get back out to The Overlook. Thistle wisely parked at the back of the inn and killed the snowmobile engine quickly. I followed suit.

"How do you think we should handle this?" Thistle asked, her face flushed from the sharp breeze that had accompanied the long ride back out to the inn. It was so red, it almost matched her windblown hair.

"Let's split up," I said finally. "I'll take Aunt Tillie in through the back door and you and Clove try to go through the front door. At least that way, we won't all be caught at the same time."

Thistle nodded and then looked around blankly. "Where is Aunt Tillie?"

I looked back toward the snowmobile, expecting to see her but finding an empty seat instead. I looked up toward the inn and found that the back door was already standing open – and Aunt Tillie was nowhere in sight.

"You've got to be kidding me," I growled.

I started toward the back door angrily. I was surprised to find Thistle and Clove close on my heels. "I thought you were going out front?"

"That was before Aunt Tillie went vigilante," Thistle said. "I'm not leaving you alone."

I sighed, shrugging off my irritation with Aunt Tillie. "We don't have a lot of choice now," I agreed. "Let's go."

We slipped into the family living quarters through the door Aunt Tillie had left open. The room was empty, meaning that Aunt Tillie had already made her way further into the inn. Clove shut the door behind us, taking care to be as quiet as possible. The three of us shrugged out of our heavy coats, but kept our boots on – just in case.

Thistle and Clove took a few seconds to look into the family bedrooms and then came back into the living room. Thistle shook her head to indicate that the bedrooms had been empty. That didn't necessarily mean anything, but it filled my heart with dread.

I led the way into the kitchen, glancing at Aunt Tillie's empty recliner momentarily, and then continued through the room. I paused at the swinging door that led to the dining room and pressed my head against the door to see if I could hear anything. There was nothing, though. That didn't have to be ominous, I knew that deep down. The inn should have been empty, except for our moms, with the hipsters out snowboarding and Byron and Lillian on their boat. Still, though, the silence of the usually bustling inn was oppressive.

I took a deep breath and swung the dining room door open and glanced around the room. It was empty, too.

The three of us stepped into the dining room, Thistle sliding around the room – sticking close to the outer wall – and heading toward the archway that opened into the main hallway of the inn. Clove and I followed instinctively.

When we still didn't hear anything, we continued moving through the inn. The main hallway branched off into three directions: the main office, the main foyer and the small alcove at the bottom of the grand staircase.

We each took a different direction. Thistle peeked into the foyer, glanced around and then turned back. Nothing. Clove glanced into the staircase alcove and then shook her head. That left the office. I took a deep breath and turned the door handle. It turned easily and I pushed the door open.

Nothing could have prepared me for what I found. My mom, Marnie and Twila were all sitting, silently, in different chairs in the room. None of them were moving, but they all appeared to be fine. I pushed the door open the rest of the way and stepped into the office irritably. "What are you guys doing?"

My mom turned to me, fear etched on her face. I knew then. *I knew*. I opened my mouth to warn Thistle and Clove to stay out of the room, but it was too late. They were right behind me, moving toward their moms with twin expressions of concern marring their features. The office door slammed shut behind us quickly, causing all three of us to spin around in surprise.

Trevor was standing there, previously hidden by the door I had opened – and he wasn't alone. He had a big knife in one hand – the butcher knife from the kitchen, in fact – and he had his other arm wrapped around Aunt Tillie, with a hand clamped over her mouth.

"Thank you for joining us," Trevor said evenly. "I've been waiting for you."

THIRTY-FIVE

*A*unt Tillie was fighting Trevor furiously. Unfortunately, he had more than two feet and a hundred pounds of muscle to make sure that he had the advantage. Of course, he didn't know about her *special* gifts, either.

"Let her go," I said coldly, meeting Trevor's frigid eyes evenly.

"Sit down," Trevor countered.

"Let her go first."

"Sit down first."

"Let her go," Twila screamed anxiously.

Thistle shot her mother a murderous look. "Calm down," she hissed.

"She's an old woman," Twila blubbered. "He's going to hurt her."

That was a definite possibility, I reasoned. It was also a possibility that she would skin him alive and leave the carcass for us to clean up.

Trevor didn't seem moved by Twila's pleas. "Then she's lived a long life."

I realized, pretty quickly, that I had to get control of this situation. "What do you want, Trevor? You want your drugs?"

Trevor didn't flinch at the question, but the slight narrowing of his

231

eyes told me that he was surprised I had the guts to ask it. I didn't know if that was a good thing or a bad thing. I was going with a good thing.

"Yeah," I continued blithely. "We talked to your grandparents."

"His grandparents?" My mom looked confused.

"Yeah, Lillian and Byron Hobbes," I continued, trying to keep Trevor's attention fixed on me.

"The Canadian couple from the boat?" Marnie asked, her eyes never moving from Trevor and Aunt Tillie.

"You know them as the Bakers," Clove supplied.

"The Bakers? How is that possible?"

"They had false identities made up," I said smoothly. "They were running from their family in Canada. They hoped to make a new life for themselves."

"They've been chatty, I see," Trevor grimaced.

"They were honest," I countered. "They told us everything, though. They told us about the money laundering. And they told us about your father and his ties to the mob."

"I didn't even know there was a Canadian mob," Thistle admitted. "It was an illuminating discussion, though."

"The best part," I continued. "Was hearing about how you took a job for a rival mobster and used their house as a drug den."

"That's terrible," Twila mused. "Those poor people."

"They were the money launderers," I corrected Twila. "It's not like they were innocent."

"They weren't bad people, though," Twila said.

"I guess it depends on what your definition of bad is," Clove said. For her part, her eyes were settled on Trevor, but they were clouded with tears. She really was a magnet for assholes.

"They certainly aren't as bad as their rotten grandson," I agreed.

"Oh, that hurts," Trevor said with faux indignation. "Did they tell you they stole my stash?"

Trevor's hand slipped from Aunt Tillie's mouth. "My nieces steal my stash all the time," she said. "You just have to get over it. Some people don't understand the sanctity of a woman's pot stash."

"You have a whole field," Clove whined. "And I only did it once."

"You only got caught once," Aunt Tillie countered. "There's a big difference."

"Yeah, we know you were taking walks this fall that often ended up in her field," I said with forced joviality.

"I knew it," Aunt Tillie muttered. "Didn't I tell you I knew it was her?"

"You said you thought it was Thistle," my mom reminded her. If she found the conversation mundane in the face of terror, she didn't let on. She was letting us lead.

"No, I said I thought it was Clove," Aunt Tillie said. She exchanged a glance with Thistle, although I couldn't read it. I didn't think it was good, though.

"You thought it was Thistle," Marnie interjected. It almost looked as if she was enjoying the game.

"That's a bald-faced lie," Aunt Tillie said.

I watched, curiously, as she shifted in Trevor's grasp. "I need to sit down."

"What?" Trevor looked frustrated.

"I'm old, I need to sit down," Aunt Tillie said. "My knees are giving out."

"Just deal with it," Trevor shook her, trying to haul her back to her feet.

"It's going to be hard to hold me up and take all of them on," Aunt Tillie said helpfully.

Trevor considered her statement for a second. He must have realized the truth behind it, because he let her go and pushed her toward us. Clove stepped forward to catch her, absorbing Aunt Tillie's dead weight as she fell forward.

Thistle and I remained standing, three feet apart from each other, neither making a move to help Clove with Aunt Tillie. Trevor noticed our stalwart stances and narrowed his eyes at us suspiciously.

"If she's such an old woman, why didn't you help her?"

"Clove had it under control," Thistle said calmly.

Trevor fingered the end of the knife thoughtfully. "What else did my grandparents tell you? Did they tell you where they were going?"

"Someplace warm," I replied. "I think there was talk of beaches and little drinks with umbrellas in them."

"And where are they now?"

"On the boat," Aunt Tillie said. "They're not leaving. Why don't you go spend some quality family time together?"

Trevor smirked. What could have once been described as a handsome feature now looked sinister. "Like I'm going to fall for that. They've left already, haven't they?"

"Oh, they haven't left," Aunt Tillie said knowingly. "I can pretty much guarantee that."

"How can you guarantee that?"

"Just call it women's intuition," Aunt Tillie said smugly.

Trevor glanced at Aunt Tillie curiously. "You're an interesting old bat, aren't you?"

"Who are you calling old?" Aunt Tillie was incensed.

"You just called yourself old." Trevor shot back.

"I did not," Aunt Tillie sniffed. "That's just a horrible thing to say. And to lie and say I would actually call myself old. That's just unforgiveable."

"You did, too," Trevor was getting visibly frustrated now. "They all heard you."

"I didn't hear her," I replied calmly.

"Neither did I," Thistle interjected. "I just don't think he appreciates a woman with wisdom on her side."

"That's just terrible," I clucked. "Just terrible."

Clove was back on her feet. She could sense something was about to happen. She just didn't know what.

"Are you going to stand for that, Aunt Tillie?" Thistle asked her pointedly.

Aunt Tillie met Thistle's challenging gaze. "What do you think?"

Thistle turned to Trevor, an evil smirk on her face. "I think Trevor's going to wish he'd never met us."

"I think he's going to wish he'd never stayed at our inn," I agreed.

"I think he's going to wish he'd never flirted with me," Clove announced boldly.

Aunt Tillie slowly got to her feet, fire in her eyes, her hands still at her side. "I think all those things are a realistic possibility," she said.

"I'm the one in charge here," Trevor said angrily, worry on his face. "I'm the one with the knife."

"We don't need a knife," I said calmly.

"I call the winds of the north," Clove sang out from the far left, reaching her hand out to grasp Aunt Tillie's waiting hand. "Let's show Trevor here what he's worth."

"I call to the magic of the east," Thistle chanted from my right, reaching her left hand out to grasp my right hand. "This will let us punish this beast."

I gripped Thistle's hand harshly. "I call to the wardens of the west," I started. "For they always find what's best."

"What is this?" Trevor looked baffled. "Are you chanting? What are you guys? Witches?"

I felt my hand slip into Aunt Tillie's, unsure how this would end and curious at the same time.

"And I call on the power of the south," Aunt Tillie said, her eyes gleaming with rage. "Let's show this lout how to close his big mouth."

It wasn't our best rhyme, to be sure, but it was effective.

Nothing happened right away, and Trevor looked triumphant in the moment. Then the power surged.

"So mote it be."

I didn't have to look behind me to know that my mom and aunts had joined hands behind us, pushing their power into our spell to tip it over the edge.

The energy in the room exploded, at this point. There was another force here now, and it was bearing down on Trevor.

I don't know what he saw with that first glimpse. The fear that washed over his face was more than enough to tell me not to look behind me, though.

There was a sudden roar and the wind spell that we had conjured moved through us with such force it threatened to wrench my arm from Aunt Tillie's grasp. I didn't let it, though. I knew that our joined hands were driving the spell.

I risked a glance to my left and saw the terrible air monster move forward. The wind was whipping through the room, driving my hair in front of my eyes. For a second, though, just a second, I recognized the figure in the wind – or at least I thought I did. I didn't have time to focus on that, though, because our spell was descending on Trevor – who was making a mad dash to try and flee from the room.

The wind monster reached out – yes, it had arms and I had no idea where they had come from – and the ethereal fingers of death now had a hold of Trevor. Trevor tried to stab the monster, but it was in vain. You can't stab the wind.

Trevor's screams were more pitiful than anything else as the wind monster engulfed him. "Help! Please, God, help me!"

"There's no help for you here, Trevor," Aunt Tillie said coldly. "I'm the god here, and I want you out of my house!"

Trevor screamed again. I couldn't see his face. I didn't want to. The mewling sounds now emitting from his ravaged throat were enough for me to know that his face would be worse. However bad he was, however terrible he was, I didn't want to see this. I couldn't look away, though, either.

"Holy shit!"

We hadn't heard the office door open. I swung in surprise when I heard the new voice and met Landon's stunned gaze from across the room. Instinctively, I let go of Aunt Tillie's hand. Thistle and Clove did the same.

The wind monster dissipated as quickly as he had formed. Within seconds, the room was empty, and Trevor was unconscious on the floor.

Landon stepped into the room, weapon drawn. He kicked Trevor with his foot and then turned to us anxiously.

"Is he dead?"

"No," Aunt Tillie said fitfully. "He just wishes he was."

Landon turned to me, sweat washing down his face. His eyes were flashing in recognition and intensity. I don't know what I expected: Questions, recriminations, outright denial? What Landon said, though, it's something I'll never forget.

"Good job, ladies. Good job."

THIRTY-SIX

*C*hief Terry didn't say anything when he entered the room. His face was as white as the snow outside, though, and I was worried he was actually going to pass out. Instead, he hauled his tall frame over to Trevor on the floor, knelt, and efficiently slapped a pair of handcuffs on him and stood back up.

"We can't read him his rights until he comes to," he grunted.

Landon was still standing next to him. The only movement he hinted at, though, was a hand through his long black hair and an occasional glance in Chief Terry's direction. Otherwise, he was frozen in his place. I felt the urge to go to him, but I kept a safe distance instead. I didn't want to push him.

Chief Terry finally could find no further reason to fuss over Trevor on the floor. He stood up, smoothed his sheriff's department issued coat down in front of him, and then turned to everyone in the room. He calmly pulled his notebook out of his pocket and raised his eyes, searching through every face assembled, before landing on mine.

"Okay," he said haltingly. "What happened here?"

Clove and Thistle both tilted their heads in my direction. They wanted to hear how I would answer. I wasn't quite sure how I was going to explain the ending, so I started at the beginning.

I told them about Lillian and Byron Hobbes and how we found them on their boat.

"I told you to stay at Hypnotic," Landon grumbled.

"I left you a note," I replied defensively.

"Well, that must make it okay then," Landon shot back. He still wasn't making eye contact.

"Where are they now?" Chief Terry interrupted.

"They're still on the boat," I said.

"How can you be sure?"

I glanced down at Aunt Tillie, who was lazing comfortably on the couch and watching the scene unfold, and merely shook my head. "I'm fairly certain they'll still be there."

Chief Terry regarded Aunt Tillie for a second, took in her smug and relaxed face, and merely grunted. In other words: He didn't want to know how we knew that Byron and Lillian would still be on the boat.

I then recounted how we got out to the inn. Landon made a motion like he wanted to interrupt me, but he must have thought better of it because he quickly stilled.

"So, let me get this straight," Chief Terry said hollowly. "Instead of calling the police, you decided to take on a crazed drug runner on your own."

"I called Landon," I corrected him. "I didn't feel we could wait, though. It was my decision."

"We all agreed," Thistle interjected tersely. "You're not taking this all on yourself," she muttered.

"No, she's not," Chief Terry agreed. "Besides," he slid a look at Aunt Tillie. "I have a feeling, even if she had thought better of coming out here, someone else would have."

He knew our family too well.

"What happened next?"

"We originally were going to split up, with two of us going in through the back and two of us going in through the front," I started, shifting a telling gaze toward Aunt Tillie. "That didn't exactly work out, though."

"Why not?" Landon asked. He met my gaze for the first time, although I couldn't recognize the emotions bubbling under his ragged surface. He was being a federal agent now, nothing more.

I pursed my lips, considering how to answer the question.

"Because Aunt Tillie snuck in the house while we were still deciding," Clove blurted out.

If I'm ever taken hostage and tortured for information, I don't want Clove with me. I'm just saying.

"Why did you do that?" Landon directed the question to Aunt Tillie.

"My girls were in trouble," she said sullenly. "I had to save the day."

"And what about the girls you had with you outside?" Landon pressed.

"They didn't have to follow me," Aunt Tillie said. "I had things under control without them."

"So, you just thought they would leave you to hunt a mad man on your own?" Landon looked dubious.

"No," Aunt Tillie said honestly. "I knew they would come. It's what we do."

"So I've noticed," Landon said dryly.

"What happened then?" Chief Terry asked.

"We searched the house and found everyone in here," I finished up simply.

Chief Terry looked like he wanted to stop, but he didn't. "And how did you disarm the suspect?"

And there it was. The question. The question I didn't know how to answer. The question I didn't want to answer. The question they – clearly – didn't want the answer to.

"We … ."

"We rushed him," Thistle interjected quickly. "Clove, Bay, and I all ran at him the same time. We kicked and hit him until he dropped the knife and passed out. That's when you came in."

My heart was hammering in my chest and my blood was roaring in my ears. Thistle had just lied to a cop and a federal agent. This wasn't going to be good.

Chief Terry swallowed hard and then turned to Landon. "They got lucky," he said carefully. "If the three of them hadn't done it together, he might have hurt one of them."

I watched Landon to see how he would react and I was surprised to see the small smile tug at the corner of his mouth. "They did," Landon said. "I still think they should probably get a proper reprimand about handling situations like this on their own, but I'm not sure what else could have been done in this particular situation."

The relief washed over me and I practically sagged to the floor. I took a hesitant step toward Landon, but my mom and aunts were herding toward Chief Terry en masse, forcing me to take a step back instead as they rushed to his side.

"We were so scared," Twila said, throwing her arms around Chief Terry's neck. "You have no idea."

"It was terrible," Marnie agreed, hooking her arm through one of Chief Terry's. "We were terrified. All I could think of was that I might never see you again."

My mom and aunts had been engaged in a battle for Chief Terry's affections for as long as I could remember. He basked under their attention – and continuous food offerings. They were clearly doing their best now to make sure he realized he had made the right decision by accepting Thistle's lie.

"I would never let anything happen to you," Chief Terry said soothingly, making room for my mom to join the fray. His gaze focused on me and darkened slightly. "Any of you, no matter how stupid you are sometimes."

"Who are you calling stupid?" Aunt Tillie huffed.

"Shut up," Thistle pinched her quickly. "Just shut up for once."

Landon moved over to me and pulled me close for a brief hug. I was relieved that he didn't seem to be pulling away, but he wasn't quite himself either. "I don't know what happened here," he whispered in my ear. "But you're going to tell me everything this time."

Landon waited for my response. Never moving his arms from my waist, but never completely embracing me either. I made my decision.

"What are you doing for dinner tonight?"

Landon tightened his arms around me in relief. "Whatever it is, it's going to involve you and me alone – with none of these crazy people within five miles of us."

Well, it was a start. I nodded in agreement.

"I told you that he would be back," Aunt Tillie said, shifting a gaze toward Thistle.

Thistle rubbed the bridge of her nose tiredly. "Yes, you know all and see all."

"And remember all," Aunt Tillie said ominously. "Don't you think for a second I will forget that you just pinched me either."

"Crap," Thistle whined. "Why is it always me?"

THIRTY-SEVEN

*T*he next few days were relatively carefree – at least for the Winchester witches. Landon and I had our first official date, which resulted in his first official sleepover. No one said much about it, even though Twila had been at the guesthouse the next morning when we walked out of the bedroom. Her eyes had widened, though, and Thistle had clamped one hand over her mouth firmly and shook her head. I knew my mom, Marnie, and Aunt Tillie knew, too. For the first time in – well, ever – I didn't care what they thought. That, of course, would probably change in the near future – but, for now, I was content.

More surprising than that, though, was the fact that I had told Landon everything. I had told him about the wind monster we had conjured and how, at that last second when it passed us, I could have sworn it looked back at me with my Uncle Calvin's eyes. I only knew those eyes from pictures, so I couldn't be sure. I hadn't pressed Aunt Tillie on that – yet. It was coming at some point.

Landon had taken the information better than I expected. Instead of freaking out, he just asked more questions: Questions about our family, questions about our history, and questions about our legacy. He seemed interested more than anything else. There was no fear in the queries, only curiosity. I felt relieved by the realization that he wasn't going to run this time. I didn't want to push him too far, though. At least not right away.

On the fourth night after our adventure, Landon had returned home to get more clothes and spend some time with his brother. He said he would be back tomorrow – and I found I was looking forward to it. Things were in a comfortable place for us right now, and I didn't think I could ask for much more than that.

On this particular evening, after a tense meal at the inn with our moms and Chief Terry – where he informed us that Byron and Lillian Hobbes had been turned over to Canadian police – Clove, Thistle, and I were relaxing on the couch in front of a roaring fire when the conversation took a turn in the direction I had been dreading for days.

"There's something that still doesn't add up," Thistle said finally.

"The Dragonfly," I agreed.

"Trevor said he didn't have anything to do with the Dragonfly," Clove said. "He said he'd never been out there and never heard of it."

"So who was out at the Dragonfly?" Thistle sipped from her cup of hot chocolate and raised an eyebrow at Clove.

"Does it matter?" Clove asked irritably. "Can't we just be happy that we're all alive and that I picked another loser? Why don't we just focus on that?"

"You'll find someone, Clove," I said soothingly. "You just need to get better radar when it comes to men."

"You didn't know that there was anything wrong with Trevor either," she said accusingly.

"We didn't spend as much time with him as you did," Thistle said.

"That's not the point," Clove said stubbornly.

"Fine, we were all wrong about Trevor," I said in a placating manner. When she wasn't looking, though, I crossed my eyes in Thistle's direction, causing her to choke on her hot chocolate as she stifled the giggle bubbling in her throat.

"So," Clove changed the subject. "What do you think was going on out at the Dragonfly?"

"Maybe we'll never know," I said thoughtfully.

"Or maybe we should go find out right now?" Thistle suggested.

"No, no, no, no, no, no," Clove shook her head. "I'm not going back out there."

I got to my feet, nodding in Thistle's direction. There was one aspect of this case that just didn't fit. The Dragonfly. We had to know. Thistle had to know. "Let's go. We're not going to get a better chance than now. Marcus is still at work and Landon is staying in Traverse City tonight."

"I'm not going," Clove crossed her arms over her chest stubbornly.

"Fine," Thistle said meanly. "Stay here where it's warm and safe. Bay and I will do all the work, like we usually do."

Clove huffed angrily. "I'll go, but I'm not going because you called me chicken."

"I didn't call you chicken," Thistle countered. "I hadn't gotten there yet."

Clove sighed in defeat. "Let's just get it over with."

We all got dressed and piled into Thistle's car. The adrenaline of another adventure was starting to pump through our veins, and it couldn't be tamped down. When we got out to the Dragonfly, Thistle parked where she usually did. As a change of pace, there was a car parked in front of the inn.

Thistle turned to me. "What do you think?"

"I think, instead of sneaking around, we should just take the bull by the horns and approach whoever is in there and ask them what they're doing," I said finally. "That would be the mature thing to do."

"I think we should sneak around and eavesdrop," Clove said. "It's safer."

Thistle cocked her head. "I agree with Bay."

"Of course you do," Clove muttered. "You always agree with Bay. Just remember, if you get me killed, I will never forgive you."

"We know," I sighed.

"My ghost will haunt your ghosts until the end of days," Clove continued.

"I get it," Thistle replied. "Believe me, I get it."

We all got out of the car and walked to the front porch of the Dragonfly. There was a light on in the foyer, but the door was shut. Thistle tried to peek in through the window, but she obviously couldn't see anything because she shook her head and moved back to my side.

"Should we knock?" I whispered.

"That will just give whoever is in there a chance to hide whatever they're doing," Thistle whispered back.

She was right. I took a deep breath, grabbed the door handle and turned it. The door opened with no effort, the light inside washing over us as it slid open.

There were three men standing in the middle of the room looking into a box. Three faces looked up in surprise when the door sprung open. One of those faces belonged to Uncle Teddy – and the other two were equally recognizable.

"What are you doing here?" Thistle strode into the room purposefully. She glanced into the box in surprise, reaching her hand in and pulling out a fistful of ... fabric samples. "With a box of fabric?"

Clove glanced into another open box on the small table next to her – a new table, with maple finishing that had just recently been moved into the previously vacant room. "And tile samples?"

"I can explain," Uncle Teddy said hurriedly. The two men with him remained silent – and stunned by our sudden arrival.

"Explain what?" Thistle charged angrily. "Why you're sneaking around out here? Why you have sample boxes everywhere?" She turned to me, the unasked question on her lips was running through my mind, too. I didn't know what to think.

"We bought the Dragonfly because we're going to open an inn here, together," Uncle Teddy said hurriedly.

"Why were you keeping it a secret?"

"We didn't want to tip your Aunt Tillie off," he replied. "She can be a little testy, as you well know."

"Why would she care?" I asked, speaking for the first time. My eyes never left the individual standing right behind Uncle Teddy. His eyes were trained on me, as well. He didn't speak, though, and I didn't address him right away.

"We'll be competition," Uncle Teddy said lamely. "It's not like she likes us anyways. This will make her go crazy. Even crazier than she is now."

"She doesn't care about competition," Thistle scoffed. "This area can easily support a new inn."

"With us running it?" Uncle Teddy looked dubious.

He had a point. Finally, the silent man standing behind Uncle Teddy stepped shakily forward. "Hello, Bay."

"Hi, Dad."

CPSIA information can be obtained
at www.ICGtesting.com
Printed in the USA
LVHW03s1344090718
583149LV00006B/1086/P